"They will just as soon kill you as they will me."

The Unravelling

BY JOANNA VANDER VLUGT

VICTORIA, BC

Carmen.
I hope you enjoy
this thriller.
Joanna Vandervlugt

Joanna Vander Vlugt
The Unravelling ISBN 978-1-9990684-0-0 (Paperback Edition)

Manufactured in Canada

Editor: Pip Wallace
Photographs by Posy Photography and Noreen @ noreen_travels
Illustrations and Book Design by JCVArtstudio
Motorcycle Model: Cathy Curti

First Printing June 2019

Publishing Support: The Self-Publishing Agency
P.O. Box 51527
West Vancouver, BC, Canada
V7T 1A0

Visit www.TheSelfPublishingAgency.com

Dedication

I wouldn't be an artist or a writer if it wasn't for my amazing mother, Mary Szasz. She was a woman before her time and she always put her four daughters first.

Always in my thoughts.

Forever in my heart.

Love, your *"Number 4 daughter"*.

Contents

Acknowledgments

Thank you to author Carolanne Papoutsis who critiqued this manuscript many times in 2006, and 13 years later she critiqued it again. Brianna and Sandi Grove-White for the critique sessions way back. Suzanne Carvell for talks over coffee and having a cat named Chin Chin. Pip Wallace for twice editing this manuscript and introducing me to Grammar Girl. My "sploosh" coffee buddy and Ashley Vander Vlugt, who both answered many questions about drugs. Kara Vander Vlugt for always asking what's my latest project, and my husband Ed for many brainstorming sessions. Belinda Jickling of Posy Photography for the fun photo shoots. Noreen of Noreen @noreen_travels whose photo of Fan Tan Alley was the inspiration for the book cover illustration. Susan Rupertus, lawyer, for checking my legalities. Katrina Maki for understanding what I was going for in the book cover when I said, "vertical." Cathy Curti, the motorcycle model, for a fun Thursday night, talking about motorcycles and taking photos. My sisters, Susan, Rose and Linda—my tribe.

Megan Watt of The Self-Publishing Agency (TSPA). Your vision and energy are contagious as you re-define the self-publishing industry. I'm proud to be part of TSPA. Laura Wrubleski and Jazmin Welch, both Illustrators and book designers for TSPA, and the TSPA team for your advice and answering my many questions.

Joanna

1

Verdict

Slithering out of bed, clambering for my clothes that had been tossed the night before.

I BLAMED IT on the dandelions.

If I hadn't been kneeling in Bianca's flowerbed of dandelions, a cold March wind pushing hair in my face as I pulled out the nasty weeds, Jules wouldn't have slammed on the brakes of his BMW, bringing the convertible to a halt at the end of Bianca's driveway, and I wouldn't have been coerced into representing my ex-husband on a second-degree murder charge.

If.

I tossed my pen on the desk and leaned forward, rubbing my temples with my fingers. I sat in Victoria's oldest courtroom with the weight of my legal career pressing on my shoulders. I detested the fact that my success piggybacked on Jules's success. The five women and seven men who made up the jury were not only deciding my ex's future, but mine. They didn't know that. They didn't know a lot of things: Jules's acquittal would guarantee me the partnership I had been coveting the last three years; the hope of an easy win had been an opiate to my deteriorating self-esteem; this case followed a string of dismal losses.

I leaned back in my chair and jabbed the end of my pen into the spine of my *Criminal Code*. Half the Crown prosecutor's office waited in the courtroom with half of Victoria's defence bar, and a small army of news anchors and camera crew were crowded on the courthouse steps. Debra Evans had flown in from the Kamloops Crown Counsel Office to prosecute Jules's case. No one in the local office wanted to go near it. I didn't blame them.

I stared at the spectators in the gallery. One lady pointed at me while whispering to her friend. Now, was she talking about my long dark hair with its two noticeable white streaks in the front, or was she chastising me for defending Jules? The side door creaked. I looked over and recognized the curly– haired reporter in his rain-soaked coat. I had been dodging the irritating man for the past five months. A stenographer's pad in his hand, he stumbled over the legs of two female law students to get to the only vacant seat.

During the last five months, Debra and I had presented our differing versions of the facts in Jules's second-degree murder charge. A small but formidable opponent, Debra had waddled around the courtroom like a wheezing penguin taking quick puffs from her inhaler. The two of us had been rivals in this courtroom. We slaughtered the criminal justice system, stabbing and slicing it to suit our purpose. It all came down to win or lose. No participation medals were handed out in court. Sure, there were rules, but we manipulated them and discarded the broken ones. It didn't matter about the facts; it was up to the players to sway the jury, or the judge, to interpret the facts his or her way. If we failed, there was always the Court of Appeal.

I leaned forward and reached for the water pitcher, sloshing water into my glass. I swallowed greedily. The ice water chilled my agitated nerves. I sat back and crossed my legs. A wise man had once told me that a good lawyer never lets the truth cloud one's judgment. The truth wasn't clouding anyone's judgment. The truth wasn't on trial. It was the obnoxious Mayor Jules Cranbury. The jurors would soon return to their twelve red seats and Jules's guilt or innocence would be determined. Could the jury put aside their political affiliations and pre-conceived impressions of Jules, and judge the facts and not the arrogant man? Had I been a good enough lawyer to cut through their prejudices and show them that he was innocent? After three days of deliberations, I sure as hell hoped so.

I glanced at the prisoner's box. Jules sat, his arm resting on the wooden side, drumming his fingers as he flirted with a rookie female sheriff. Dressed in an Armani suit—expensive clothes for a garden snake—he looked good on the stand and he gave an Oscar-winning performance.

My ex-husband had blown into my life during my first year of law school. He partied and got top grades. I studied. My mistake had been showing him a little courtesy during a wicked rainstorm that drenched the university campus. I had just settled into an over-stuffed chair in the library, fat raindrops pelting the windows, when Jules had come running to the door. His t-shirt clung to his skin, and his blonde hair made wet streaks on his forehead. He yanked on the locked doorknobs and pounded on the window, shouting to be let in. I sat in my chair, hiding behind my torts text, wondering if I should ignore the twit. Little did I know that when I opened the door for that young man, I had invited him into my life. And Jules Cranbury the wrecking ball swung in.

Jules was charged with the second-degree murder of twenty-year-old Swedish actress Anna Von Altman. I had received threats via Twitter when Jules made his $50,000 bail. Jail-breaker Jade had been the hashtag. The RCMP claimed he had shot Anna during a lover's quarrel. A horrendous charge, considering Jules didn't have a violent bone in his body, just an adulterous one. He had a weakness for blondes and blood, both made him weak in the knees and found him horizontal in someone's bed. Jules denied screwing Anna Von Altman, or murdering her for that matter. Instead, he bragged about his engagement to Olive Aubischon, my boss's daughter.

The Crown prosecutor had an informant who placed Jules at Anna's home two hours before her death, but he couldn't testify as to when Jules left. Jules's fingerprints had been found on a few of Anna's belongings, plus a hair sample with his DNA on her clothing. Oddly enough the revolver had never been recovered just the shell casings. I argued against the fingerprint evidence, saying that if Jules had been seeing Anna, who knew when the fingerprints could have been left, thus raising reasonable doubt in the jury's mind. The hair sample evidence had been a little more difficult. The Crown's case focused on one informant, a number of forensic cops, scant physical evidence, and a truckload of circumstantial evidence. The informant never showed up at the trial. I punched holes in the testimony of a number of the police officers, and because of improper procedures, I managed to get most of the forensic evidence thrown out.

My defence had been that the trumped-up murder charge was nothing more than an attempted political coup orchestrated by the leader of the opposition party to bring Jules's downfall. A simple argument which I hoped the jury would grasp. I have defended hundreds of deadbeats over the last five years, ninety-nine percent of them guilty of the charge brought before them, but not Jules. My ex-husband was not a murderer, and in the city of Victoria I may be the only person who believed in his innocence.

I picked up my pen and glanced again at the gallery and then across to the rafters. According to myth, hanging ghosts haunted this courtroom, supposedly knowing ahead of time if justice had been served. If the rattle of chains was heard, the ghosts were laughing because an accused was to be set free. If one heard nothing, the ghosts were mourning the death of the one about to be hung.

"Jade."

I jumped.

Beatrice, the court clerk with starched grey hair and skin as coarse as the sandstones of the courthouse, nodded her head and mouthed, "Time."

I looked at Jules. As if sensing my silent communication, he turned away from the young sheriff and looked at me. His smile faded. I nodded.

I grasped the leather armrests and pushed myself out of the chair. Weighted down by my robes and legal obligations and strangled by the white tabs around my neck, I glanced once more at the carved wooden beams, straining my ears for the sound of chains. I heard nothing.

"Ready, Jade?" Beatrice asked.

I nodded.

"Debra?"

The Crown prosecutor stood.

Beatrice looked at the rookie sheriff, who spoke into the microphone clipped to her lapel.

A wooden door opened and one by one the twelve members of the jury filed into the courtroom. Three women had flushed cheeks and bloodshot eyes. They must have been crying, or had a lack of sleep.

"Order in court," the sheriff said.

A shuffle of chairs and the entire courtroom was on its feet. The wooden prisoner's box creaked. I looked at Jules. A faint smile on his lips, but his eyes were cold. I closed my eyes and swallowed. *Acquit. Acquit. Acquit.*

With his swirling black robes and triple chins, the Honourable Mr. Justice "Acquit" DeWitt swept into the courtroom and resumed his position on the bench.

"Mr. Cranbury." Justice DeWitt glanced over his bifocals at Jules.

"My Lord." Jules nodded.

DeWitt turned to the jury. "Mr. Foreman, have you reached a verdict?"

A balding man, dressed in a plaid shirt and Levis, stood. "Yes, we have, My Lord."

Beatrice flipped back a page in her file and read from the Indictment the charge of second-degree murder.

I turned my attention to the foreman.

"Does the jury find the accused, Jules Cranbury, guilty, or not guilty?" Beatrice asked.

The foreman cleared his throat. A sheen broke out over his balding head, and he gripped the oak post at the end of the pony wall that separated the jurors from the rest of the courtroom.

Beatrice eyed him over her glasses.

I sucked in my breath and looked down at the handwritten notes and stacks of case law strewn on the desk. Come on. Spit it out.

The foreman cleared his throat again. "We, the jury, find Jules Cranbury—"

I glanced at Jules. His Adam's apple bobbed.

"—Not guilty, My Lord."

Cries of jubilation punctured by shrieks of blasphemy shattered the courtroom.

I closed my eyes and dropped my head forward.

I did it.

My body swayed.

I did it. Despite pressure from the Crown, the leading opposition party, women's advocate groups, and the media, *I did it*. Jules was a free man. A whooshing sound filled my ears, and I pressed my hand to my forehead.

"People. People," DeWitt bellowed, "settle down." DeWitt looked at me. His jaw muscles clenched and his eyes glared into my soul as he shook his head. He returned his gaze to the jury. "To the members of the jury, I thank you for your service and hard work on this difficult trial." DeWitt looked at Jules. "Mr. Cranbury?"

"Yes, My Lord."

"You have been found not guilty of the charge brought before this court." DeWitt frowned, he glanced at me, then looked back at Jules. "You are free to go."

Jules smiled. "Thank you, My Lord, and—" he looked at the jurors, "—thank you."

DeWitt pushed back his chair.

"Order in court," the Sheriff said once again.

Justice DeWitt marched down the steps. The door of his chambers slammed shut.

I collapsed in my chair. The courtroom erupted as spectators shuffled out. I propped my head up with my hands, trying to numb the throbbing.

A hand slapped my shoulders, and I jumped.

"Congratulations, Jade," said one legal counsel.

"Knew you could do it, Jade," said another.

I sat back, fanning my face with my notepad. I had to get out of there, away from the noise, the people, the legal ramifications that circled me like a bee ready to sting. I tossed my files into my briefcase, trying to block out the sound of Jules's voice, choking back the nausea that rose in my throat. I grabbed my *Criminal Code*, stood, and pushed my way through the spectators.

Jules stepped in front of me, his arms outstretched. "Jade."

"No." I shook my head. "Not now, Jules."

He wrapped his arms around me. "You did it, girl. You could always get me off."

He laughed as he mashed my face into the fabric of his double-breasted suit. I tried to breathe. The intoxicating spice of his cologne pierced my brain and spots flashed before my eyes. He had to let go. He whispered something in my ear, but I couldn't hear a thing. It was as if my head was under water.

I pressed my briefcase against his leg and pushed back. "Jules, no."

"Jade, you did it." He had the excited face I remembered from our wedding day. "You—"

"No." I pushed past him, squeezing between spectators. I needed air, space. I squeezed past another suit. Someone else patted me on the shoulder and then I looked up and from the corner of my eye spotted a dark image at the aisle seat of the last row.

I stopped.

His hair was darker and long. Clean-shaven, tall, piercing eyes. The same eyes which, after one or two gin and tonics, could melt any resolve, resulting in a morning-after tirade of "I should have known better," while slithering out of bed, clambering for my clothes that had been tossed the night before. My mind removed him from the courtroom and from the long black leather coat, black pants and black shirt he wore, and he stood before me, in front of the shelves in the campus bookstore, in blue jeans and a white shirt, telling me how all the books were catalogued. The young face of a handsome twenty-five-year old man melded with the mature man before me. A harder man tainted by the stresses of his work. Wide across the shoulders, he had spent his teenage years in a boxer's gym, so he could fight off his father's drunken blows and later fight off the blows of drug lords and gang leaders. He unhinged every nerve in my body.

Osmond.

He frowned.

I opened my mouth to say "Hello," but words tumbled like dominoes. I clutched at my confidence, which evaporated in thirty seconds. An elderly man and woman stepped into my view, giving me a few seconds to drape a fake calm over my body. I moved around the old couple, and caught a glimpse of the retreating black leather coat, its tails flapping before the swinging courtroom doors closed him out all together.

Someone bumped into me. I looked up.

Sergeant Stone, the lead investigator on Anna's murder. He scowled, then stepped past. Men and women moved around in slow motion, shimmering like heat waves rising up from streets in mid-August. I pressed trembling fingers to my cheek, my skin clammy and cold.

Osmond.

I had to get out of the courtroom. My mind unhinged from my body, I planted one foot in front of the other. My cell phone vibrated in my suit pocket. I stumbled down the aisle, banging against chairs. I barged through the courtroom doors, pulling out my cell.

I did it. The realization buzzed like my cell in my hand.

Osmond.

What the hell was he doing in my courtroom?

More spectators scattered from the gallery. Cold sweat prickled my face and dampened my armpits. I bumped along, ears ringing, the sound of Jules's voice cutting through my brain like a hangover gone wrong.

Buzz. Buzz.

My stomach heaved and a wave of nausea washed through my body. I barged through the crowd to the washroom. The rookie sheriff gasped at my rudeness. Spots flashed before my eyes. My stomach heaved again. I clenched my jaw and dropped my shoulder against the bathroom door and pushed.

Dirty white tiles and pale green walls blotted with dark splotches. Nausea swept through my body a second time. I lurched into a cubicle, banging against a door. My briefcase crashed onto the floor and my cell splashed into the toilet, flashing *new message*. My legs buckled and I fell to my knees. Clutching cold porcelain, I groaned as bile spewed out of my mouth.

The bitter taste of victory.

2

Aftermath

Your charade will last only so long, sweetheart, and then you'll be needing something stronger than Vicodin.

I SLAPPED MY CHEEKS.
Curdled milk.

I slapped them again, but my pale reflection in the mirror still didn't improve. I tucked my dark hair behind my ears. Feeling like a mop, I propped myself against the sink and splashed water on my face. I gasped at the ice coldness and fumbled for a sheet of paper towel. My skin looked as white as my white streaks. I thought I had overcome this nervous reaction from childhood—vomiting when stressed. Obviously, Jules's case had restored every ugly insecurity.

I filled a paper cup with water and rinsed my mouth. Jules's case. So bloody much riding on it. His career. My career. If I had lost, I would have lost everything. A partnership would have been the least of my concerns. No doubt, Jules would have sued me, and with much publicity, placed blame on my misrepresentation. New counsel would have been hired to conduct his appeal. Aubischon, Thyme and Bastine would have offered me a nice settlement to quietly disappear, and no other law firm in Victoria, or Vancouver, for that matter, would want anything to do with me.

I leaned over the sink and spat. I rinsed my mouth a second time. I had made it through this trial with my reputation and law practice still intact. My cell phone—not so lucky.

I spat again, scrunched up the paper cup and tossed it in the garbage. I tugged on the buttons of my robe, and a shroud of black material slipped from my shoulders, taking with it the stress of the last six months. My black bolero-style jacket and skirt, which also made up the court attire, hadn't been soiled by my mishap, not the same with my tabs, which I removed from around my neck and dropped on my robe. I dug through the pockets of my jacket and found a half roll of Tums and a small container of Vicodin. Perfect. I tossed one of each into my mouth and that's when I noticed *her* in the mirror.

I spun around. The roll of Tums flew from my hand. The bathroom stalls tilted and slid. A humming in my ears, I closed my eyes and clutched the sink. *No. Not again.* The humming subsided. I opened my eyes.

She was gone.

Damn it! I slammed my palm on the basin. I hated this. On shaky heels, I wobbled across the floor. I stood in her spot, rubbed my arms and shivered. I eyed the perimeter of the washroom—sinks, drains, mirrors and a tampon machine. Yet *she* had been here, wearing her pink rhinestone bodysuit—the clothes she had died in.

The first time I saw Anna's ghost was the day Jules entered his not guilty plea. She sat on the corner of his Lordship's bench in her burlesque costume—a sparkling pink bodysuit embroidered with rhinestones and a pink boa draped over her shoulders. The left side of her face was a bloody pulp from where the bullet had taken fragments of bone as it exited her skull. I had nearly fainted, and during the break I suggested to Jules that he obtain new counsel. I was not up to the task. Jules laughed off my fears. As the months passed, I stumbled through fixed dates, trial confirmation hearings, and pre-trial conferences with no sign of

Anna. It wasn't until I fixed the Supreme Court trial date that she reappeared, this time sitting in the prisoner's box beside Jules, sipping a martini and wearing the same sparkling bodysuit. It seemed Anna was hanging with a new crowd.

I grabbed my briefcase and gathered up my gown. I threw back one more Vicodin before dashing out of the washroom.

Successful partners did not see ghosts. Successful partners did not hallucinate unless they indulged in copious amounts of alcohol. I squeezed between lawyers and court clerks, sidestepping skinheads and hookers. I raced through the metal detector, tripping the alarm, but I ignored the sheriffs' shouts and pushed through the glass courthouse doors.

A cold wind hit me straight on as I lurched down the steps. My papers flapped and my hair swept back from my face. I dashed across the street, trying to blend with the other suits clutching briefcases. A semi-truck roared past. Mud splashed from a puddle onto my legs and skirt. I gritted my teeth and flipped my hair over my shoulder.

"Spare change?"

A street person stood, leaning one hand on a cane, while the gnarled fingers of his other hand held out a tattered hat. Grey stubble grew on his tarnished skin. Behind cracked glasses, vacant eyes reflected a vacant soul.

"Spare change?"

I fished out a coin and went to toss it.

"He didn't do it."

I stared. "Excuse me?"

The man shook his hat.

"He didn't do what?" I repeated.

"Spare change."

The hat trembled and the man teetered. I became aware of his bony frame protruding through his dark coat. I dropped the coin into his hat and marched down the street. Everyone had been swept up with Jules's case. I made it a habit to disregard the tweets about the case. The tweets about me were not that easy to ignore.

I passed St. Peter's Cathedral with its sandstone archways and steeples, one of the many Gothic structures that decorated Victoria's streets. I marched across the cobblestone courtyard to the office and looked up at the trees' swaying crooked branches and pink candy-tuft blossoms. Spring was determined to come early. I caught my reflection in the glass building. The gold letters that spelled Aubischon, Thyme and Bastine were printed like a scrolling marquee across the glass. Hopefully, my name would soon replace Bastine's. At 33, I would be the firm's youngest female to make partner.

Norman Bastine had defended the most notorious of criminals. A skinny and unassuming man, he'd hidden his incredible mind behind a façade of John Lennon glasses, wrinkled suits and bow-ties. Living life by instinct and a bottle of vodka, he'd never write much on paper. What little he had written was incomprehensible. He'd spend hours staring at the walls of his office, thinking out entire legal arguments. Many times I had spotted him tapping his temple, a gesture, I guessed, to make sure everything fit in.

But whether it was the booze or his own demons, Norman had disappeared twenty-four hours after his biker client had been found not guilty of murder.

I walked through the glass carousel doors to the bank of shiny elevators. One opened and I hustled in. I dropped my briefcase and pressed fifteen.

I won. My losing streak was over. A partnership within my grasp. For once I'd be recognized for my name and work, not my father's. He had a knack for attracting attention.

The elevator pinged and the doors opened. I scooped up my briefcase. The firm's name was etched in the two glass doors leading into the office. Internationally known, the firm had offices in Hong Kong, Toronto, Vancouver, Sydney and Seattle. When Jules sauntered into my office, the partners took notice.

I pulled open the door to find our receptionist speaking Mandarin to a suited man at the counter. An Asian woman sank into one of the leather sofas, her small frame reminded me of a bird.

I trudged past three wooden desks, where secretaries sat, their fingers dancing over their keyboards. I passed off their congratulations with a wave. Loud voices and laughter rang out from the conference room at the end of the hall, and I saw a camera flash.

"Mayor Cranbury, can you comment on—"

One of a handful of reporters, no doubt, and Jules was buying them off with champagne. The buzz of a blender broke the hum of printers and the ringing of telephones. There was another flash, then high-pitched squeals. I ducked into a back office.

Kate, my secretary, a short-haired platinum blonde, crouched underneath her desk. Shoes kicked off, the telephone receiver pressed against her ear, she brandished a screwdriver as if it were a weapon. She roughed up the back of her hard drive.

"I don't give a rat's ass what's wrong with the server! Put me on the other server."

I bit back a smile. Kate had once told me while she manipulated my frozen computer that I was a virus! If Kate was at her wits' end, something had to be wrong. I pressed my briefcase against my body, grappled for the doorknob and banged into my office. I kicked the door closed, shutting out the sound of success and jubilation.

Jules's case was over.

My briefcase tumbled to the floor and I dropped my robe. I'd won. I rested my elbows on the back of a blue velvet chair. So why the hell didn't I feel like celebrating?

Because Anna's murderer still walked free.

I grabbed a bottled water from my mini-refrigerator and walked over to the window. A red and white seaplane bobbed in the harbour. I twisted the cap off the bottle and took a swallow.

Osmond. What was he doing in my courtroom? His ancestors dated back to the Hungarian throne and were rocked with scandal, although one would never guess it talking with the man. He had a quiet understated strength. At university, he had been an outcast, scorned by the rich male jocks who played on the various teams. His rebel attitude had attracted a flock of young female students, including myself.

The rumbling of a seaplane's engine seared through my thoughts. I took another swig of my water. Maybe the time had come to stop defending hookers, impaired police officers and crooked politicians. In a city known as The Bermuda Triangle of the criminal justice system where everything from files, guilty pleas, witnesses and accused mysteriously disappeared—and now dead victims reappeared—maybe the time had finally come for me to—

A sharp knock at my door made me jump, spilling water on the hardwood. "Damn."

My door swung open and crashed against the doorstop. "Hey, baby." Jules stood, a lecherous smile on his face, his teeth clamped around a cigar. He held out a champagne bottle. "How's my girl?"

Kate burst in after him, still wielding the screwdriver. "I tried to stop him, Jade." She jammed one fist on her hip and pointed the screwdriver in Jules's direction. "But he wouldn't listen!"

"It's okay, Kate. Thank you."

Kate glared at Jules, then turned, slamming the door behind her.

"She's a tight ass," he grumbled, stepping around my briefcase and robe.

"Show my staff some respect," I said, walking over to my desk and ripping a tissue from the box. I kneeled and wiped up the water. "What do you want, Jules?"

"I've got champagne, Jade." He placed the bottle on my desk. "Or did having a good time get beaten out of you in law school?" He dropped into the other blue velvet chair, his legs sprawled in front of him.

A good time? With Jules? "The media are here for you, Jules, not me. You're the star. The one up for re-election."

"You saved my ass, Jade, granted it's not as nice as yours."

I spun around.

Jules puffed on his cigar, a slimy smile on his face. He hadn't always been like this, or maybe when I had been an inexperienced twenty-year-old, I had mistaken his arrogance for confidence.

"Come on, Jade." He gripped his cigar between two fingers. "You're my girl. Always have been. I want you out there. Rejoicing in my victory."

His victory. "I'm not your girl, Jules. I never was your girl." I stepped toward my desk and tossed the wet tissue in the waste paper basket. "If you don't have anything further to discuss, you'll excuse me—" I sat in my leather chair and reached for my telephone "—I have to get a new cell phone from IT."

Jules, his blue eyes cold, reached across and grabbed my wrist. A dark curl slipped over his forehead, and his breath smelled of alcohol and his Cuban cigar. I thought of pirates and the rumours that he had been involved with insider trading.

"Don't—" he tightened his grip, pinching my skin "—brush me off."

My wrist tingled.

"We go back too fucking far, Jade."

I looked at his hand gripping my wrist—the gaudy signet ring hinting at its owner.

"Let go."

He stared at me and I stared back. A muscle twitched in his cheek.

"Win yourself an election." I tugged my wrist from his grip. "This is your spotlight." I leaned back in the chair. "Time to reap the rewards."

He sat back and puffed on his cigar. "Why did you do it?"

"Do what?"

"Defend me."

I leaned forward in my chair and tapped my water bottle on the blotter. "What does it matter? We won."

"I'll invite in the press and they can ask you."

I rolled my eyes and swivelled around so I looked out the window instead of at him. The harbour with its buoys, sailing ships and yachts being batted around in the wind wasn't quite postcard perfect. "I believed you were innocent."

"And."

I turned and looked at him "I was also offered a partnership if I won."

He leaned forward, resting his elbows on his knees, a slick smile on his face. "Work for me again."

I stopped tapping the water bottle. "Excuse me?"

"I'll employ you. Double your salary. Bonuses. Extended vacations. Get you that Honda 500 Rebel motorcycle you've always wanted. But work for me."

I stared. What trouble had he gotten himself into? "I ride a Triumph Bonneville now."

"Oh. I can take care of you. Come on, Jade, or is there more at stake?"

I picked up a file. "I don't need taking care of."

Jules sat back, a slow satisfied smile crept across his face. For some reason I felt like a canary and Jules the cat had just swallowed me whole. "Still wearing the blinders, Jade? Believing the office mission statement?"

"Now you're just pissing me off."

He snickered, then stood and walked over to the window. "When was the last time you talked to Pappy?"

I gnawed on the inside of my cheek and looked over at my law diploma that hung beside a large picture of my father and me dressed in our robes. Jules loved drama. He couldn't get right to the point. He enjoyed watching people squirm. "Two, three years ago."

"You work in the same frigging company and you—"

"—He's retired. Hardly ever shows up. Too busy lecturing."

Jules leaned against the window. "So you don't know?"

Don't take the bait. "Know what?"

He puffed on his cigar. "Ever wonder why those male university students came to your house?"

I shuffled files together. "Jules, my father is a law professor.

Students always came by. Now you'll have to leave. I have work to do." I grabbed a pen.

He stepped away from the window and in two long strides stood before my desk, his palms pressed flat against its surface. "Your Pollyanna charade will last only so long, sweetheart, and then you'll be needing something stronger than Vicodin. You know that in this office, in this legal community, there is more going on behind those Q.C. appointments. The shit's going to hit the fan, and when it happens, you don't want to be buried with these cocksuckers. *Work for me.*"

Some days I swear Jules did not play with a full deck. I leaned back in my chair. "What are you up to?"

Jules straightened and tugged at his shirtsleeves. "The bastards thought they'd shut me up, stick me with a murder charge. Surprised they didn't string me up, but then again they didn't anticipate I'd go to you."

"I defended you because I believed in your innocence."

"They thought you would lose. Did you know that? Brilliant move you electing trial by judge and jury. I applaud your change of venue application, even if we didn't get it. Your famous law partner, Mr. Keith Aubischon. I bet he's pissing his pants right now, because I'm in here talking to—"

I stood. "—Get out!"

"You're not safe here."

"And you sound paranoid. Out!" My hand trembled as I pointed to the door. Keep it together. Do not throw my *Criminal Code* at him.

Jules took a slow drag of his cigar. "No more secrets, Jade." Smoke billowed from his nostrils.

I pointed again.

He strolled toward the door. "Anna found out about them. What they did to Norman, and they blew her brains out. That doesn't bother you?"

I swallowed.

"Sure as hell bothers me, but unlike you—" he pointed the

cigar "—I'm going to do something about it."

The pen shot out from my fingertips.

Jules opened the door. "Have fun at the courthouse centennial tonight. I'll talk to you later at Aubischon's after party. Around 8:30, his study. I have a thumb drive. You need to see what's on it."

3

Punishment

Eyes frantic and unfocused, she leaned against the door, flattening a bloody hand against the door jamb.

IN THE BUZZING warm air of James Aubischon's living room, I squeezed past two men in black suits, who with greasy smiles blatantly sized me up. I reined in my irritation and told myself not to stomp on their feet with my spiked heels. They were not worth wrecking my Jimmy Choos. I stepped over to the bar where wine glasses were stacked like a pyramid.

"A bohemian, please." I was in the mood for a pretty pink cocktail to match my pretty pink dress.

The bartender nodded and brought up a martini glass from under the bar. Perspiration gleamed on his face. The collar of his shirt cut into his neck, and it looked as if his head would pop off like a cartoon character.

I watched as men in designer suits and women in cocktail dresses wedged beside each other at the multi-tiered buffet table, all reaching for the scallops wrapped in bacon. Another wave of lawyers swarmed around the dessert table, balancing their wine glasses with meaningful conversation. One guy I recognized from my days doing kiddy court pushed in beside me.

"Eh, a Molson's." With no hair except for the fuzzy growth on his chin, he turned and smiled.

I moved over to make room for him.

"Bohemian." The bartender passed me my cocktail.

"Thank you." Drink in hand, I slipped away from the suit with the chin stain and stepped past the circle of legal assistants surrounding Troy Reilly. Troy, the ink still wet on his law diploma, had impressed the partners at Aubischon, Thyme and Bastine with back-to-back wins on three high-profile fraud cases. A genius in court, this California surfer softened the most brittle of trial coördinators. I figured he would make partner before I did.

I stepped around the other side of the buffet table and plucked a shrimp-filled mushroom cap from a silver platter. I pressed between two legal secretaries who ogled Troy.

The centennial photo session had taken longer than anticipated. I had stood in front of the one-hundred-year-old courthouse with my fellow colleagues, a fixed smile on my face and chattering teeth. I waited, as did four hundred other lawyers, for the photographer, who stood in a white bucket at the end of a crane, to stop playing with his camera lens and take our picture. While I stood in the tenth row—my face would be the size of a pinhead—Jules had stood in the first, laughing and joking with the Supreme Court Justices. The boys from the old school liked him because of his grandfather's reputation—an opium smuggler in Victoria's early days. The new school of lawyers liked him because of his wealth and power, and before he became Mayor, he was an excellent defence lawyer.

After the picture taking and paying homage to the beautiful courthouse dedicated to the brutalities of mankind, Victoria's legal community disbanded for drinks and good food at James's home. I caught a glimpse of Jules making his way to James's Mercedes and tried to wave him down, but a sea of black robes had sucked him in.

I picked up a plate and cloth napkin and from a passing waiter's tray snatched a deep-fried oyster covered in Brie. I took a sip of my bohemian and squeezed my way among more bodies.

The strong scent of expensive perfumes and colognes mingling with the heat caused a thud in my head. I meandered through the French doors and stepped out onto the stone deck with its multitude of pots and shrubbery. I drank a mouthful of my drink, trying to dull my anxiety, then walked over to the rock in the stone wall that looked like a map of Australia. I stood in that spot and gazed over the kidney-shaped pool. It had been a few months since I last stood here. Would she even show? Or had my mother given up hope of ever seeing me? I was a fool to think this could happen again. I took another sip and leaned my forearms against the wall. I glanced at my watch. I should be meeting with Jules, not trying to conjure up images of my dead mother. I seriously needed a shrink. I glanced at the pool. The water glittered and the lazy lapping soothed my raw nerves. The orchestra under the blue striped canopy in the corner struck up a seductive rendition of Gershwin's *Rhapsody in Blue*. The romantic notes stirred the shadows in my soul. A breeze brushed my shoulder and as the violin section played the glissando, the water bubbled into foam. Instead of a swamp monster, my mother's ghost, violin tucked under her chin, rose from the deep end of the pool.

My cocktail glass trembled. I watched my mother, eyes closed, a beautiful smile, the bow of her violin gliding across the strings. An accomplished violinist, she had given up her career when I was born.

It had been six months since her passing, but still, words could not explain my loss. There were tears. Often. It was the hollowness. I was present, doing my morning routine, running, but I was emotionally gutted, and what was left was raw. I don't know what beat in my chest, because my heart had been taken when my mother breathed her last breath. Besides these ghostly visions, she visited me in my dreams. The first dream she had been well-dressed, playing her violin and I had said, "Welcome back." Then I woke. Sad, and gutted again, I had wiped my tears with my palms and for a moment thought *take me with you.*

I shook my head, clearing the memory but also losing the

vision of my mother. No. Come back.

Water drops sprayed against my skin. I touched my cheek. The water glittered in the pool and a circle rippled over its surface and spread to the outer edges. *You don't know how much I miss you.*

I looked at my glass. I had tried to avoid the Aubischon residence like the dreaded stirrups on a doctor's examining table. Mom had died here. I was angry that no one could save her and I wanted to kick the crap out of James's leather-upholstered seats.

"Jade Thyme."

Jesus. I closed my eyes and swallowed.

"Jade."

I stood, clearing my throat. I took another gulp of my bohemian. The lights around the swimming pool blurred.

"Jade. How the hell are you?"

Crown prosecutor Bianca Taylor leaned a hip against the stone wall. She was wearing her famous red suit which accented every curve, and caused young male articling students to drool. She tossed a mane of blonde hair over her shoulder as she stirred her Caesar with a celery stalk. "God, you look like shit."

I dabbed the corners of my eyes. "Thank you." I cleared my throat. "Just trying to get over a little burn out."

"More likely getting over working with Jules."

The blunt truth, as always, coming from Bianca. It was her blunt truth that landed her in trouble a number of times with the Law Society. This month a disgruntled witness had filed a complaint about her bullying him on the stand.

"So—" Bianca crossed her arms before her "—do you think the trial killed or boosted his chances of getting a second term in office?"

"What do you think?" I said, my voice laced with sarcasm.

Bianca's seductive smile slipped across candy-apple lips. "With you defending him, honey, say hello to another term." She bit the end of the celery stalk. "I was shocked that you took the case," she said between noisy bites. "You didn't strike me as the type to put up with his cesspool attitude. At least, you didn't before."

I rubbed the skin between my eyes. "And ditch a possible partnership and an exceedingly gross amount of money? Remember—" I clinked my glass against hers "—I'm a lawyer."

Bianca dropped her head back and laughed. A few suits standing around the pool looked at her, shook their heads then resumed their conversations.

"It's your fault that I defended him," I said.

"My fault!"

"If I hadn't been house-sitting for you while you soaked up the sun in Mexico, Jules wouldn't have seen me weeding your front garden. Do you know how many times I've said, 'if!'"

Bianca smiled. "You could have said no. Is it true? James, Keith's dad, sunk a whole lot of money into Jules's re-election campaign?" She chomped on the celery stalk.

"You're not supposed to know that."

"Hell, everyone knows."

I leaned my forearms on the stone wall. A woman in a dark sequined dress squealed and fell into the pool. The man who stood beside her also fell in. It was as if an invisible hand had pushed him from behind. I shuddered and wondered if my mother was still here working the party.

"A lot of partners backed him. Then I stepped in and cleaned up his mess, so it didn't look as if they were backing a criminal."

Bianca finished the last of her celery. "Damn shame what happened. Anna couldn't hurt a fly."

No, she just scared the hell out of opposing counsel.

"Doesn't look good on the Crown. We're supposed to uphold and enforce the law. Jules going free doesn't help the cause, or put the Criminal Justice Branch in good light. Guarantee you the Deputy will be calling." She pulled out a pack of cigarettes from an inside breast pocket. "Speaking of which, where is our man of the hour? Bonking the hired help?"

"Actually—" I glanced at my watch "—damn. I was supposed to meet him a half hour ago."

"Sounds like trouble," Bianca said, as she placed a cigarette between her lips. She fished out a lighter from her inner coat pocket.

"He's offering me a job," I said, turning around and trying to spot him in the crowd.

Bianca flicked her lighter. "More trouble." She tilted her head and blew a stream of smoke.

"I'm not representing him."

Bianca looked at me, one eyebrow arched. "Keep telling yourself that. You'll be his fix-it in a skirt."

I frowned and looked at my drink.

"Honey, defence lawyers cater to the scum of the earth. Your clients are too stupid to not get caught. That's how you make a living, Jade. But in Jules's case, your mandate is more damage control and slopping up the garbage left behind. Not an easy task and worth every God damn cent the jerk gives you."

I swirled the gin in my glass. Ever since I had left the prosecutor's office, Bianca never missed an opportunity to take a jab. Having gone through law school together, I had at first found Bianca's coarse and abrupt demeanour offensive. While I spent my free time going to the theatre and jazz clubs, eating steak and prawns and doing the appropriate things expected of a rich man's daughter, Bianca had waited on tables to fund her university education. I didn't worry about books, tuition fees or a car. My father just scribbled out another cheque much like he scribbled out his love.

While in law school, Bianca had acquired the nickname of "Bianca the Bitch", a name she still lived up to in court. Women and men were intimidated by her, so they labelled her. Five foot six and one hundred and twenty pounds, she could drink the boys under the table on wing night and still be able to drag her skinny butt into the office the next morning. Bottle-blonde hair and six thousand dollars breasts—care of an illicit affair with an L.A. surgeon—Bianca coughed like a seal, stunk of cigarettes, and threw files across her office. Many of the higher echelon frowned upon my association with her.

"It's crazy," I said, shaking my head. "My making partner hinged on whether I got Jules off. Forget that I negotiated the settlement during the airline strike, or that I negotiated the merger between Cranbury Plastics and Johnson Plastics. My success hinges on him. What is so important about him? Some days I think I'd be better off in Disneyland, dressed as Snow White, waving to the kids."

"No," Bianca said, blowing another stream of smoke. "Walt, or his successor—" she waved the hand holding the cigarette "—would give you a pooper-scooper and tell you to scoop up Mickey's shit."

I stared at her for a moment, then burst out laughing.

Bianca laughed too then broke into a coughing fit. She pounded her fist against her chest, and once she stopped, inhaled from her cigarette. "Have you heard the latest gossip about Olive Aubischon?"

"No."

"Olive chucked Jules's ten-thousand-dollar engagement ring into his Wheaties this morning."

"Olive's calling off the wedding? But Jules was found not guilty."

"My sources haven't been able to confirm, but it looks like Olive saw a sex-text from Troy on Jules's cell phone."

"Seriously?"

"That's what I've heard." Bianca leaned back against the stone wall.

"Jules is onto something. He mentioned Norman Bastine to me."

Bianca quickly looked at me. "What did he say about him?"

"Not much, but that Anna had found out what they had done to him. Whoever *they* are. He insinuated—"

"—What?"

"Nothing. You know Jules, all cloak and daggers. He wants to meet me."

Bianca took a long drag of her cigarette. "You did your part, Jade. Don't get sucked in by him. Accept the partnership, keep your nose clean and stay away—"

"Taylor!"

Bianca and I jumped and at that moment the first firecracker went off. The party-goers oohed and ahhed. Some ladies clapped. We turned.

Keith Aubischon's father, James, lurched upon us, dragging one leg behind as if it were attached to a ball and chain. His robes long gone, and his shirtsleeves rolled to his elbows, his tie swung like a pendulum. His name, along with my father's, Charles Thyme, pulled in clients from all over Canada, and certainly, having *MacLean's* magazine tout him as one of the top ten lawyers in the country hadn't hindered his, or the firm's, success. But right now, his aura seemed as sloppy as his untucked shirttails.

Bianca straightened. "Hello, James."

He placed an arm around her shoulders and leaned into her cleavage. "T-T-Taylor, with those titssh, you'll make it to the Supreme Court bench."

Bianca's eyes bulged from their sockets. Anger flashed across her face and she opened her mouth—

"James!" I jumped in, trying to save my friend from saying something that would get her in trouble, although James was being the letch.

"Yessh, Jade," he said, stealing his eyes away from Bianca's breasts.

Bianca slid me a lethal glare as more fireworks screeched into the air.

"Have you heard anything more about Norman Bastine?" I asked him.

James's eye twitched. He slugged back a mouthful of his drink, wiping his mouth with his forearm. He leaned into Bianca, forcing her to place her hand against the rock wall.

His head lolled in my direction. "He alive?"

"Jules had—"

"Jules. Conniving shon-of-a-bitch."

Several more fireworks exploded, lighting up the sky with star bursts of pink and purple.

"Not the thing to sh-sh-shay to Crown prosecutor Bianca Taylor." He squeezed her shoulders.

"James—" I reached for his drink.

James pulled his hand away, slopping alcohol onto the patio. "Hey. D-drunkenness as a defence. And you, Madame prosecutor—" he spoke to Bianca's breasts "—can't do a damn thing about it. Jade—" he pointed the hand holding his glass "—defend me. Sh-she got that prick off."

"Come on, James." Bianca tried to pry his glass from his hand.

"God damn cocksucker!"

A half dozen fireworks illuminated the sky in bursting colours.

I put an arm around James's shoulder, trying to usher him away from the people and the pool before he made a greater fool of himself. Where the hell was Keith? He could deal with his drunk father.

"How could you marry him, Jade?" James asked, leaning on me, causing me to step to the side in order to keep my balance. "His dick?"

Not likely. "Come on, James." I stepped away from the stone wall.

"I, I sh-should have killed the f-f-fucker when—"

A scream shattered the evening. Bianca and I, with James in between us, bumped into the glass table.

"Olive," James belched. With unexpected strength, he lurched out of our grasp, lost his balance and fell. He grabbed Bianca's arm, pulling her down on top of him and they both crashed through the table, sending glass shards everywhere.

Olive Aubischon burst through the French doors, dark hair hanging in messy strands, one strap of her white sequin dress hung from her shoulder. Eyes frantic and unfocused, she leaned against the door, flattening a bloody hand against the door jamb.

"He's dead."

I dropped my martini glass.
"Jules—is—dead."

4

Crime Scene

In their uniforms they swept over the scene like an ant invasion, contrasting with the glitz of gowns and tuxedos.

NEVER DISTURB THE scene of a crime. Never. A reasonable person calls 9-1-1, but lately, I had fallen a little short in that department.

I blasted past James and Bianca sprawled on the deck, and I dodged Olive, who hung like a rag doll over Troy's arm. My heels scraped the hardwood of the long formal hall as I made a sharp turn and barged into the study.

Silence.

I took a step, eyeing the floor, steeling myself for the sight of Jules's bloodied body. I stepped around the Persian carpet—nothing—no bloodstains, no trail of blood, not even a flipped over rug corner. The old-fashioned oak desk and antique leather armchair stood undisturbed and the globe in the corner slowly stopped spinning. Someone had knocked over a glass on the corner table beside the sofa. It lay on its side, water and ice soaking into the cherry wood. An ashtray lay upended, cigarette butts and ash dusting the hardwood. Something had happened.

But still, no *body*.

Where was he?

The room didn't smell of gunpowder, or released bowels which occurs when a person dies. Instead, I smelled *shellfish*.

I turned. At the far table: crystal plates displayed tortes and cream-filled cakes; cups stacked beside coffee and tea urns; behind me the white damask covered buffet table with ornate silver platters of roast beef, lamb and squab. In the centre, arranged amongst the shrimp and calamari, sat Jules's severed head. His glazed eyes stared at me from a tangled nest of prawns' whiskers, mussels and lobster claws.

I screamed.

Stumbling back, I crashed into the side table, knocking a lamp over. My legs buckled and I fell. With horror I flung a dangling lampshade from my wrist. My nails scraped the floor; unable to crawl away fast enough, I faceplanted into the hardwood. I pushed myself up and saw blood. I groaned, my eyes rolled and my body convulsed.

The second time that day I threw up.

"Holy shit!"

Back arched, hands pressed against the floor, and arms ramrod straight. I braced myself as another wave of nausea seized me and I threw up again.

"Jesus, Jade."

I rubbed my coat sleeve across my mouth. Blood.

Strong hands clamped my shoulders, hauled me to my feet and spun me around. Jules's head with torn flesh flashed before my eyes. "No!" I screamed, batting my hands at the image.

"Jade. Jade. It's me. Keith." He shook me.

Keith.

As I gazed at him, his dark eyes and strong features came into focus.

Keith. Law partner. James's son.

My knees gave out. He grabbed me and flung one arm over his shoulder. My legs dangled as he dragged me away from the buffet table. "Have to get you out of here."

I pressed my face into his shoulder and squeezed my eyes shut, scared of seeing Jules's eyes and what was left. Sirens rang in my ears. I squinted over Keith's shoulder and through the window saw the flashing red and blue lights of police cars.

Code three.

D.O.A.

Jules.

I sobbed and whispered, "No."

"It'll be okay," Keith grunted, hauling me around a corner. "I can't have you found at the murder scene."

I gazed at Keith, breathing vomit breath in his face. His dark eyes stared back—so much worry. He'd help me get out of this mess.

He looked away and dragged me through a stone archway that led into a large stainless steel kitchen. Three chefs in tall white hats mused over a cookbook. All three looked up and their mouths dropped open. Keith shouted orders—something about water and a towel.

He deposited me in a chair, then kneeled and placed both hands on my shoulders.

"Don't say a word."

I nodded.

"To anybody. Don't talk to the cops. *Any one.*"

I nodded again.

A chef placed a glass of water on the table. Keith reached for it and cradled it in my hands. "Drink this." He pushed the glass at me.

I slurped. The cold water iced my nerves. I shakily put the glass back on the table and saw blood on the rim. Jules's blood?

"No!" I swiped my hands across my mouth.

"Jade." Keith grabbed my wrists. "It's your blood. You bit your tongue. Where's that towel?" he shouted.

I swallowed, wincing at the bitter taste of blood and the pain in my mouth.

"I've got cops pounding on my door, Jade. Stay here. Don't move, don't say a word."

"Okay," I whispered, my voice sounding far away, not my own.

Keith gave my shoulder a squeeze, then brushed my hair back from my face. "Remember, not a word. I'll be right back." His knees cracked as he stood and left the kitchen.

With trembling hands I brought the glass of water to my lips again, trying to wash away bile and despair. Cold water dribbled down my chin and onto my pants.

A fourth chef tossed a washcloth onto the table. I pressed the washcloth to my mouth, then pulled it away. Blood smears. So much of it. Dear God, *Jules*. What had happened? Why had it happened? I was supposed to meet him.

Outside, the Victoria Police Department and the RCMP were already gathering and herding witnesses. They swept over the scene like an ant invasion, contrasting with the glitz of gowns and tuxedos.

Despite what Keith had said, I had to explain. They'll think I'm hiding. I dropped the cloth and jumped up when a firm hand on my shoulder pushed me back down.

"Where you going, Thyme?"

I opened my mouth but couldn't speak.

I heard loud steps circle the table and glimpsed a grey tweed jacket with matching grey slacks. The man pulled out a chair, propped his foot on it and leaned forward. "We meet again."

Sergeant Stone. Of all the men on the homicide unit, why him? Who had tipped him off?

His gaze shifted from me to the chefs. "You people follow Constable Green."

That would be the young officer standing in the doorway. Chef hats were flung on the counter, and I heard grumbles in broken English about roasting chickens and rising egg whites. They had no clue about Jules's murder.

The Sergeant tapped his notebook on his knee as he waited. "Goddamn refugees," he grumbled.

I dabbed my mouth. *Bigot.*

"I thought criminal lawyers had tougher stomachs, Thyme.

You should know better than to barge onto a crime scene." He tossed his notebook on the table.

I looked down and swallowed, trying to will the nausea back down my throat.

"Is destroying evidence how you get your clients off?"

I picked up the water glass and took a few gulps. I put the glass down and swiped at my cheeks. My skin was sore and tender around my eyes.

"That's—" I swallowed "—m-m-my ex-husband."

Stone's mouth twitched. "I know that's your ex." He looked over at the counter cluttered with lobster, clams, mussels, prawns. He reached over and snatched a prawn, biting into the fleshy meat. My stomach lurched. I swallowed once, then twice. Stone discarded the shell on the table. "A dead ex. He looks like a mutant sea urchin." He licked his fingers.

I gagged and pressed my hand over my mouth.

He reached for another prawn. "Unfortunately it's my job to find the person who killed him, and you just made that much more difficult by contaminating the crime scene, unless you did it."

Clamminess settled on my skin and soaked into my dress. I shivered and hugged myself. "What do you want? I should be outside with them." I nodded toward the French doors overlooking the pool and beleaguered guests.

Sergeant Stone grabbed a napkin and wiped his fingers and mouth. "Why aren't you? Why were you in the study, Jade?"

Don't talk to the cops. Keith's words echoed. "I want a lawyer."

"You are a lawyer. You do something wrong, Jade?"

"I'm not talking to you."

"You're not? Well you have no goddamn choice. Your blood and vomit is on the floor. What the hell were you doing in there? Did Jules take a swipe at you, counsellor? Is that why you have—" he pointed with his pen at the bloody washcloth on the table "—that?"

I glanced at the washcloth. "I bit my lip."

The Sergeant smiled. "Really." He picked up his notebook and flipped it open. "Two m's in Thyme or one?"

I remained silent.

"Fine," Stone mumbled. "Home address and telephone number?"

I looked over at the kitchen island with its silver trays of lobster and crab, and remembered how Jules's face had stared back at me. I looked back at the table. "I want a lawyer."

"Did Jules refuse to pay his account, Thyme? Is that why you were in there? Settling your account?"

I leaned forward and grabbed the water glass, but it was empty. I slammed the glass down on the table. Where the hell was Keith? I should leave. Get up and walk out, but my legs felt weak and I feared that Sergeant Stone wouldn't hesitate to slap on some cuffs and charge me with obstruction. Cooperate. I had done nothing wrong.

Stone leaned closer, his breath reeked of prawns and cigarettes. "Or did you walk in on Jules screwing the party planner?"

I pressed my hand against my forehead. He was trying to bait me, and I knew it. But it was working. "We've been divorced for three years."

"So? You still could have ordered the hit."

I stared. "I didn't kill him!"

"But you definitely checked to make sure he was dead."

I opened my mouth then quickly shut it, biting my tongue again. I winced and swallowed fresh blood.

"You were the closest person to Jules and—"

The Sergeant's cell phone rang. "Shit." He unclipped the phone from his belt and flipped it open. "Stone."

Whatever the conversation, it was bad for Stone. He closed his eyes, pinched the skin between his eyebrows, and turned his back.

"That's because all the judges are at the crime scene!" He walked over to the counter. "Bring the warrant down here, and I'll get one to sign it, or get me a telewarrant." He walked toward me. "I don't care. Wake up one of those snotty-nosed justices. I have Jules Cranbury's head on a silver platter. I want the rest of his damn body! I want a warrant!" He tucked his notebook under his arm and picked up a stuffed mushroom cap and popped it into his mouth. "Yes!" he shouted, mushroom bits sprayed from his mouth. "Now!" He pressed a button, tapped his flip phone against his bald head then clipped the phone back onto his belt loop.

"Good luck," I said.

Stone stopped chewing.

"There's no way in hell you're going to get a warrant to search this place."

The complexity of what he was involved in seemed to have finally hit him. "I have a dead mayor. I'm getting a warrant."

The phone call had given me a chance to regroup. I sat back in the chair, my confidence slowly returning. "You think a judge is going to sign a search warrant so your men can search the residence of The Honourable James Aubischon? Get real, Sergeant."

"These assholes have something to hide, Jade? Or do you?"

I looked at the discarded prawn tails on the table. I had nothing to hide, but Stone wouldn't believe me. He itched to stick me with a murder rap. Hell, he'd hoist me up. Jules's death had slotted me into the role of witness, or worse yet, suspect. My actions and conversations would be recorded and later probed, analyzed and manipulated in a court of law. I knew the game. I played it every day.

I closed my eyes, trying to block out the image of Jules. He would be reduced to autopsy and crime scene photos in a police exhibit book. A dozen close up pictures would show the stump of his neck. I placed my hand over my mouth. The torn flesh.

Why hadn't anyone heard his screams? Dear God, Jules.

"Look, Thyme, I know you're tired and want to get out of here. A little cooperation is all I'm asking. Someone put Jules Cranbury's head on that table, and I know it wasn't you. Help me and we can put the sick bastard who did this behind bars."

"Don't say a word, Jade."

Keith stepped up to the table.

Stone removed his foot from the chair. "Jesus Christ! Who the hell are you?"

"Keith Aubischon. Ms. Thyme's lawyer. Are you questioning my client, Sergeant Stone?"

"She's your client? Then that would make me Frank Sinatra."

"Is she a suspect?"

Stone's mouth twitched again.

"Has she been chartered and warned?"

"No," I replied.

Stone tapped his notebook against his knee. He glowered at Keith.

"Sergeant, I'm tired of your harassment and witness bullying. My father has friends on the force."

"I have friends too, Aubischon. Don't threaten me."

"Ms. Thyme will voluntarily give a statement. Right now she needs medical attention, so stop wasting your time and go secure the crime scene. This is a case you don't want to lose."

The colour drained from Stone's face and his mouth twitched again.

An RCMP officer stormed into the kitchen. "Sir—" he looked from Keith, to me, to Sergeant Stone "—the coroner's here, and you should come look at this."

Look at what?

The Sergeant scowled and flipped his notebook shut. "Here's your time to speak with your client, Aubischon. I'll be sending another officer in to take her statement." He marched out after the RCMP officer.

I swung around. "They think I killed him! They think I ordered a hit!"

Keith knelt. "Jesus, Jade, you're bleeding again. Here." He grabbed the cloth and pressed it against my lips. "Did you tell him anything?"

"No," I mumbled.

"Did he charter or warn you?"

I shook my head.

"Good."

I pulled his hand holding the cloth away from my mouth. "I didn't kill him!"

"I know, but you've pissed off the wrong cop. What were you doing in there?"

I leaned sideways against the chair and looked around at the deserted kitchen. Spice jars were strewn on the counter. A barbecued chicken still rotated on a skewer in the oven. Everything seemed normal but was far from it. Jules had been murdered and mutilated. His head . . .

An RCMP officer shouted. I jumped. I looked out the window at the swimming pool with its moonlit ripples. More uniformed officers appeared, shepherding guests, sealing the residence off with yellow crime tape. Pain. So much pain.

"Jade!"

I looked at Keith.

"What were you doing in there?"

"He wanted to see me."

"Jules?"

I nodded. "He had information about Anna and Norman Bastine."

Keith again pressed the rag to my lips. "Did you touch anything? Did you touch —?"

Jules's head. "—No!"

"Did you go anywhere near the buffet table?"

"No. I saw him and I got scared, fell against the side table, then got sick."

Keith rubbed his chin, then dropped his hand to his side. I knew what he was thinking. My fingerprints on a lamp near a severed head in a home I hardly frequented. Not good. But physically, I didn't have the strength to swing an axe or sever a man's head. Jesus. I was already planning my defence.

Keith tossed the washcloth onto the kitchen table then looked at me. With his dark eyes and dark hair, he had a toughness about him. He would help me out of this mess.

"I didn't kill him, and I didn't order a hit."

Another RCMP member walked into the kitchen and up to the table. "Sir, we need that." The young rookie nodded at the washcloth. "Evidence."

"Fuck," Keith whispered.

The rookie took the washcloth that had my blood on it and dropped it into a plastic exhibit bag before marching out. One of many exhibits to be logged and tested—I never thought that my blood would be the subject of a forensic report.

"Your blood is at the crime scene, Jade. They're going to want a blood sample. You're their number one suspect, spouses always are, and they're going to spin this case around you. I don't want you giving them anything until we see a warrant."

A tear ran down my cheek. "I didn't kill him, Keith."

"I know, Jade." He brushed the hair back from my face. "Now, come on, you're a lawyer, the burden to prove is always on the Crown."

5

Investigation

And here I thought he was hatched from a buzzard's egg.

FEELING LIKE a three-day-old pizza, I shook the rain from my umbrella as I trudged down the long corridor to my office, brushing aside hushed whispers like the raindrops from my overcoat. I couldn't wait for Jules's funeral to be over, so the office could return to its normal bustling self, and my behaviour, as it had been for the last week, would no longer be gossip around the water cooler. Yes, I had been married to the man, but no, I hadn't killed him.

I turned the corner and stepped around the photocopier repairman who knelt on the floor, the guts of the machine strewn across the carpet. Everything around me: people talking, doors slamming, espresso machines hissing sounded so loud. Each file I picked up had a missed deadline date. My body ached and if I got prompted "incorrect password try again" one more time, I would throw whatever device I held in my hand out a window. Now was not the time to lose my shit.

My father's name had opened many doors for me, but once in, I still had to prove myself. I worked hard, did extremely well in court, and clawed my way to the top like the rest of my colleagues, stepping on a few fingers and toes in my ascent. My association with Jules had provided me with an unspoken protection. Not something I sought or flaunted, but a consequence. I did not suffer backlash from disgruntled colleagues. If a senior partner wanted to get rid of me, he or she would factor Jules's reaction into the equation. I had been labelled an elitist. But now with Jules dead, all that had changed and everyone knew it.

I turned another corner. I never ran to Jules for help, but many suspected I had. I fought my own battles. Yet this morning, as I straightened my black suit and pinned a gold scales of justice brooch on my lapel, I couldn't help but feel that I would be fighting more than just a battle, I'd be fighting for my life. My foolish action of barging onto Jules's crime scene played like a Shakespearean tragedy.

I stopped at my office door, passed my raspberry truffle mocha from one hand to the other, and placed my briefcase and umbrella on the floor. I turned the doorknob, catching sight of Kate's abandoned desk. She had mentioned she had a dentist's appointment and would be late. I glanced at the collage of photographs on her bookcase—niece, nephew, brother, sister, aunt, uncle and grandparent—and felt a pang of envy. I grabbed my umbrella and briefcase and stumbled into my office.

A heavy wind splattered raindrops against my window, rattling the pane, as well as my nerves. Quite the day for a funeral. According to the perky weather forecaster, Victoria was being hit with the worst rainstorm in seventy years. During the next twenty-four hours we would go through every weather condition known to man: rain, hail, gale force winds, sun and at higher altitudes—snow. The west coast, or as some called, "left-coast."

I hung my umbrella on the coat tree and shrugged one arm out of my black overcoat and then the other. I stepped around the glass oval table in the sitting area of my office, knocking my knee on one of the blue velvet armchairs. I flicked the switch on the stereo. The *Sound of Silence*, an arrangement for two cellos played.

Bianca knew I hated funerals, so she agreed to attend Jules's with me, which fit nicely between my 10 o'clock chambers application and 1:30 trial. Bianca had said that my presence would give her strength to deliver the eulogy. What did one say about one of the city's most obnoxious and repugnant lawyers? That he had dirt on three-quarters of the politicians in the city? That he prided himself on his exploits in bed? That he had slept with half the paralegals on this side of the Georgia Strait! I groaned. I had to get rid of my wicked thoughts. Jules had been brutally murdered. The grass seeds hadn't even sprouted on his grave.

I walked over to the window and leaned against it. Outside, people huddled under black umbrellas, leaping puddles, diving for cover. The Canadian flag atop the building next door snapped and unfurled in the wind. It was as if Jules's restless spirit had escaped and ran wild, seeking revenge on those who had killed him.

Hard to believe a week before he had stood in this office, asking me to work for him. Who had he pissed off so much that he or she had killed him? Brutally. A harsh wind slammed against the building, blurring the windowpane with rain.

I jumped, spilling hot coffee on my hand. "Shoot!"

The lights flickered.

"Jade?"

Keith stood in the doorway, briefcase clutched in hand, looking dashing in his charcoal suit and teal shirt.

"Hi."

"How are you holding up?" He glided into my office.

I shook coffee drops from my hand. "I've been better."

He put his briefcase down and slid his hands into his pockets. "Sergeant Stone been bothering you?"

"No." I walked over to my desk and snatched a tissue. "At least not yet. I haven't seen him since the night of the murder."

"Good. If he harasses you, call me."

I nodded and wiped my fingers.

"Look—" he rubbed his jaw "—I have this search warrant hearing of a law office. I know you're grieving and should be on leave—"

"When is it?"

"In three or four weeks."

"I'm free. Are we acting on behalf of the Crown?"

"No. We're defending another lawyer—Clive Vandenberg. He's accused of swindling money from a client's trust account while he was drawing up her will. I need research done but I'm running out of time."

"I can do it. The research. I'll email your assistant."

"Seriously, are you okay?"

"I'm good," I lied.

"If you want time off—'

"—I'm good." I forced a smile. "Thank you."

Keith grabbed his briefcase. "I'll see you at the funeral."

I waved.

Keith walked out of my office, nodding at Kate who stood at the door. Dark shadows and swelling marred her face.

"You're back. Are you all right?"

She rolled her eyes.

Kate hated dentists. She'd rather fight it out with the Canada Revenue Agency than set foot in a dentist's office.

"I have 'o go back."

"No."

She nodded. "Sergean' Swone is in da foyer," she said, trying not to move her lips.

"What does he want? I gave him my statement, an audio and video statement."

She frowned. "He wan 'o spik 'o you." She slurped and dabbed her lips with her fingers.

Couldn't the man leave me alone? "Does Keith know he's here?"

She shook her head.

"All right. Show him in." I walked over to my desk. "Kate?"

She stopped.

"If you want to go home—"

She shook her head then groaned. She held her hand to her cheek and walked out.

I placed my coffee on the blotter and reached for another tissue. I dabbed at the coffee stains on the pocket of my coat and pants. From the corner of my eye I saw Sergeant Swone, as Kate said, standing in the doorway.

Raindrops dripped from his black leather coat and his slacks were wet midway below his knees. With the palm of his hand he wiped the rain streaks trickling down his bald head.

"Don't you have an umbrella," I said, dropping the tissue in the waste paper basket.

"I was conceived in this weather."

And here I thought he was hatched from a buzzard's egg.

He closed the door behind him and walked toward my desk.

"What can I do for you, Sergeant."

He removed my briefcase from the blue velvet chair and sat down. Immediately my office smelled of rain, aftershave and leather.

He leaned forward and tossed an envelope onto my desk. "Guest list."

I picked up the damp envelope and pulled out two folded pieces of paper.

"Go over it carefully. Tell me if anyone listed there had it in for your ex."

Listed were the names of my colleagues. I flipped the first page over. My eyes faltered at the sight of my own name underneath my father's. Murder suspects, and Stone expected me to be the snitch, disclosing my colleagues's individual fears and insecurities, which he would manipulate into motives for a criminal investigation. I was no expert on relationships, my own relationship with my father non-existent. I had no right to verbalize my interpretation of my colleagues's behaviour.

I stuffed the sheets of paper back into the envelope and tossed the envelope onto my desk. "And why should I help you?"

Stone arched his eyebrows. "Because you know what I'm up

against. I want to know who's who in the zoo, Jade, and I figured you'd want the bastard caught."

Hand it to Stone for zeroing in on my sensitivities. "When do you want this back?"

"End of the week."

I nodded.

"You have time for a few questions?"

I was taken aback by his polite manner and wondered if he had been reprimanded for his behaviour on the night of the murder. "My lawyer tells me I'm not to speak to you."

"Are you guilty of anything?"

"No. Am I a suspect?"

Stone hesitated. "You're a person of interest along with one hundred and ninety-nine other guests."

Keith would freak if he knew I was talking to this man. I checked my watch. "I have a six-year-old witness I need to prepare for a trial, so make it quick."

He reached into his inner coat pocket and pulled out his notebook.

I sat in my chair and sipped my coffee.

"What do you know about Anna Von Altman?"

"Besides the fact that she was an aspiring stage actress who was murdered a year ago, not much more than your police file. She was a private person, yet a lot of rumour and speculation followed her. You know that, Sergeant. You were the lead investigator on her murder."

"We found pictures of her on Jules's phone."

My eyes widened. "What kind of pictures?"

Stone arched one brow and frowned. "Nothing sordid. Pictures of her at parties; pictures of her talking to James Aubischon." Stone stood and strolled over to the bookshelf that took up one wall of my office. "Any idea why Jules would have these pictures?" He pulled out a book from the bookshelf and read the cover.

I picked up my pen and wove it between my fingers. "No. They were friends, that's all. If you're still trying to prove that

Jules murdered her, you're wasting your time. He was found not guilty and now he's dead. You should be focusing on his murder."

Stone slipped the book back on the shelf. He leaned forward, looking at the plaque I had received three years ago from the Nanaimo RCMP in appreciation for my work as a special prosecutor on a double homicide file. "The man is killed eight hours after a jury finds him not guilty of Anna's murder, and on that same day Olive Aubischon breaks off her engagement to him. What's the connection? You'd think Olive would be overjoyed that her man was cleared of the murder charge."

I sat back. "Maybe Olive stayed with him for moral support. Standing by her man throughout the trial didn't hurt his image."

Stone moved over to a photograph of me windsurfing in Hawaii.

"When was this taken?"

"Four years ago."

"Maui?"

"Waikiki."

"Boyfriend?"

"Ex-boyfriend. I thought I cut him out."

"You have quite a few of those."

"He's still living."

Stone nodded. He moved over to the picture of my father and I in our robes just after I had been called to the bar. "Do you have any idea why your father would be involved with Anna?"

The pen flipped out of my fingers, hitting the wall. I leaned forward on my chair. "My father? With Anna? No."

Stone looked at me from the corner of his eye, a sardonic grin on his face. "Rumour has it she was hot stuff. Nobody could resist her."

"Really. That's the only compliment you can say about her."

A smile cracked Stone's lips. "Maybe your father wanted a companion."

My pulse pounded. Sergeant Stone had no clue what my father wanted. I had no clue what my father wanted.

"He's been widowed—"

"My father—" I bit my tongue and looked out the window, trying to swallow the tremor in my voice. The succession of young men, university students, who had sauntered through the family home the last couple of years, like models on a catwalk, played through my mind. Everyone liked Dr. Thyme, legal professor. All hoping my father could fast-track their legal career in a city that was saturated with lawyers, some were even articling for free. That was the first time I met Troy. He had been one of father's students. "My father—" I jabbed a pencil against the blotter. Why was I defending him? "—is extremely busy."

"Are you saying he was never interested in her?"

"I don't know and I don't care. That's something you need to ask him."

"That's where I have a problem, Ms. Thyme," Stone said, placing his hands on the back of the blue chair. "He won't return my calls. He's never home when I go to his residence."

I scoffed and jabbed the eraser end of the pencil against my desk. "Not my problem. He probably wants to talk to you as much as I do."

Stone sighed and leaned forward, his forearms pressed on the back cushion. "That's where you're wrong, Ms. Thyme. The more you talk, the sooner I cross your name off that list. The same with your father. He knows something. That's why he's not talking. Get him to talk, Ms. Thyme. Like you, he knew both victims. Jules had cozy pictures of him with Anna. Jules's phone records show a number of telephone calls between your father's residence and Anna's."

"That doesn't make my father a murderer."

"Did I say murderer, Ms. Thyme?"

Shit.

"Your father and James are neighbours. Their houses next to each other. Do you remember seeing your father on the night Jules was killed, Ms. Thyme?"

No. "He was there."

"Where did you see him? What time?"

"I can't remember. There were two hundred guests."

"Were the three of them involved in some sort of love triangle?"

"Involved? Love triangle! My father and my ex-husband! A few phone calls doesn't make someone involved!"

"Did you know your father was seeing Anna?"

"No—"

"Why won't he cooperate, Ms. Thyme?"

"I don't know."

"Right now he's classified as a hostile witness, who doesn't want to cooperate with law enforcement—"

"—He's a busy man!" *Why was I defending him*?

"And if he doesn't start cooperating, I'll haul his ass down to the detachment for questioning!"

"Do it!" I slammed my hand against my desk, launching myself out of the chair and spilling coffee over the rim of my cup. "You're badgering me because you can't get to him. Do you have physical evidence linking him to Jules's murder besides some drunken party pictures? Or is this all superficial speculation. So what if Jules spoke to him, he was once his son-in-law. Did you ever think that Anna wanted legal advice!" I paced between the desk and the window. "And why have you come across this information now? None of this was ever mentioned in the initial investigation of Anna's murder! If I had known my father was involved with Anna I wouldn't have become involved in her case!"

"So you're confirming he was involved."

"I'm saying if he was involved."

Stone tapped his notebook against the palm of his hand. "Tell me Ms. Thyme, why, after a five-year absence of doing criminal work, did you put aside your litigation practice and take on Jules's case? Maybe you did know your father was involved. Just whose ass were you trying to save? Your ex's, or your father's?"

I gritted my teeth. "I believed in Jules's innocence."

"You do know that we have fresh evidence and we've re-opened Anna's case."

I had defended Jules of Anna's murder. I never fathomed that the suspicion would shift to my father.

"And in terms of physical evidence with respect to Jules's murder, we have your blood smeared on a broken lamp near the deceased, your blood on a cloth that you touched, unknown fingerprints found on the lamp which we suspect are yours, you want to tell me what's really going on, Ms. Thyme? Why a defence lawyer who's just come off a criminal prosecution would go busting into a crime scene? I can't see you yielding an axe, but I can see you protecting someone."

I walked to the window and stared at the whitecaps and a lonely boat bobbing in the harbor. Keith was right, Stone was trying to pin a murder rap—manipulate the evidence to fit his theory. He probably already had my motive worked out, but he was fishing for my father's, hoping I would spill something useful.

I pulled my hair back from my face. Who was I to say what my father would do, or had been doing on the night of the murder? I didn't know the man anymore. I hadn't talked to him in a couple of years except for the occasional 'hello' at an office function. What was he, a semi-retired sixty-four-year-old, doing with Anna and how had Jules become involved? Jules had hinted at a conspiracy, not a love triangle. And why wasn't any of this brought to my attention during the initial investigation into Anna's murder? I pressed the palms of my hands together in front of my face and expelled a long uneven breath. I didn't want to wade into this pool. My father was a grown man who could look after himself. He wouldn't want my help, and he was arrogant enough to believe he was above reproach. "You should leave."

"Anna's best friend told me that Anna had an appointment on the day she died."

Another sheet of rain pelted the building. I looked at the veins of water running down the windowpane. Across the city my condo peeked out of grey murky clouds. "Who was the appointment with?"

"Your father."

"Is this so-called friend credible?"

Stone stepped up beside me. "Very. She's Olive Aubischon. Your boss's daughter."

6

Funeral

Outside the black cemetery gates, leaning against a maple tree, stood Osmond.

RAINDROPS GLITTERED like diamonds and dripped from the oak tree branches while the sun's warmth caused a mist to roll off the headstones and rise to the heavens.

I stood like a sentinel amongst a spectre of black suits at the Ross Bay Cemetery. Gathered around Jules's casket with its plume of white gladiolas and calla lilies, I couldn't help but feel that if I stood too long among the towering angels and granite crosses, or stared too hard at one of the mausoleums, that Jules, his head haphazardly placed on his shoulders, would walk around a corner and say, "Hey, baby. How's my girl?"

Jules's mother, Candace Cranbury, sat on a white fold-out chair sobbing behind a black veil. Franklyn Cranbury patted his wife's shoulders, while trying to control his own emotions, an occasional tear slipped down his wrinkled cheek. As reckless and as pompous Jules may have been, Mr. and Mrs. Cranbury had still lost their son. Although his body had not been found and there was nothing in the casket except Jules's head, his parents wanted a proper burial. I wasn't going to pass judgment. I understood the need for closure, and at the wake, I would express my condolences to them.

The minister's humble words dispersed into the air and settled on our mortal shoulders. Politicians and city councillors stood together. The legal community had descended upon the cemetery and we stood eight deep. The secretaries gathered in bunches, dabbing their tears with tissues. The young lawyers stood, heads bowed, a cocky set to their shoulders, while the retired ones clutched canes, their shoulders stooped from years of stress and legal responsibility. My father stood with the retired lawyers. I wondered if these men were secretly rejoicing Jules's death, or feeling genuine sorrow for the loss of a colleague. Lawyer wives dabbed their false tears of grief.

I hugged my elbows, to ward off the feeling of guilt. Could I have done more? If I had been on time for our meeting, instead of trash-talking him with Bianca, would Jules still be alive today?

Why hadn't anyone heard his screams?

I thought about Sergeant Stone with his innuendos and suspicions and a bitter indifference rippled down my spine. I sighed.

Bianca patted me on the shoulder. The smell of alcohol mingled with her perfume. She had given a beautiful eulogy about Jules. Her voice only cracked twice, and at the moment when I thought she'd completely break down, she clutched the podium, thrust out her chin, and ploughed on. Too bad her tight black suit and the three swigs of vodka in Troy Reilly's Corvette earned her disparaging remarks from the wives.

Keith looked at me softly over the casket. I remembered as kids, we'd play with his matchbox cars, and later as adults, we walked around the university campus–that is, before Jules swept into my life. Olive stood next to Keith. She looked at him, looking at me. Scorn obliterated her tears. She had always been possessive of her older brother even when we were young, kicking our matchbox cars, destroying our make-shift cities made from wood blocks. Given that they had lost their mother to cancer at a young age, I could understand why. Keith and Olive were from mixed cultures. Keith's mother had been East Indian and he had inherited her gorgeous complexion. James was Caucasian and Olive looked a lot like her father. Today, her black suit gave her skin a grey-white hue, and her cheekbones and jaw cut harsh angles. So much for the bereaved fiancée. Personally, I wanted to take her behind one of the mausoleums and interrogate her. Why was she cooperating with the police now, when throughout Anna's murder investigation she had been labeled a hostile witness? Why was she pointing the finger at my father?

I blinked and brushed the tears from my cheeks. I shoved my hands in the pockets of my leather suit.

The minister raised his hands and the mourners sang a hushed rendition of *Ave Maria*. I swallowed hard and lip-synced the lyrics, staring at the treetops and drifting clouds. The minister blessed us all and then we dispersed.

Bianca lit a cigarette as she waited for Troy, who was expressing his condolences to Mr. and Mrs. Cranbury. I blended among the black suits, focusing on putting one foot in front of the other. Twigs and pinecones crunched beneath my feet. Jules was gone. His absence scarred our lives. Every lawyer present felt vulnerable and the unspoken question lingered. Had he been killed by one of us—a lawyer—sworn to uphold the law?

I looked up and froze.

Outside the black cemetery gates, leaning against a maple tree, stood Osmond. Wind tugged at his coat tails, as if coaxing him to leave. Even from this distance, his caring look rattled me.

"Osmond," I whispered. We stared at each other. He stepped away from the tree. My chest heaved. I was in a trance—hypnotized by his image. The closer he stepped the deeper the trance. I've had men woo me, others flatter me; Osmond just had to look at me. I took a small step, the ground uneven beneath my feet. So much I wanted to ask him.

Osmond stopped at the open iron gate, his expression sullen.

A voice came from behind. "You look like you could use a drink."

I swung around, my hair whipping me in the face. Keith stood with his hands in his pockets.

"Jesus," I whispered.

"No, the name's Keith Aubischon, but you're in the right place if you want to see the Almighty."

I smiled.

Keith stepped forward. "There are drinks at the golf club, Jade."

"I—" I looked back at the gate but Osmond was gone. I heard a car start and then accelerate onto the street. "—I don't think so, Keith."

He glanced down the street. "Are you expecting somebody?"

The black hearse drove past behind Keith. A tear slipped from my eyes. That's all it took, seeing a black hearse, and the pain of my mother's funeral returned. I dabbed my cheeks with a tissue, blotting mascara and foundation. God, to be seventeen again.

Keith slung his arm around my shoulders and walked me to my car. "It was a beautiful funeral, Jade. This must be very hard on you. I can't imagine what you're going through."

I groaned. Keith's sympathy didn't help my situation, just made it worse. "I've got court."

"No you don't. Your client's been arrested for breaching his curfew. The police picked him up last night. He's not going anywhere except to jail. Kate was denotifying witnesses when I left the office, and the articling student is adjourning the trial to the next Supreme Court fix date." He gave my shoulders a squeeze.

"How do you know all of this?"

He smiled. "I know many things, Jade Thyme."

I touched the iron railing where moments ago Osmond had stood. As we descended the steps, we walked in unison. We stopped at my car. I looked at Keith's face, dark complexion, jet-black hair stylishly cut, and dark eyes that had caused many legal secretaries to swoon. Longing mixed with sadness. I looked down the street. Car doors slammed as lawyers slipped into their Mercedes and BMWs. No sign of Osmond.

"One drink, Jade." Keith took the keys from my hand, unlocked the passenger door and pulled it open. "Give me an excuse to drive this thing," he said, looking at my car.

"You once told me you would never drive an import."

"Jade," he said, leaning toward me, his tone dropping a notch, "there are imports and then there is your Audi TT."

My soul lifted. "All right."

"All right to what?"

I stepped off the curb and sat in. "The golf club."

He winked, closed the door and walked around to the driver's side.

In a matter of minutes we were whipping through Pearl Estates. After a few quick turns, Keith turned onto the Patricia Bay Highway, weaving through lanes of traffic and dodging maniacal yellow cabs. Keith made comments about the front suspension and independent twin wishbones and 290 horsepower. I just nodded as merge lanes and white lines blurred into each other. I liked the heated soft leather seats and the fact that my car handled like a charm.

We pulled into the cobblestone parking lot of the Silver Creek Golf and Country Club, parked, and were soon trailing a line of black-clad mourners into the lobby. After signing the guest book, we entered the lounge with its oak-paneled walls, smoke grey furniture and large tree ferns. I followed Keith, manoeuvring between tables. Any sombre traces of the funeral had been replaced with clinking glasses and seductive jazz melodies. Two female lawyers with drinks in their hands laughed and pointed down the fairway at the first hole. The old boys' club, which included a number of fossilized lawyers, stood in a circle on the patio, puffing cigars. I spotted Bianca, her delicate foot poised on the brass rail, throwing back a drink while she listened to surfer boy Troy. Unease crept over me as I walked among my fellow legal practitioners. Keith must have sensed my discomfort for he turned and placed his hand on my back, and guided me to a corner table which overlooked the pond on the eighteenth hole.

"White wine, Jade?"

"Yes. A Gewürztraminer." I sat, pulling in my chair.

Keith ordered my wine and himself a rye and seven. I slipped my feet out of my high heel pumps and looked outside at lawyers and secretaries. I hoped like hell I wouldn't see my father. The thought of him seeing Anna . . . Jules seeing Anna. I shivered and refocused my attention on the stainless steel trays of seafood on the side table and remembered Jules's head. *Damn it.* I looked at Keith. "Whose idea was this?"

He leaned forward, rubbing the palms of his hands together. "I have no idea. Troy, or was it Bianca, sent me an email asking for a donation. Check with Troy."

I looked around the room at the circles of men and women, young and old, the joviality on their faces. A cold chill seeped through the windowpane. I rubbed my hands over my arms. The voices in the lounge blended into an incomprehensible noise, and my mind receded as if sucked into a vacuum. The suits acted their parts, nodding their heads, discussing points of law, commiserating over their last win or loss. Was I one of them?

"Jade?"

I jumped.

Keith rubbed his hand over mine. "You all right?"

I averted my eyes to the well-trimmed greens and the mallards gliding on the pond. "I'm nothing but a fraud, Keith."

"What?"

I pulled my hand back from his and tapped the cardboard wine list against the table. He wouldn't understand. Years of trying to prove myself, to gain acceptance, do the right thing, be the right person. Did I really want to be like them, given one of them was a murderer? Where was that glass of wine?

Sergeant Stone expected me to burrow through a working environment I had been a part of for so many years, exposing people's secrets, maybe even my own. Already I looked around, not trusting a soul, wondering who could swing an axe and cut off . . .

"What's wrong, Jade?"

"I don't know." I ran my hands through my hair and looked outside again. Mr. Cranbury, wobbling on his cane, and Mrs. Cranbury, holding his other arm, wandered over to the old boys' club. "Sergeant Stone visited me," I said.

"What? When?"

"This morning. After you left."

"I told you not to talk to him."

"I handled it."

"Like hell! The man's hungry for a conviction to make up for his botched job on Anna's case. Did you say anything?"

I looked down at the table.

"Shit." Keith dropped back in his chair and rubbed his eyes. The waitress arrived with our drinks. Keith straightened and moved his leg as she placed two coasters, his rye and seven and my glass of wine on the table. She moved on to the next table. Keith leaned forward. "What did you tell him?"

I picked up my wine glass and sipped. "Nothing."

"Try again counsellor. What did you tell him?"

I placed the glass on the coaster. "Nothing. He told me more than I told him." I rotated the stem of the wineglass. "My father is a suspect. Seems he was seeing Anna."

"Your father?"

"Yes. Stone says he has pictures of him and . . . her. Do you know how sick that makes me? To think that Jules and my father could have been—" *sleeping with the same woman.* I shook my head. "Why was none of this brought up in the initial investigation?"

"Because it's a—" Keith took a long swallow of his rye.

"A what?"

"The cops figured Jules had killed Anna. They focused all their manpower on digging up evidence and following tips against him. With Jules being found not guilty, it's forced them to back up and follow the tips they may have disregarded. Also Jules's death puts a new slant on what happened to Anna. Did Stone tell you where he got his info?"

"Yes. Your sister."

Keith's eyebrows rose. "Olive?"

"Miss Uncooperative throughout Jules's trial. Now that the man's dead, she's opening her mouth." I sighed. "I just about had to get a witness warrant for your sister. Strikes me odd that she breaks off her engagement to him in the morning and twelve hours later she finds him dead. And now she's cooperating with the police."

"Olive gave Stone the pictures?"

"They were on Jules's cell phone. I'd like to know what else he found."

"Cell phone." His face paled. "Did they find his body?"

"He didn't say. There was nothing in the papers."

Keith sat back. "Hold back information. I'll see what I can find out."

"How?"

A smile tugged at the corners of Keith's lips. "I know how to manipulate the police and my sister."

I sipped my wine. "It's a charade, Keith." I glanced around the room. "A bloody charade. Nobody is who they say they are. Sometimes I wonder if Jules had been found guilty, would he still be alive?"

"What else did Stone tell you?"

I looked out at the putting green. "He wants me to look over the guest list and tell him if anyone had it in for Jules. Then in the same breath he tells me that I'm still under investigation."

Keith placed his hand over mine. "Where's this list?"

"On my desk."

"When we get back to the office, give it to me. As far as I'm concerned, Stone can shove his list up his ass. If he wants to talk to you, he goes through me. Got it?"

"I handled him."

"You're too emotionally involved." Keith slugged back a mouthful of his drink then placed his glass down hard on the table. His father, the Honourable James Aubischon, walked across the fairway and joined the judicial circle. James patted Franklyn Cranbury on the shoulder, then moved over to Mrs. Cranbury and, taking both her hands in his, leaned in and kissed her.

Had Jules figured out at the last moment who had killed Anna? Is that why he had wanted to see me? These suits. Who were they protecting? It was like a political party and they were forever loyal to their leader. They'd sworn allegiance to the system. Yet, my actions were being questioned. My wineglass tipped. I grabbed for it, but the glass hit the table, and my Gewürztraminer spilled onto the burgundy tablecloth.

Keith jumped up.

"Crap." I grabbed a napkin and dabbed at the wet puddle.

"No problem, miss," the waitress said, offering me a smile as she picked up the glass and mopped up the wine. "I'll get you another one."

"No. No. I've had quite enough." I slid down in my chair and pressed my hand to my forehead.

Keith sat down again.

Outside, Mrs. Cranbury clutched onto James's hand and by the tender expression on her face, she was saying something nice to the scumbag. "I wonder if she knows."

"Knows what?"

"That James wished her son dead."

Keith removed the unlit cigarette from his lips and leaned forward. "What did you say?"

I realized that I was talking to Keith about his own father.

"What did you say?"

I looked at James, then back at Keith. "The night of the murder I saw Jules get into James's Mercedes. That was the last time I saw Jules alive. Then, at the party, your father said he wished he had killed Jules before. Before what? And when? Bianca—" I nodded toward Bianca who had one arm resting on Troy's shoulder as she whispered something in his ear "—Bianca heard him."

Keith's face paled. He leaned over the table. "Did you tell Stone?"

"No."

"Jesus." He looked out at his father. "Jesus Christ." He tapped the unlit cigarette against the table. He looked at me. "Don't say a word to anyone about Jules's death or who—" he looked at his father then at me "—said what to whom."

"Jules knew, didn't he? He knew who killed Anna. That's why he wanted to meet me. That's why he got killed."

"Jade, I'm warning you, not a word about any of this to anyone. Let me deal with this." He rubbed his hand over his chin. "Deal with my father."

7

Tension

"How's your Cantonese Buddhist Delight?"

THE TINY PRINTED words blurred into one. My head bobbed as my hand slipped across the page. I jolted. Sleep. I needed sleep. I rubbed my cheek as I looked at the case book I had been reading. A warrant. Yes. A warrant to search a law office, that's what Keith had me researching. I reached for my mug, wincing at the taste of cold coffee. Yuck. I put my mug down.

Keith and I were defending Clive Vandenberg who had been accused of defrauding a client. The RCMP had illegally searched his law office. I had gathered some information during the two hours I sat cooped up in the office library. The RCMP needed a special warrant, which they didn't have, before they searched Clive's office. The documents they had seized, Clive claimed solicitor-client privilege, so those documents were sealed and had been given to a judge. The Crown wanted to use those documents, which we believed they didn't have the right to use, in the upcoming trial, the reason for our hearing. Should a ruling be granted in the Crown's favour, Keith and I would appeal the judge's decision, delaying the trial at least another six to eight months.

I stood up, gathered my pages, and clicked them into my binder. Tomorrow I would give Keith a briefing note. I tossed my binder and file folder into my briefcase, snapped it shut, and turned to leave. Troy Reilly walked in.

"Troy!"

"Jade." His tie loose around his neck and his blonde messy hair even more disheveled, he looked as if he had crawled out of hibernation. He slammed his briefcase onto the table, walked over to the bookshelf and pulled out a few law books.

Our office had a no smoking policy, but that didn't stop any of our die-hard smokers from sneaking a puff, or smoking a celebratory cigar after a win. We ordered a lot of air freshener. Troy didn't smell of cigarettes, he reeked of pot. Cannabis is legal, but showing up at work reeking of it is against office policy.

"What are you doing here?" I asked. "It's past six."

"Research." He tossed the books onto the table and grabbed another. "You?"

"Research. The Vandenberg file. Keith and I are doing it. The Crown wants to use documents the police obtained during an illegal search."

Troy grunted and flipped open a book. "The case I was supposed to do."

Troy and I never did get along. No matter what I did to ease the tension, he always held a grudge. "What are you doing?"

"An impaired driving charge," he said, sounding disinterested.

I nodded. "There are some excellent cases on Quicklaw."

"My computer crashed."

"Oh."

"Besides, I'll be getting Dr. Reed off on a technicality. The technician's breathalyzer certificate had expired when he took the good doctor's readings." He flipped a page in the case book. "Saw your father at the funeral reception yesterday."

"Really? I must have missed him."

Troy leaned his hand on the table as he flipped through more pages. "He came in just after you and Aubischon left. You like your men trailing on your heels."

My spine stiffened. I placed my briefcase on the table. "Excuse me?"

Troy looked up. He adjusted his glasses and snorted. "Right. Whatever you have to do to score a partnership."

"I don't need to score anything. My work speaks for itself."

He pushed the book aside and flipped open another. "With the name Thyme and your connection to Jules, I'm sure your work screams brilliance."

I placed my hand on my hip. "If you have a problem with me, then spit it out instead of these immature innuendos."

He straightened and I was taken aback by the anger in his eyes. "My billable hours have gone through the roof. Westwood Lumber has contracted all their litigation to me!" He stabbed his pencil against a book. "I'll make this firm hundreds of thousands of dollars but all that doesn't mean shit!"

I stepped back.

"You have the name. You screwed the mayor, and now you're screwing Aubischon!"

I clutched the back of a chair, digging my nails into the cushion. *Easy. Don't rip his throat out. Typical response.* He thinks I slept my way to the top. I did not have to waste my time defending my work ethic. "When you were an undergrad—" my voice trembled "—I negotiated the merger between Cranbury Plastics and Johnson's Plastics! When you were doing your articles, I was negotiating the airline's strike, and before that, I prosecuted the Hatchet Murderer. So don't talk to me about billable hours or what *you've pulled* into this company. Success you have to work for. It's not a photo op so you can update your Instagram feed. There are much smarter lawyers in this firm who deserve the partnership more than you!" I marched towards the door. "And another thing." I turned back. "I risked *everything* because I believed in Jules's innocence. I'd like to see you do the same."

Troy's face flamed. He clenched and unclenched his fists and I thought he was going to throw something.

"If you want the partnership so damn much, Troy, learn the rules, play the game, and stop blaming everyone else for your inadequacies!" I turned.

Keith stood in the doorway. He arched one eyebrow. "Is there a problem?"

Oh crap.

"What the hell do you want?" Troy shouted, turning around.

Keith stepped into the library. "I work here."

Troy swallowed. "Keith. I, I thought you were—"

"—Someone else?"

Troy placed his hand on his briefcase, steadying himself.

Keith leaned against a bookshelf, arms crossed.

Troy tapped a pencil against the table.

Good Lord, someone say something.

"Troy, do you remember anything peculiar from the night of Jules's murder?"

"Not a damn thing. I got wasted."

That was a brilliant answer.

"So, why did you sneak upstairs that night?" Keith asked. "Were you looking for Olive? Or were you looking for Jules?"

Troy's face paled.

Oh God. He was looking for Jules. Bianca had said Olive found a sex-text from Troy to Jules. Or was Troy angry with Olive?

"Actually—" he rotated his shoulders and shifted his weight from one foot to the other "—I did go looking for Olive."

"Because?"

"Your sister wants legal advice, Aubischon."

Keith frowned. "What the hell for?"

I edged toward the conference table. I wanted to make a quiet and quick exit.

Troy pushed my briefcase out of his way and out of my reach. He stood, legs apart, arms crossed. "Solicitor-client privilege, and I don't think you want me breaching that. A man of principles such as yourself."

"We're talking about my sister, Reilly. She has no principles. Tell me and save us a lot of headaches."

Troy looked long and hard at Keith. "Olive was involved in a business transaction."

"What kind?" Keith asked, strolling over to the window.

"Ask her."

"I'm asking *you*."

The edge in Keith's voice made the hair on my arms stand up. Outside, the shifting wind slammed sheets of rain against the windowpanes. I wanted my briefcase.

Troy took a coin from his pocket and tossed it in the air. "Anna and Olive had plans to open a performing arts studio in Sweden." He caught the coin and tossed it again. "Anna had the money to do it."

"How much money?"

Troy shoved his hands back into his pockets. A blonde curl slipped over his forehead.

"How much?"

Troy looked at me, then at Keith. "Two hundred and fifty thousand."

Where the hell did she get that kind of money? I looked at Keith.

"Did you know about this?" he asked me.

"I had no clue. I wish I had."

Keith looked at Troy. "Where the hell did she get that kind of cash?"

"I don't know, but she made an offer to buy a small studio in April. The closing of the deal wasn't until July. She got murdered in June. If she hadn't stuck around for that prick—" he glared at me as if it was my fault Anna was dead "—never mind. We all know Jules got what he deserved. The Soc—"

"Troy!" Keith shouted.

I jumped, banging into the chair. It rolled back and collided with the bookcase.

"Where did she get the money?" Keith demanded.

"I don't know! And why do you care? It's not as if the sale ever completed."

"So where's the two-hundred and fifty thousand now?"

"I don't know."

"What do you mean you don't know?"

"It's gone."

"What?"

"It's gone!"

"A quarter of a million dollars?"

"Yes. That's why Olive wanted to see me. The money was in a safety deposit box. Only Anna and Olive had keys. When Olive went to get the cash it was gone."

"Who else knew about the cash besides my sister?"

"No one."

"You knew."

Something dangerous flickered in Troy's eyes. "I'm not a thief."

I stepped away from Troy and stood closer to the bookshelf. I didn't feel safe near him.

Keith must have seen the expression on Troy's face, for he paused before asking his next question. "Were you seeing Anna?"

"That's none of your business."

Keith stepped forward. "I've got Sergeant Stone breathing down my neck, wanting to interrogate every lawyer in this firm. Be straight with me and I can be straight with him, at least get him off my ass. Then the lawyers in this firm can do what they do best."

"No. I wasn't seeing her," Troy said, a cocky lift to his chin, "but she was seeing—" He looked at me.

Who? Jules? My father? Were they each a Tinder swipe? I had to stop thinking like this.

"There was nothing Anna wouldn't try once. Although, for awhile there—" he picked up the pencil "—she started seeing Jules and the game changed."

"She dumped you," Keith interjected.

Troy glared. "We weren't an item. Why didn't she and Olive leave when they were supposed to?" He tossed the pencil onto the table. "I'm tired of this shit. I've got a trial tomorrow." He grabbed his briefcase and marched out of the room.

Keith waited a few moments, then walked over and closed the

door. He turned to me and scratched his head. "We hired that pothead?"

I couldn't help but smile. "I'm sure he wasn't stoned when he came for his interview."

Keith groaned.

"He's very intelligent, very full of himself. He has a great career ahead of him if he stops sleeping around, mouthing off partners, and maybe kick the cannabis during work hours."

Keith strolled over to the window and looked out at the darkness and the lit buildings next door. "I'm trying to protect this firm from a cop who wants to pin Jules's murder on you, Troy or my father. You believe a word he says?"

"Some of it. Trying to figure out what's truth and what's gossip."

Keith rubbed the back of his neck. "What do you think is truth?"

I walked over to the credenza stacked with legal texts. "I think Troy's seeing your sister. Or at least was."

"And now that Jules is out of the way, my sister's his fast track to success."

I hadn't thought of that.

"My father's an alcoholic," Keith said, looking out the window at the Parliament Buildings. "The bottle is his escape. It makes him say things that he wouldn't normally say and act like an ass at parties. He hated Jules."

"Jules was–" *say something nice* "–Hate is a strong word, Keith."

Keith's jaw clenched. "After my mom passed, Father had fallen in love with Jules's mother. But Mrs. Cranbury loved Mr. Cranbury and would have nothing to do with my father. Father saw Jules as the offspring from a love he could never have."

So that was his excuse for being an alcoholic? Having his heart broken? At least he had never been dumped via text message. Jules being engaged to Olive, Aubischon senior's daughter, probably made for many awkward family dinners. "I won't say a word, Keith."

"With you, Stone has no motive," he continued, "you're not the jealous type. You helped Jules. With Troy, Stone can allege that with Jules dead, Troy had improved his chances of pursuing Olive and his progress in the firm. You and I both know Troy hasn't been silent about wanting the partnership."

"And if Troy was seeing Olive while she was engaged to Jules—"

"Both Troy and my sister would make perfect suspects."

I believed Jules's and Anna's murders were connected, but I lacked the energy to connect the dots. "What are you going to do?"

Keith stepped away from the window and circled the conference table, looking at the legal texts and file folders. "Protect my family, protect the staff in this office. I am a senior partner. I consider it my responsibility. Hopefully I can get to the bottom of this before Stone wrongfully accuses someone else." Keith picked up photocopied pages of case law and tossed them into a pile. "And if I'm lucky, find a quarter of a million dollars. Where do you think Anna got the money?"

"That's a question for Olive. The thing is, who took it?"

"God, I don't need this shit. Have you eaten yet?"

"Who? Me?"

"No, Jade. Mr. Pothead. Of course you."

"Well, no, I haven't."

"Are you up for some Asian fusion cooking?"

"I have fuzzy ravioli and a slice of toxic pizza in my refrigerator, at home, what do you think?"

Keith smiled and for a moment the stress lines creasing his face faded.

I grabbed my briefcase and coat, and Keith and I made our way out of the office. We said hello to the security guard on the first floor before dashing outside into the freezing rain. Running from awning to awning, dodging street-people and puddles, Keith held his coat over both our heads.

The fluorescent purple lights spelling "Ginger Lee" flashed in the fogged up windows. The trendy restaurant had opened a month ago and was frequently attended by lawyers, artists, and writers. Keith and I splashed down the cement steps. He pulled open the heavy wooden door, and we walked in.

Stir-frys hissed and dishes clattered accompanied by animated voices and laughter. I soaked up the warmth and breathed in the smell of curry and ginger. A young Asian woman dressed in black slacks and a white shirt, her hair pulled back in a bun with chopsticks sticking out of it, greeted us with a smile and led us to a corner booth.

I slid over on the cushions, placing my briefcase beside me, brushing rain from my face. Keith hung up his coat and then sat across from me. Raindrops speckled his hair and trickled down his cheeks. Another young woman in black pants and a white shirt introduced herself as Ming and said she would be our server for the evening. She gave us menus and recited the specials.

I flipped the menu open and immediately scanned the combination dishes. I spotted my all-time favourite—chicken wings, Taiwanese sweet buns, pho and egg rolls. I closed the menu.

Keith eyed me. "Decided already?"

"Yes."

He smiled and wiped another raindrop from his forehead.

Ming returned, placing two glasses of water on the table. She took my order and turned to Keith.

Keith closed up his menu and placed it on top of mine. "I'll have your Cantonese Buddhist Delight." He reached for his glass.

Ming nodded, took the menus and scurried off.

"So tell me Jade, seriously, why did you defend Jules?"

I shrugged out of my coat. Why was everyone asking me that? "I believed in his innocence."

Keith held the glass to his lips, an incredulous smile on his face. "Had nothing to do with pissing off your father?"

I smiled and picked up a chopstick. "No, although the thought did occur to me."

"How is your father? Enjoying semi-retirement?"

"I don't know. Ever since—" *mom died.* I tapped the chopstick on the table. I didn't want to get into this. "—It's been awhile."

"Still not talking to him?" he persisted, putting his glass down.

I weaved the chopstick between my fingers. "Mom died six months ago, and my father pretended her death was a subtle inconvenience in his all important life." I looked over at an aquarium where goldfish swam through bubbling water. "Sage and I are over it." *Liar.*

"You and your sister will always be his girls, Jade, and as far as I'm concerned—" he reached forward, his fingers caressing mine as he untwined the chopstick "—you are the most amazing woman I know."

I looked into his dark eyes, shadows flickered over his face from the candle light. Seeing him in this relaxed atmosphere enhanced his casual sex appeal, from his rolled up shirt sleeves to the tie that hung loose around his neck. I had to be careful not to fall for those eyes and easy smile.

Ming arrived with the Taiwanese sweet buns.

"Sweet bun?" Keith offered.

I couldn't help but feel that he was offering something more. I reached for one. "Thank you."

"You may have to make the first move."

"Excuse me?"

"Your father's a proud man, Jade. He won't take the first step."

He was still talking about my father. I was a little disappointed. "Well that's his problem. Now let's talk about something else." I picked up the chopstick and weaved it between my fingers again.

"How's Sage? Is she still riding that bike?"

My sister liked living on the edge. I also rode, except there was a big difference between my Triumph and her Harley Davidson.

"She's busy running her own personal training business."

"She's still doing the fitness thing?"

"Yes. She kicks ass, and some days I'm jealous."

Keith laughed. "And the research on the Vandenberg file?"

"Good. The RCMP screwed up. They needed a special warrant to search Clive's office, which they didn't have, and—" the chopstick flipped from my fingers.

Keith caught it. "You're trying to kill me with this thing."

I laughed. "I'll get my notes." I pressed the catches on my briefcase. "Anything the RCMP seized would not—" I froze.

Where were my notes? Where was my wallet?

I scrambled through the impaired driving case law, and case law on charter arguments. I picked up a plastic baggie containing three joints. Dammit! This wasn't my briefcase. This was *Troy's*. He had walked out with mine!

"Jade?"

I dropped the baggie and looked up.

"What's wrong?"

I looked back at the baggie and that's when I noticed the pictures slipping out of an envelope. "This isn't my briefcase."

"What do you mean that's not your briefcase?" Keith peered over the table. "It looks like a company issued—"

"—It's not mine! It's Troy's. He grabbed the wrong one. This is impaired driving case law." I picked up the pages and dropped them on the table. "And his notes." I held up a scribbled on legal pad. "And his pot and these pictures."

Keith scooted around, placing his arm on the cushion behind me. "Quite the loot for show and tell."

"Keith!"

He grabbed the case law from the table and tossed it on top of the baggie, burying it. He slipped the photos out of the envelope. Anna. Her head tilted back, she looked over her shoulder at the camera.

I looked at Keith.

He slipped that picture behind another. One of her and Olive at a barbecue. He slid that one behind the first. A few more pictures of her and some cast mates in costume, and then one of her and Troy.

"Those should be given to the police," I said.

Keith flipped through a few more pictures of lawyers from our firm. A picture of Keith holding a pool cue, hosting his weekly Friday night pool party. His father, James, proudly standing behind him, his hand on his son's shoulder.

"These were taken at the office," Keith said. "There's one of you."

Sure enough there was a picture of me talking to Kate.

Keith slid that one behind the others. Anna and my father. He had his arm draped over her shoulders. A full smile on his face, his eyes twinkled.

"Where did Troy get these?"

"I don't know. They're of different functions."

Something about Troy having these pictures seemed wicked, deceiving. Keith flipped the second-to-last picture to the back and stopped. James Aubischon was holding his wine glass towards the camera. To the side of him stood a tall and healthy Jules, loathing and hate filled Jules's eyes. "Jesus."

"You okay?" He looked at me.

I pressed my hand to my lips. "He's whole." I could only remember him as . . . a head. "We shouldn't be looking at these." With trembling fingers I grabbed the photos and tucked them back into the envelope. I noticed written in the top-right hand corner in Jules's handwriting 'Members'.

"Members." I said.

Keith's face paled.

"These aren't Troy's pictures. They're Jules's. How the hell did Troy get them?"

Ming arrived with our food and placed each dish before us.

Keith moved back to where he had been sitting. A few of the pictures had slipped from my hand. I gathered them together except the one of Anna and my father, which I tucked into my purse. I returned the pictures to the envelope and put the envelope on top of the briefcase.

"Tomorrow morning I'm talking to Troy," Keith said, picking

up his spoon and dipping it into his hot and sour soup. "His conduct was totally unprofessional and—" he eyed the briefcase "—I want answers."

"I'll work from home."

"I'll take Troy's briefcase, exchange it for yours. Give him back the pictures and the other stuff."

I slid the briefcase across the cushions, when something dropped to the floor. I leaned over and picked up one last picture. Anna had her arm casually looped over Olive's shoulders as she kissed Olive on the cheek. Olive smiled at the camera. I wouldn't have recognized where the picture had been taken if it wasn't for the swing in the background. The very swing my mother had died in.

"Jade?"

I looked at Keith.

He put down his spoon. "Everything all right?"

"Yes." I smiled as I slipped that picture beside the other one I had taken. "How's your Cantonese Buddhist Delight?"

8

Accident

I leaned on the horn but the Corvette with its tinted windows came straight at me.

MY MORNING BEGAN with a violent swipe at the alarm clock. I dragged my body upright in bed and peered at the red digital numbers winking at me from the night stand. Lately, I had the sleep patterns of a hamster. Blinking heavy eyelids, I wished the numbers would flick back an hour so I could crawl back under my duvet. But my good Catholic upbringing forbade such laziness, and I whipped back the blankets, annoying my cat Chin Chin, who had, during the night, curled up on the foot of my bed. Stumbling through an obstacle course of discarded clothes, tasseled pillows, and spiked heels, I barged into the bathroom and began my ritual: shower, dress, and straighten hair while mentally reviewing my submissions on sentence.

It had been three days since Jules's funeral and the wheels of justice continued to turn. I would be up against Jonah Aristotle, Q.C., one of the Crown's oldest yet respected prosecutors, on a theft charge of a five thousand dollar diamond ring. My client, a kleptomaniac, who also happened to be the daughter of a Member of Parliament, had walked out of Lady Claire Jewellery with the rock on her finger.

Jonah wanted jail time. I wanted a conditional sentence and

counselling.

And at 10 o'clock that morning, sitting in Madame Justice Smither's courtroom, I got what I wanted.

I gathered my pens, tucked my file under my arm and cruised out of the courtroom. The courthouse halls were crowded during the morning break. I squeezed past beer-smelling bikers speaking with suits and teenage boys, the crotch of their pants hanging to their knees. Crown Counsel Bianca Taylor nodded at me while maintaining a conversation with a teary young mother clutching a baby. I pushed through the courthouse doors escaping the pandemonium of guilt and innocence, good versus evil, right against wrong. All that mattered was that my client was happy, my client's father was happy, and I was happy. I had nailed another small victory.

I spotted my Audi, one in a string of vehicles parked along the street, and pulled my car keys from my purse. That's when I glimpsed the picture of my father and Anna. I tugged it out, glancing at it as I marched toward my vehicle. She looked so damn happy. So did my father. When had they become an item? Was Anna mistress number two, three, or four? I put the photo back in my purse. I should feel pity for this dead woman but instead I now felt anger. How dare she disrupt our lives? Technically, my father hadn't cheated. My mother was dead. But still, why did Anna have to become involved with him?

My purse strap slipped from my shoulder. I flung it back over. Memories of my parents's late night screaming matches, shattering dishes, and my father storming out of the house not to return until morning replayed in my mind. On those terrifying evenings, my miniature Schnauzer, Pogo, would slip into my room and crawl under the covers, calming my fears.

I pressed the fob to disarm my car alarm then shoved the key into the lock. I looked over the roof. A red and blue double-decker transit bus laboured up the street. Silence no more, Father.

I opened the car door and sat, tossing my purse and file on the passenger seat. I dug out my cell phone and called Kate. I would be out of the office for a few hours. I had an appointment. I lied. I tossed my phone onto the passenger seat and pulled onto Quadra Street. After a fifteen-minute drive, I found myself cruising down Pearl Drive. I passed mansions behind wrought iron gates. The Aubischon residence was next door to my father's. My mother had died in James Aubischon's backyard and Jules had been murdered in his study. I was never stepping foot on that property again. I saw the cobblestone driveway of my father's residence. I slowed.

The driveway stretched and curved, disappearing into a maple grove. Childhood memories knocked, wanting to be let out. No time to play.

He'd deny his involvement. Give me a bullshit excuse wrapped in a condescending smile, and ask if I was fabricating stories again. I'd end up storming out.

I gripped the shifter. I didn't need his crap. But Jules and Anna were dead. *You're in danger, Jade*, Jules had told me. I shifted into first and pulled into the driveway.

Home. I cruised under the forbidding wrought iron archway.

Father's black Ferrari was parked outside the three-bay garage. He still had a flare for Italian sports cars. I drove around the circular garden and parked. Tulip stocks pushed out of the ground and under the large oak tree purple, and yellow crocuses sprinkled the lawn. I remembered picking crocuses for my mother, but they always wilted by the time I got them into the house. I removed the key from the ignition and undid my seat belt. I grabbed my purse and stepped out.

Robins twittered, reminding me of a time I chose to forget. The smell of the freshly cut lawn softened my hard city edge. I used to stumble and roll over these lawns. Pogo bouncing at my heels. No family pet ran to greet me now.

I dug my heels into the cobblestones, straightened my spine and swung my hair over my shoulder. An image in black in my dress slacks and suit coat, I climbed up the stone steps of my father's stone castle, breathing in the crispness of a lingering winter. I reached for the doorbell and stopped at the sight of the scales of justice depicted in brown and gold stained glass.

Justice.

My finger stretched and curled.

Justice for whom?

I pressed the doorbell. Chimes echoed.

Footsteps thumped down the hall then the door swung open, and Edith stood in her black uniform. Her dark hair, streaked with grey, was pulled into a bun. Her skin, sagging and wrinkled, had lost the battle with time. Had I been away that long? Lifeless eyes assessed me at first and then sparkled.

"Jade." She stepped forward, then back, opening the door wider. "Come in, dear, come in."

I stepped across a checkerboard marble floor into a world of walnut trimmed archways, mahogany spiral staircases, twelve-foot ceilings and heart pine panelling. My father's antique chair and bureau were still flush against the east wall, under the oil painting of Great Uncle Thyme. Legend had it that Great Uncle Thyme had worked as a police officer and had been a friend of Judge Begbie, the hanging judge.

Home.

"Jade, you look beautiful," Edith said, taking my cold hands into her soft warm ones. "Your hair is so long, and you have your mother's white streak."

I smiled. "How are you, Edith?"

"The arthritis is getting worse. In two months I'm having my second knee replacement surgery. But your father takes good care of me. He installed an elevator so I don't have to use the stairs."

"How considerate."

"Is he expecting you?"

"No."

Apprehension flickered across Edith's face, but she quickly hid it with a smile. "Why don't you wait in the library. Come."

She led me down to the other end of the house, commenting

on my appearance on the national news during Jules's trial.

As I followed her into the labyrinth of my father's home, the old owl of foreboding perched on my shoulder, digging its talons into my skin. I should have made an appointment. I should have called ahead of time. I should leave.

Edith opened the mahogany library doors. I smelled leather–bound books, old wood, and my father's musky pipe smoke. I gripped the door frame, choking back the overbearing desire to run.

"Have a seat, Jade." Edith waved me in.

I took a few hesitant steps.

"I'll get your father." She walked out of the library, closing the door behind her.

Trapped. I crossed my arms.

Sage and I were never allowed in this room, which might explain my reluctance to enter it. We had walked past it many times, peeking through the slightly open door, listening to voices, trying to identify to whom our father was speaking. But Father always picked up on our presence. It didn't help that Sage always stepped on the creaky spot on the floor. Father would only have to bellow our names and we'd run.

I slung my purse over my left shoulder and approached the bookshelf: photos of my father and James; my father and Judge DeWitt; my father and the old mayor of Victoria; my father and the university rugby team, not one picture of my mother, or Sage and me. My fingers traced the gold lettering on the spines of *War and Peace*, *Macbeth*, *Julius Caesar*.

I walked over to the window seat and stared at the terraced gardens, the rhododendron bushes, and the ornamental maple trees. How many times had he stood in this spot and watched us? Never a smile on his face. Never a wave of recognition, only . . . resentment. Sage and I weren't boys. We knew from a young age that we occupied a small portion of his life—a pink wedge in dad's life game of Trivial Pursuit. I stepped away from the window, trailing my hand over the uneven surface of the hand-painted globe. I turned and that's when I saw above the fireplace the large oil painting of my mother.

My heart stopped.

I told myself to breathe and reached a hand out to the back of the sofa. Her blue eyes, so clear, so caring; her smile; the locks of hair that curled around her face. She wore cream pants and a cream sleeveless shirt and sat on the Persian rug before the fireplace, hugging her knees. She was so beautiful. I didn't look at all like her. I had my father's looks—same nose, same chin, same smile. I couldn't walk past a glass paned building without seeing shadows of him.

The floor creaked.

I turned.

Father stood in the doorway.

Age had not shown him any favours. His sharp chin and wide jaw were now hidden under pillows of pale, pudgy skin. Broad shoulders stooped, he had shrunk in height and stature. He tried compensating for his aging body by wearing expensive, well-cut clothes. Hair greyish white, stylishly cut and spiked. Female court reporters had once told me over a beer after a long laborious trial, that my father made them feel *naked, sexy*, when he looked at them. I had nearly spat out my beer. He made me feel like I was nine years old.

Father walked across the room and stopped in front of me. "Jade," he whispered.

My body tensed.

He held out his hands. "You look stunning."

I wrapped my hands around my waist. "Father."

His discomfort at my lack of affection showed briefly in his face. He placed his hands in his pockets. The floor creaked and he turned. "Edith, tea."

She shuffled from the doorway.

He looked at me again, a smile on his face. "Come sit down, Jade." He indicated the cream sofas. I sat on the edge of one, relieved he sat on the other.

"What brings you home?" He rubbed the palms of his hands together.

I cleared my throat and with shaking fingers pressed the catch on my purse. "I have—" I cleared my throat again "—a picture."

"A picture? You drove out here to show me a picture? You couldn't email it to me?"

No. I wanted an honest explanation, not a liability-free one. I pulled the picture out of my purse. "I need to know what your relationship was with her?" I sucked in my breath and flung the picture across the table.

My father took his glasses from his shirt pocket. He flipped the picture around. He whipped the glasses off and glared. "Where the hell did you get this?"

"I found it."

"Like Hell! Jules gave this to you!"

"Was he supposed to? Supposedly you and Anna saw a lot of each other." The cork removed, my anger fizzed out like cheap champagne. "Did you sleep with her?"

My father dropped the picture on the table and stood. "That is none of your business!"

"Father, she's dead. The police—"

"—The police can't prove anything! They're incompetent fools who don't know how to dig their heads out of their asses." He marched over to the bar, dropped two ice cubes into a tumbler, and poured himself a drink. "We wouldn't be having this conversation if they had done their job right the first time."

He threw back a mouthful of Jack Daniels but didn't offer me one. I could have used a drink. "You're being investigated for murder—" I stood "—a little cooperation would help."

He spun around. "Your insinuation, Jade Thyme—"

"—Insinuation! You're a *murder* suspect."

"I don't need to prove my innocence to you, or any one else!"

"Then stop acting like you've got something to hide."

He fired me one of his cutting looks, but I didn't waver.

"Anna and Jules were *murdered*. The police think you did it.

They've reopened Anna's case."

He took another mouthful of his drink. "People die, Jade. Final lesson of life."

I grabbed the photo and held it out. "Who killed her? Who killed Jules? He was once your son-in-law. Your Thursday morning golf buddy."

My father scoffed and walked over to the fireplace. He leaned his elbow against the hearth.

"Was Norman involved with her? Jules? Troy? What was going on among all of you? Why won't you say *anything*?"

"God dammit, Jade, stop!"

I stared.

He walked over to me and grabbed the photo out of my hand. He looked at it. "Anna needed legal advice. Our relationship was strictly professional." He flung the photo back. "Why are you involved with this?"

"Because I'm a suspect too."

He clinked the ice cubes around in his glass. "If the RCMP are looking at you and me, then they have no idea who committed the crimes."

"Was Jules blackmailing you?"

My father froze. "No."

"Then what are you hiding?"

"Nothing!"

"Someone murdered Jules and Anna, and you know why. How can you protect such a person?"

My father's dark eyes bore into my soul. If I had been twelve, I would have run, but I stood my ground.

He thumped his glass on the table, and straightened to his full height. "You have no clue what you're involved with. Neither did Anna, neither did Jules. The Society is invisible. You think you know where they are? You think you know who's a member? They're a plague. Norman thought he knew, so did Jules, and they're both dead! Stay out of this, Jade. The police won't touch you. You're too valuable for both sides."

The Society? I had to get father to spill. Get him riled. The only way I'd get answers. What did I have to lose, he didn't like me anyway. Change tactics. "How many others, Father? Is that why Mother died? Of a broken heart?"

My father clenched his fists. "I know what you're doing. It won't work." He walked over to the fireplace. "Even if you do find something, no one will believe you."

"You—" I walked after him "—a man of the court, a professor of law, how can you protect this person? Or is it persons?"

"What I know will be of little use to you or anyone! If anything, it will only destroy you. Jules knew that, but he thought he was invincible. He thrived on other people's pain, used it for his own means." My father looked me up and down. "You should know that."

"He was going to expose them, this group, this, what did you call it, a *Society*? That's why he was killed."

"Jade, drop it!"

"Why should I?!"

"Because they'll kill you!"

A disjointed, surreal feeling came over me. *Kill me.*

"Leave this alone. And the next time you visit, make an appointment. You can show yourself out." He walked toward the door.

I tapped the back of the couch and looked over at the bookshelves filled with legal tomes. "Did you have a mistress before, during, or after you buried Mother?"

My father stopped. He turned, his expression livid. He marched up to me and backhanded me across the face.

I toppled over the back of the sofa.

Edith screamed. There was a crash.

My face pressed into the sofa cushion, my cheek tingled as if pricked by needles. I dug my nails into the piping and hauled myself up. Blood flowed from my nose and left a stain on the cushion. I brushed the hair back from my face and groped around the pillows for my purse. I snatched at the leather strap.

"Jade, I'm—" my father stepped forward.

I stumbled from the sofa. "Don't—" I choked back a sob, swallowing blood.

"Jade—" he stepped closer.

"Get away from me!"

"Jade, please—"

Wobbling on my heels, I made for the door.

"Jade. Why are you doing this? Jules is out of your life!"

I pushed myself away from the doorway and stumbled down the hall. Edith sobbed, holding her hands to her cheeks.

"Jade. *Jade.*"

My hip collided with the armoire. I heaved open the front door and stumbled down the stone steps. I pulled my keys from my purse and jammed the right one into the lock. I tossed everything into the car, including myself. Horror and shame swallowed me up and spat me out. Body trembling, I gripped the steering wheel. Past images of my father, drunk, his black silhouette stumbling up the stairs, bellowing my mother's name. Another sob wracked my body. I slammed my fist against the steering wheel. God damn him. God damn him to Hell! Why didn't Mother pack us up and leave? I wiped the blood from my nose then turned the key in the ignition. The Audi purred to life. I dropped the clutch and screeched down the drive. Trees flashed past my windows and rearview mirror as I made my way to the gates.

I was in control. I repeated the words over and over again. I wouldn't let him steal what I had, what years of therapy had given back. I wouldn't let him diminish my self-worth. I wouldn't let him. I was in control.

I swallowed and brushed at my eyes. The Audi gripped the curve and I shifted into second. The wrought iron gates stood open. I whipped past them and out onto the street, shifting into third. I glided down Pearl Drive, trying to paste together the pieces of me that had fallen apart. My therapist had said I would need to confront him. Well, I had. I didn't feel any better.

I shifted into second as I turned a hairpin curve. That's when I saw the deer. I slammed on the brakes. The tires screeched. The Audi veered to the left before stopping across the centreline. The deer leapt into the trees.

I pressed my hand against my forehead. Jesus. I ran my hand through my hair and that's when I saw her. *Anna.*

Wearing her rhinestone pink bodysuit, she placed a calla lily across the hood of the Audi. She smiled and mouthed something.

"What?"

She spoke again and pointed down the road and made a rocking motion as if rocking a baby.

I looked down the road. Nothing. I looked back at her but she was gone. I was losing my mind. I shifted into reverse and backed up and turned so I was facing in the right direction. I then shifted into first and drove. I needed a vacation. I leaned my elbow against the door as I safely drove over hills and past multi-million-dollar homes. I sat back in the leather seat.

My father knew who murdered Jules and Anna, so the murderer had to be somebody close. Why else would he protect the person? Or, was it persons? What was this Society? At any rate, the motive had to involve him, that's why he was uncooperative and refused to tell me, or the police, anything. I sighed. My body shuddered. I pressed the button of the CD player and Beethoven's *Moonlight Sonata* filled the interior of the Audi. So how was I going to uncover the motive? If I exposed Anna's murderer I would expose Jules's. Who were the people involved with Anna? My father, Jules, Troy, and Norman Bastine. The missing law partner. My father and Troy wouldn't tell me anything. Jules was dead. That only left Norman.

I glided through an intersection, running a stop sign. I had to be more careful. Thank God nobody had been coming the other way. A long stretch of road ahead, I breathed deeply, trying to release tension. I would think about all of this later. Right now I had to get back to work. Safely. I stretched my neck to the left and then to the right. Up ahead, a black Corvette swung around the corner.

"Idiot."

The Corvette accelerated.

"Maniac." I checked my own speed.

The Vette cut into my lane.

"Shit!" I pressed the brake and shifted down. I leaned on the horn but the Corvette with its tinted windows came straight at me.

I laid on the horn again but the vette didn't stop. I cranked the wheel. The Audi spun. Moss, rocks and shrubs swirled before my eyes along with the ghostly smeared image of Anna's face. A tearing crunch ripped the side of the car, and I was thrown sideways. My head hit the side window.

9

Prescription

Or did she want me dead, like she was?

VOICES FADED IN and faded out.

A doctor was paged to emergency.

Dishes clattered.

Trolley wheels squeaked.

I rolled my head from side to side, trying to deaden the noise but that only made it worse. What were those sounds? I wanted them gone but they only grew louder, and that—that *smell*? A disinfectant smell mixed with *roast beef*? I moaned and raised my hand to my temple and instead touched a bandage. What had I done?

My eyes fluttered open. The brightness hurt and sliced across my forehead. I squinted. Everything teetered—the walls, bed curtains, food tray. I looked over at the window. Through gauzy curtains streetlights shone. A name band around my wrist, and a blue gown on my body, I was in a hospital all right. But how the hell did I get here?

Screaming brakes, the flash of a vehicle, my car spinning.

"Oh God." My shoulders and neck ached. I tried to sit but the thumping in my head raced into double time. I had no broken bones that I was aware of and none of my limbs were strung up in a harness or hanging from pulleys. I should consider myself lucky. I was just very sore. I touched my cheeks, feeling tiny cuts. Thank God I had been wearing my seat belt. But what about the other driver? He had come at me. Cutting straight into my lane. Had he been drunk? Had he survived?

I looked at the hospital window again. Five bright flower arrangements decorated the windowsill and more arrangements were lined up on the floor. I wasn't dead. I closed my eyes and released an unsteady breath. I looked back at the arrangements. The last one caught my eye. Calla lilies with white gladiolas. What one would find on a casket.

Calla lilies. Was someone trying to send me a message?

Anna had placed one calla lily on my car. Why was she tormenting me? I couldn't help her. Or did she want me dead, like she was? Had she sent me the arrangement—a rehearsal for my own funeral?

I stared at the calla lilies.

She was dead . . . but . . . I had spoken to her.

I placed my bandaged hand over my eyes. Faces of deranged colleagues scrolled by like 'wanted' posters. Was this how it started, losing one's mind? Seeing and talking to dead people. Would criminals I had once defended now haunt me? Was I really trying to solve Anna's and Jules's murders, or had I become fixated with their deaths? I was already a manic wretch who triple-checked the locks on her windows and doors in an attempt to keep the bad guys out. Or was it an attempt to keep my sanity locked in? Would I soon blow bubbles and babble about discarded victims and abandoned cases? The words *conspiracy*, *cover-up*, and *corruption* dominating my thoughts. Would my friends dash across the street to avoid me, or politely nod when I spoke to them for fear of "disturbing" me?

My arm slipped to my side. Anna had spoken to me even if she was dead. Her voice had sounded muffled but she had spoken, and I had responded. I had crossed that cellophane barrier that separated rational thoughts from irrational thoughts.

"No."

I stared at the calla lilies. I had to get out. Before interns jabbed me with needles and wheeled me up to the fifth floor—the psych ward.

I pushed myself up. The walls tilted to my left and the pounding in my head caused black spots in my vision. I waited for the spots to disappear. I had to get my feet on the floor. Walking would be another challenge, but I had to move. I flipped back the blankets.

From the corner of my eye, a dark image appeared in the doorway. *They're here to take me away.* I looked up. The image blurred. I blinked once, then twice, and regained my focus.

Keith stood, one hand in his pants pocket, the other holding a small vase of purple and pink flowers.

"Jade." He walked toward me.

I couldn't move.

He stepped over to the bed, placing the vase on the side table. The smell of his leather coat combined with the smell of his cologne hushed my fears. He gave me an assessing look. "What are you doing, Jade Thyme?"

Escaping.

He picked up my bandaged hand and caressed it, then gently placed it back on the bed. He pulled the blankets over my legs. "Speeding on Pearl Drive as if you're in the Molson Indy is not a smart thing to do, counsellor. You nearly killed yourself."

I touched his arm. "Keith, I have to get out of here. You have to help me."

"Jade—" he gently pushed me back "—calm—"

"—No!" I clutched his arms. "They'll take me away!" Oh my God. I sounded like a crazy person.

"Who will take you away?"

The Society. Keep that thought to yourself.

I pulled the blankets up to my chest, twisting the wool material around my fingers.

Keith sat on the side of the bed. "No one's going to take you away, Jade. You're in a hospital. You're safe. You've been in a horrible accident, and I thought it best you stay overnight for observation." He leaned forward and brushed a strand of hair away from my face.

"I can't stay here. They'll, they'll—"

"—Make you better." He cupped my face in his hands. "You're lucky to be alive, Jade. I shouldn't even be here, but the doctor agreed to let me have a few minutes. She said you might be disoriented."

Disoriented? So that's how they were categorizing me? Did that mean I was a level one, two, or three security risk?

"Why were you driving so fast?" he asked.

I wasn't.

"Jade?"

I looked at Keith's flowers. "I visited my father."

"And?"

I bit my lip.

Keith touched the tender area of my cheek where my father's hand had left his mark. "Your father?"

I nodded.

Keith's jaw hardened. He knew my history with my father. The violence. He was the only one who knew. He had witnessed it one Christmas Eve when James had come to visit. I had been a teenager at the time, and I was fed up with Father bullying my mother.

"He knows, Keith." I looked at him. "My father knows who killed Jules and Anna."

The colour drained from Keith's face. "He knows?"

"I showed him the picture of him and Anna—"

"—What picture?"

"The one that I got—" from Troy's briefcase. I looked down at my name band.

"What picture, Jade?"

"The photo I had taken out of Troy's briefcase the night we were at the Ginger Lee. It was just a photo of my father and Anna. I shouldn't have taken it, but—" I sighed, feeling very tired and worn "—I wanted to know . . . know why he loved her and not me. Has Troy asked about the photo?"

Keith lifted my chin with his thumb, forcing me to look him in the eye. "I haven't returned Troy's briefcase yet. He's out of town interviewing clients. What did your father say?"

"Nothing. He—"

"Hit you?"

I nodded and sniffed. "He knows, Keith. He knows who killed them!"

"Did he tell you?"

"No."

Keith sat back, his body relaxed. "Then what makes you think he knows?"

"He said Jules and Anna didn't leave well enough alone, that's why they were killed. He doesn't care that he's being implicated for their murders. He just—" I shook my head and then groaned "—he doesn't care!"

Keith ran his hand over my matted hair. "Have you shown the picture to the police?"

"No."

"Don't."

I looked at him.

"You can't trust them, Jade. They want to tidy these murders up nice and quick. Get their man, be it your father, Troy or you. Do you have the picture now?"

"No. When Father—hit me I dropped it." I was sort of glad that Keith was present, but ashamed that he was seeing me in this state—physically and mentally BandAided together.

"Did your father give you any clue as to whom this person may be?"

"No. He told me not to get involved or else—"

"Or else what?"

I whispered. "They'd kill me." I brushed my hand over my cheeks, wincing at the pull of cuts.

"Who's they?" he asked.

Don't say it. Don't. "The S-Society," I whispered again.

A hardness set in his jaw. He cupped my face in his hands again. "No one will lay a hand on you, Jade Thyme."

I tried to smile.

Keith looked deep into my eyes. "I promise you." He kissed my cheek. "You are not alone," he whispered. He pulled me in for a hug.

I eased into his embrace and every anxious nerve relaxed.

"You promise not to talk to anyone about the picture or the Society."

"Yes."

"Say it."

"I promise. Who are they, Keith?" I pulled away. "Do you know?"

His eyes softened. "People you don't want to know."

I looked at my hands. "So they really exist."

"Too much so."

"Have you ever been threatened by them?"

He looked down at the blanket. "No." He cleared his voice. "But I've heard stories. Rumours."

"Such as?"

"Stories about Norman and his disappearance. But I don't want you thinking about that."

"How did you know I was here?"

"Sergeant Stone. I was at the courthouse talking to Bianca about the search warrant hearing, when Stone interrupted us. He said he had received an anonymous tip that you were in a car accident."

"Visiting hours are over, sir," an authoritative female voice interrupted.

Keith and I looked at the doctor standing in the doorway.

"You have to go," she said to Keith. "How are you doing, Jade?" She walked into the room.

"I'm feeling okay. I want to go home."

The doctor glanced at Keith before looking at me. "Best you stay overnight. Press the button if you need anything. Good night." She walked out of my room.

"I better go." Keith removed his hand from mine. He picked up a pill bottle and read the prescription. "Vicodin. You're feeling no pain. Get some rest, Jade, and tomorrow I'll spring you from this joint."

But I want to go home now.

Keith gave my good hand a little squeeze then reached forward and clicked off the bedside lamp.

"Keith."

"Yeah."

"How's the other driver?"

There was a moment's silence then the black outline of his body leaned forward and he clicked on the light. "What other driver, Jade?"

"There was another driver."

"Stone said it was a single car accident."

Single car accident! I stared at the ceiling.

"There was another driver?"

"Yes. He came straight at me. I spun out of control trying to avoid him."

"What was he driving?"

"A black Corvette. It all happened so fast. I'm not lying." My voice rose. "I know what I saw!" I had also seen a ghost.

"We'll talk about this. Keep that information to yourself, right now, all right?"

I couldn't tell anybody anything.

"I'll find out what's going on."

I nodded.

He stepped to the foot of the bed. "Get some rest, Jade." He gave my foot a squeeze. "We'll get to the bottom of this."

10

Job Offer

"Watch yourself, Jade, because the Society will be watching you."

I DREAMT ABOUT Osmond last night. He had stood over my hospital bed, his hand caressing my face. I had tried to speak but no words came out. He had leaned over and kissed my forehead then whispered something in my ear before I faded into sleep.

My cell phone trilled.

I jumped, scratching a red pen line across the police report I had been reading. I groaned and dropped my head into my hand. The fourth time that day—being startled. The first scare was walking across the street after Keith had dropped me off. A Trans Am slammed on its brakes at a red light. The second scare had involved my own reflection in the bathroom mirror. The third had happened when I'd given Chin Chin her supper and she'd hissed and arched her back at her food dish.

I reached for my cell but it stopped ringing. I sat back, releasing a deep breath, and slipped my index finger behind the lenses of my glasses and rubbed my eyes.

My frazzled nerves were the result of long hours in the company of murder scene photographs—eight-by-ten glossies gruesome in their detail and lurid in their sprawl across my dining room table. I wasn't scheduled to be back at work yet, but as a favour to Bianca, who was short on prosecutors, I had agreed to take on a few charge approvals. I glanced at the macabre display. It wasn't the first time my dining room table had been witness to such crimes.

No, Jade. It isn't the photos and it isn't the police report that goes with them. Talking to myself again. The real reasons for my fears had to do with the accident and seeing Anna's ghost.

I had tapped into a spiritual world beyond my control. I hadn't asked for this psychic excursion that came free of travel insurance. And what the hell, I had more than my share of living humans to deal with, might as well add a couple of dead ones to really muck up my mind. Yet I couldn't help but wonder if through me, Anna was making her presence known. I dropped my hands to the arms of the dining room chair. Chin Chin, a Himalayan cat, poised on the back of the leather sofa, blinked and swished her tail.

"You're not allowed up there."

She flicked her tail.

"Are you sensing her too?"

She pounced off the sofa and sauntered across to the chair where I sat. She rubbed her body against my leg. I reached down and scratched her back. "You and me both."

My cell phone rang again. I picked it up. "Hello."

Bianca's husky voice crackled in my ear—someone living! She was in her Corvette on her way home from a boxing class. Would I be interested in a coffee? I agreed to meet her at the coffee shop on the bottom floor of my building.

I glanced at the photograph of Colton Yorke, his lifeless body sprawled on a restaurant seat, his chest and head riddled with bullet holes. Things could be worse. It could be me. Dead. I flipped the file closed and made a quick change into jeans and a black cardigan. I slipped on a comfortable pair of knee-high boots, threw Chin Chin a kitty treat, and was out the door.

Jabba Java hissed from the sound of espresso machines, loud voices and jazz. Musicians with dreadlocks and ragged clothes slouched over the coffee table near the main counter while near the front window, a half dozen university students in turtlenecks and Tommy Hilfiger jeans sat in a booth.

I waited in line with other die-hard coffee fans and eyed the list of mochas and special teas written on the chalkboard behind the wooden counter. Jabba Java, having been designed in colours of lime green and tangerine and with modern stainless steel lamps hanging from ten-foot ceilings, reminded me more of a nouveau art gallery than a coffee shop. It had recently been written up as the "in" spot in *Boulevard* magazine. I placed my order with a young woman with vampire red hair and a number of rings in one eyebrow, then strolled over to the wood counter flush with the other front window. I slid onto a lime green stool just as Bianca pulled open the door and glided in. Dressed in a white sleeveless belly shirt and low-riding tight jeans, her platinum blonde hair swayed in time with her hips. She waved then weaved her way between chairs and tables, stirring up lustful glances from the male patrons.

I never looked like *that* after a fitness class. I ran my fingers through my hair and sat straighter. Vampire Red pushed my Tazo Chai tea across the wooden counter. Foam slopped onto the saucer.

"Jade, honey." Bianca slid onto a stool. She looked at Vampire Red. "I'd like a tall and dark—just like my men. Not that decaf shit."

Vampire Red spun on her heels and marched over to the university guys.

Bianca turned to me. "How the hell are you? I heard about the car accident, and by the look of your face—"

"—Some jerk thought he was driving in England and wanted to use my lane."

"Brutal. Any word on criminal charges or whether the lout will pay for damages?"

I stirred my tea and glanced at my bandaged hand. "First the cops need to find him."

"Shit. Otherwise you're all right?"

All right? I see dead people and I pop a lot more Vicodin. I forced a smile. "The accident triggered an old running injury in my lower back from high school. I have a prescription. How's work?"

She rolled her eyes. "The special prosecutor who took a one-year leave of absence because he wanted to trek across the Sahara on a camel?"

"Yeah."

Vampire Red brought Bianca her mug and snatched the five-dollar bill Bianca held out to her.

"Tom likes riding that camel so fucking much—" Bianca reached across for a bowl of artificial sweeteners "—he's not coming back."

I dropped my spoon on my saucer. "He's not!" I, and another lawyer had taken over Thomas's workload, hence the reason for the Colton Yorke charge approval on my dining room table.

"That's right. Tom, bless his Godforsaken soul—" Bianca ripped open a packet and dumped the fine white powder into her mug "—was our designated special prosecutor. Anything too big or showed possible bias on the Crown, Thomas took on. He prosecuted the cabinet minister on sex charges. He approved the murder charge involving the owner of Jenny Jiggle Escorts."

I brought my tea to my lips. "What are you going to do now?"

Bianca stirred her coffee. "Ask you to take over."

I froze. The heat of my tea burned my lips. I put my mug down. "What?"

Bianca sipped her coffee, made a face, and grabbed another sweetener. "Think about it, Jade. It's not a glamourous job. No bonuses, partnerships, extravagant parties, or vacation packages in the Dominican Republic." She dumped the second sweetener in her coffee and picked up her spoon. "You're day in and day out dealing with a two-tiered justice system. If you prosecute a wealthy man who has political affiliations, hope like hell you get a conviction, because the next day he's going to sue your ass. Judges hate you, victims hate you, the police hate you, accused hate you. But—" she placed her spoon on the saucer "—if you want an awesome office with a view, migraines, ulcers, the chance to work with experts in the forensic field, and have the satisfaction of putting animals like the university strangler behind bars, well, do I have a job for you." She lifted her mug in a mock toast.

A smile cracked my lips and I picked up my own mug. "And why am I supposed to take this job?"

"Because both you and I know prosecuting is what you do best."

"Really?"

"You got it." Bianca swallowed a gulp. "Ah, wonderful."

I leaned my elbows against the wooden counter and looked out the window at the passing headlights. "Your timing sucks, Bianca. You know I have this partnership hanging over my head."

"Aubischon hasn't confirmed anything yet?"

"He's been busy, and then the murders."

Bianca eyed me. "Fine. It's your future." She leaned against her elbows and sipped her coffee.

Unease slithered up my spine. I looked at her. "What's the real reason for the job offer?"

"There's no other reason."

"Then why do I get the feeling you're throwing me a life-preserver, not an opportunity?"

Bianca placed the mug on its saucer and flipped her blonde hair over her shoulder. "Look, Jade, I never liked Aubischon."

"Which one?"

"Both. Your partnership should have been made public by now."

"Keith told me it's mine."

Bianca leaned back and crossed her legs. "Lawyers spew a lot of shit, Jade. You know for sure you're in and Reilly's out?"

I hesitated. "Y-y-yes."

Bianca picked up her spoon and pivoted it on its edge against the counter. "Then why hasn't Keith made the announcement?"

"Work, Bianca. It's been nuts."

"It's an announcement, Jade, not a goddamn merger. Aubischon's secretary could type the thing in five minutes."

I squirmed on my stool. "You know something, don't you?"

"Nope."

She had said 'nope' a little too quickly. I stared at her, her face expressionless. She could very well be lying. I couldn't tell. She was that good.

"I have a partnership, Bianca."

She remained silent.

"Thank you for considering me."

She pivoted her spoon from tip to tip.

"What's really going on, Bianca? Somebody doesn't want me at the firm?"

"I need another Crown, Jade."

I gulped my tea. Its spicy warmth did nothing to soothe my edge.

"Jade, you're a damn good lawyer."

I speak with ghosts.

Bianca's violet eyes sparkled like a prism. High cheekbones, cupid lips, she wasn't wealthy, Crown prosecutors didn't get paid that well in B.C., but she was in the right occupation to meet influential people. During her various trysts, she had picked up a lot of information from her sexually delirious bed partners. She knew *something*.

I placed the mug down hard. A Vicodin would be good right now.

"Look Jade, how about you tell me what's going on?"

That I was going crazy? Or that Anna visited me on occasion?

I tapped my finger against the counter. "The cops say my accident was a result of my poor driving and that no one else was involved."

"But you said—"

"—there was another car, Bianca. Keith's trying to get me a police file number, but he keeps hitting dead ends." I looked outside. Sergeant Stone stood across the street next to a lamppost, watching me. A semi-truck rumbled down the road and stopped before the coffee shop, obliterating my view. The truck hissed and rolled back then slowly pulled forward into traffic. Stone was gone.

"Jade."

I stared at the vacant spot. *Was Stone watching me*?

"Jade!"

I looked at Bianca.

"So what are you going to do about the accident?"

"I don't know." I swished the tea around in my cup then looked her in the eye. Time to drop the bomb. "I think the Society's involved."

Bianca's cheeks drained of colour and her eyes quickly scanned the coffee shop. "Jesus, Jade." She lowered her voice. "Watch what you're saying."

"So you know of them."

She was silent.

"My father believed Jules and Anna had uncovered something about the Society."

"And you think the Society's involved with your accident?" she whispered.

She wasn't denying their existence. "Or caused it. A black Corvette, like yours, came speeding straight at me. An anonymous tip called in the accident. Victoria police have no record of it ever happening. The insurance company is giving me grief because I can't provide them with a police file number or a name. It makes a big difference on my claim if I can prove fault on the other party, instead of the incident being regarded as a single-car accident. But that's not what's bothering me."

Bianca sat still. Not a usual endeavor for this Crown prosecutor.

"What do you know?"

She took a long swallow of coffee and focused her gaze outside. "Nothing."

I'd try another tactic. "Why do you think Norman Bastine disappeared?"

Bianca frowned. "I don't know."

"I think you do."

Bianca pulled a cigarette out of her pack, then cursed, realizing the coffee shop was a non-smoking environment.

"Anna and Jules found out about the Society and their practices. Whatever the Society is involved with it's more than illegal bingo. Norman knew something, didn't he?"

Bianca said nothing.

"If I can find Norman maybe he can give me answers, because you know what, I think he's alive. Hiding."

"Look, Jade—" she held her hand out towards me "—they're dangerous."

"Who?"

She leaned over her cup. "Norman is alive. And yes, he's hiding, but because of them."

"The Society?"

"Yes."

"Where's Norman, Bianca?"

"Around. He—" she glanced over her shoulder again, an action which coming from Bianca seemed bizarre and frightening. If she was looking over her shoulder, what should I be doing?

"He doesn't have a permanent residence," she whispered.

"Where does he hang out?"

"Jade, leave this alone. Even if you do find out something, what are you going to do? You're not a cop. We lose cases even when the police follow the correct procedures. You go in solo, the legal ramifications, your life. Whatever you find out will never make it into a courtroom and neither will you."

"Are you threatening me, Bianca?"

Her eyes widened, and she shook her head in disbelief. "For Christ's sake, Jade. I'm warning you."

"They have to be stopped."

"But you're not the one to do it."

"Then who is?"

Sergeant Stone walked up behind Bianca and placed his hand on her shoulder. "Bianca."

She looked up and he kissed her on the forehead.

Oh my God.

Bianca averted my gaze. "Jade, you remember Sergeant Stone?"

"You two are an item?" I asked. I was tired of niceties, and I couldn't believe Bianca was with *him*.

Stone smiled. "We're friends."

God help me if he said "with benefits", I would throw up.

"How have you been feeling, Jade?" Stone asked, rubbing Bianca's back.

"Couldn't be better. I'm having difficulties getting a police file number for my accident. Supposedly, you got the call."

"The report must be getting transcribed."

"What are you doing here, Sergeant Stone? You're not using my friend—" I looked at Bianca, who wouldn't look at me "—as an excuse to question me?"

"I'm not questioning you, Jade."

Bullshit.

"But now that you bring it up, I find it odd that Jules's head was placed on a dining room table, not seen by anyone and nobody heard his screams. Do you find that odd, Jade?"

Bianca still wouldn't look at me. What the hell was going on? What did Stone have on her?

"Yes, I do. Just like I find it odd that the police can't locate the black Corvette that ran me off the road. What type of car do you drive, Sergeant Stone? Or did you borrow Bianca's Corvette yesterday morning?"

Bianca glared.

Stone shook his head and chuckled. "Now that I think about it, Jade, I did see the police report. I'm sure your insurance company will want to know, that you were under the influence of prescription drugs when you had your single vehicle accident."

I was stunned.

Stone smirked. "Well, love, you and Jade have talked long enough. It's time to get home."

The arrogant prick was shutting us down.

Bianca threw back the last of her coffee.

Stone was about to say something when his phone buzzed.

1-800-SOC-IETY I wanted to ask.

"Excuse me, love," he said to Bianca. He walked outside and stood on the steps.

Bianca looked me straight in the eye. "Norman's a transient," she said quickly. "He never stays in one place too long. Try Fan Tan Alley." She stood.

"Bianca, what does he—" I nodded at Stone who had finished his call "—have on you?"

Bianca pulled car keys from her pocket. She leveled serious dark eyes at me. "Some lawyers are granted privilege in court, while others have their asses chewed off. Watch yourself, Jade, because the Society is watching you."

11

Fan Tan Alley

"I've seen the friggin' Pope and the Kardashians."

THE SOCIETY IS watching you.

Bianca's warning from the night before rang in my ears, stirring up unease. I still couldn't believe she was hooked up with Sergeant Stone. Tough, take no prisoners Bianca had slipped into a shadow of herself as soon as Sergeant Stone had shown up. What did he have on her? Unlike Bianca, I was not going to let Stone intimidate me, no matter what was written in that police report.

High on a prescription confidence, I was out to play detective with two bottles of cheap wine and a loaf of bread tucked into my large shoulder bag.

If bread and wine were good enough for Jesus, why not the denizens of skid row? I wanted to narrow down my search for Norman and had an old photo of him on my phone. I, a single white female, would be the obvious minority in Chinatown.

I weaved my way along Douglas Street between men and women in suits, street people and university students. Dressed in jeans, sneakers and a sweatshirt, I blended in with the crowd. I didn't want to be recognized by one of the suits, or anyone else for that matter. My car accident had awakened a new sense of caution, and my survival depended on my anonymity.

I stopped at a crosswalk along with a half dozen other pedestrians. Cars and trucks, their tires slurping the wet pavement, whizzed past. A horn blared as a taxi made an illegal left-hand turn. Somewhere someone swore. Raindrops splattered and umbrellas popped open, my fellow Victorians looking like green, black and yellow toadstools. Across the street a man holding a tin cup sat on the cement steps of St. Peter's Cathedral. Hunched over, he serenaded a lamppost. The light changed, the chirping alert for the blind sounded, and I dodged a grated manhole cover and crossed the street.

A small Chinese woman hauled a bucket of flowers out of a grocery store and onto the sidewalk. She rearranged two rows of buckets with their pink, purple and red blossoms and then with an unsteady heave, lifted the bucket she had brought out and placed it with the rest. I crossed another crosswalk and eyed the queue of customers waiting inside the newest trendy coffeeshop. Victoria was all about trends. I turned left on Fisgard and looked up at the red flared archway stretched across the street. The ceramic-tiled Gate of Harmonious Interest with a hand-carved stone dragon on either side guarded the entrance to Chinatown.

Flashing lights, pagoda roofs, and the dissonant sound of plucked strings, Fisgard Street housed a community and culture where I was the foreigner. During the late 1800s, Victoria's Chinatown was the largest one north of San Francisco, housing nearly ten thousand Chinese immigrants. Some of the people worked in the coal mines, others on the railway, while the more adventurous searched for gold. I walked past the open window of a spice shop, and breathed in a bizarre mixture of pleasant and repugnant odours. Two old women spewing rapid-fire Mandarin tugged on a bag of potatoes in front of another grocery store. A handful of giddy teenage girls bustled out of a trinket shop. I skirted around a large assortment of stacked wicker baskets and spotted a woman sleeping under a newspaper blanket.

My first candidate.

I slowed my step. This is what I had come for. But did I have the nerve to do it? Did I really want to talk to this creature who might spit on me?

No. But I knelt beside her.

"Hello."

The woman didn't move. I wasn't going to touch her.

"Excuse me—" I raised my voice and held out my phone "—have you seen—"

"Buzzsh off!" A leg kicked out from under her newspapers.

I jumped back. Okay. I stepped around her and walked further down the street. I told myself to remain calm. No harm done. I had dealt with worse in court. I got a better grip on my loot, when I noticed a man huddled under a blanket, slouched inside a covered doorway. Wearing a tattered coat, his toque pulled low over his head, he held out a dirty hat.

"Spare change?" he asked the people marching past him. "Spare change?"

I walked up to him and knelt. The homeless drug addict smell is unique. Body fluids mixed with dampness, cigarettes and alcohol, topped with B.O. The sad smell of neglect. I took the bottle out of my shoulder bag. "No change. But how about a bottle of red?"

His eyes glimmered.

"And a loaf of bread. Good enough for Jesus. Maybe get you a little redemption?"

"What do ya want?" he asked, his voice a dry croak.

I showed him the photo of Norman on my phone. "Have you seen him?"

He glanced at the picture. "You a cop?"

"No. Why?"

"They lookin' for him."

I arched my eyebrow. "They? The police?"

He slouched his shoulders.

"Have you seen him?"

His eyes shifted to the bottle. He swallowed. "Maybe. Don't know." He eyed me, his alcoholism overshadowing his street-earned wariness. "You, you wit' the other guys?"

I straightened my back and the hand holding the bottle dropped between my knees. "What other guys? Someone else is looking for him? What do they look like?"

The derelict looked around at the people walking on the street. One lady with long stockinged legs, chatting on her phone, nearly tripped over us. She looked back in disgust, before whipping her hair from side to side and continuing her catwalk strut. The derelict huddled down in his blanket.

"Please," I said. "I'm in trouble. I think he is too. I wouldn't be doing this otherwise."

He looked at me. Swallowed. "Lady, they kick the shit out of me and leave me for dead. You think anyone would notice?"

Sadly, no. Just another street person who got himself in trouble. "Who are they? The cops?"

He tugged on his blanket, tripping over his words. I had a hard time understanding what he was saying. His eyes wandered, always returning to the bottle in my hand. Finally, addiction won out over caution and he spat out, "Piccadilly. Salvation Army. Fourth Street. Bottle."

Despite its quaint country name, Piccadilly was Victoria's most gruesome neighbourhood. An area which many of Victoria's elite refused to acknowledge while enjoying afternoon tea at The Empress Hotel. An area not featured in tourist magazines. An area most definitely not visited by the Queen when on official tour.

"You're sure that's where I'll find him?" Bianca had said Fan Tan Alley. She also said he moved around.

He nodded, extending a shaky hand covered with scabs.

"B-bottle?"

I held out the wine bottle and the loaf of bread, which he snatched from my hands. "Thank you," I said, standing up.

The man stashed his loot under his blanket. "Noxzema man."

I stopped. "Noxzema man?"

"Nox for short." He huddled under his blanket, turning his

back to me, ending our conversation.

I walked past another homeless person who cuddled up to a dog. "Eh, I tell you things," dog-man called out. "I've seen the friggin' Pope and the Kardashians."

Together? I wondered. I smiled, thinking of the easiest and safest route to Piccadilly. I shouldn't even be going there alone. *Don't do anything stupid*, Bianca had said. Yeah, right. I was sure listening.

A few other derelicts watched me from under coats and sleeping bags. One woman shouted at me that hair dye was on sale for $4.99. Others shook their fists at imaginary enemies.

Across the street, five Chinese men with identical leather jackets, sunglasses, and spiked hair with blonde tips stood in a circle watching me. I glanced around, hoping they were watching someone else but there was no one around. Great. A gang. My steps became shorter, faster. Glancing behind, I saw them tracking me from across the street. Dammit! I thought of all the things to do if being followed: be in a crowd, be in bright places, and go where people can hear you scream. I pulled open the door to a butcher shop. Chimes clanged against the glass, announcing my arrival.

Wooden counters, dirty windows and worn spots on the floor, I spied dismembered chicken feet on a plate on the counter. Large destructive meat cleavers and an odd assortment of knives stood blade up against the back wall. I breathed in the smell of curried meat and age. A grandfatherly figure stood behind the counter, swiping a cleaver at a chunk of meat as he spoke Chinese to another elderly man.

"Can I help you?"

I stared at a tiny Chinese girl who looked about fourteen. Maybe the older man's granddaughter. I might as well get something while I was here.

"Yes. Two pounds of your barbecue pork."

"Barbecue pork. Two pound," she said in her broken English.

"Yes." I glanced out the front windows but because of the

sudden rays of sunlight, I couldn't see a thing.

"Twenty dollar."

The chimes clanged again. I jumped. A stocky woman laden with plastic bags bustled up to the counter. She eyed me through thick glasses.

The older man laughed and waved to his elderly customer, then lay a sheet of brown paper on a scale and unhooked the barbecue pork from the window. "Two pound?" he asked me.

The chimes clanged a third time.

"Yes."

"Twenty dollar," demanded the young girl.

I slipped my fingers into the front pocket of my jeans trying to pull out my money, when the exotic fragrance of designer cologne wafted over my shoulders, and a dark figure loomed to my right. I didn't have to look up to know that one gang member stood beside me. He wasn't here for the barbecue pork or the chicken feet. I glanced at the young girl.

"Twenty dollar," she said impatiently.

At that moment, the sunlight disappeared and the butcher shop grew darker. The meat cleavers, hanging carcasses and tastefully arranged delicacies looked grotesque. I thought about Jules and his missing body and myself going missing. No one knew I was in Chinatown. As far as the office was concerned, I had taken a couple days sick leave. I pulled out a twenty along with ATM receipts and Kleenex tissue. I held it all out to the girl, the twenty trembling in my hand.

The girl's face flushed. She quickly looked at the young man looming over my shoulder, grabbed my twenty and stashed it in the cash register.

The old man lumbered over and gave me a package wrapped in brown paper and a plastic bag. "Thank you," he said.

I took the package, nodded, and hustled around the woman and out the door. I stepped amongst school children and young mothers pushing strollers. I breathed in the musky air, relieved to be in bright open spaces. Steam from the quick rain shower rose from the street. No one would touch me out here.

I marched past another corner grocery with an obstacle course of produce boxes littering the sidewalk. A man wearing a green apron stood by one box, bunching up radishes. I picked my way around carrots and bok choy, wanting to put distance between me and the butcher shop, only to run into a sea of babbling tourists pouring out of a dim sum restaurant. I squeezed my way between excited patrons, almost walking into a red telephone booth. Piccadilly. The Salvation Army. *Please Norman—be there.* I stepped around a box of cantaloupe when up ahead I saw the five gang members. I stopped, stepped back, turned and collided with another wave of chattering patrons exiting the restaurant. Through a narrow clearing of the darkly clothed bodies, another gang member appeared. I pushed, bumped, and jostled my way through the crowd, my ears bombarded by excited Mandarin voices. I looked over my shoulder. Three more gang members closed in from behind. I looked ahead. Another gang member was coming toward me. *Shit.*

I wrestled myself free from the crowd and dashed into Fan Tan Alley, splashing through puddles. I skidded around dark corners, as I grasped my barbecue pork in one hand, and pushed away from the brick walls with the other. A side door opened and I ran into it, banging my head. I grabbed onto the edge. A young woman shouted in Mandarin, dumped a bucket of water at my feet, then slammed the door shut. My head spun. I leapt over the puddle, one hand still clutching my barbecue pork. I glanced over my shoulder. Two of the guys were catching up and that's when I fell. Arms outstretched, my barbecue pork flew from my hands, and in those brief moments my life dropped into slow motion as I became airborne and the muddy pavement rushed up to greet me. I hit hard, flat on my stomach and chest.

I couldn't breathe. I couldn't move. But I heard shouts—Mandarin—and steps, pounding on the pavement. And then I heard the revving of a throttle. I looked up. A biker sat on a Harley at the other end of the alley. The rider turned the front wheel so he faced me. I had to move. I dragged my arm forward, sloshing it and my shoulder bag through a puddle. The voices grew louder. I gasped, propped myself up onto one elbow when an arm slung around my waist and hauled me up.

"*No*!" I wheezed.

A hand slapped over my mouth.

Breathing hard, I smelled odours of dank effluent and garbage, and of leather. No cologne. I squirmed and kicked as I was dragged into another alley and through an open door. I bit and clawed at the hands.

"Stop it! I'm trying to save your life!" A voice hissed.

My captor kicked the door shut and dragged me down another dark alley and through another door and another. He finally propped me onto my feet. Unbalanced, I pitched forward onto dirt and gravel.

I squinted at the brightness of being outside again. My hands scraped gravel and grass blades protruded between my fingers. I turned and looked over my shoulder as my kidnapper jammed three worn dead bolts across the door.

Osmond.

He grabbed my hand and lurched me to my feet. "This way."

We ran across the gravel parking lot, ducking between parked cars. Seagulls perched on a dumpster screeched and flapped their wings. I heard gunshots, then the splintering of wood.

Osmond pulled me down another alley, dodging Chinese lanterns and wall hangings draped in a row. One old woman shrieked as we charged past her, knocking an armful of boxes out of her hands. A few old men stared through windows. A shot fired and a paper lantern by my head exploded. I ducked. Osmond tugged my arm and whipped me around another corner.

Out of breath, a stitch in my side, I was going to throw up. Osmond hauled me out onto a street, slinging his right arm around my shoulders. We walked.

"Jesus," I puffed. My lungs felt as if they were going to burst.

Men in suits made a wide detour around us.

I recognized designer clothing stores and shops such as Villeroy and Bosch. We were on LoJo, Lower Johnson Street, by the expensive clothing stores. I looked at my mud spattered sweatshirt and felt the caking of mud on my face. Not quite the spa treatment today.

"Osmond," I gasped, taking two steps for his every one. "Slow down."

Long leather coat, black shirt, jeans and long hair, he looked like a drug dealer. "You're alive, Jade."

I swallowed, tasting grit between my teeth. My heart pounded and my blood whooshed in my ears. Osmond and I stopped at the intersection of Douglas and Fort Street.

He looked at me. "Shit." With his hand clutching my jaw, he turned my head from left to right.

"What?"

"What the hell happened to you? You're bruised and cut. I know some of the glass got you, but—"

"I was in a car accident. That's all." I heard the defensiveness in my voice and I knew Osmond had heard it too. I was too ashamed to tell him that my father had hit me. "Really. I'm fine. I can't feel a thing."

Osmond didn't look convinced, but he respected my privacy and didn't push for an explanation.

The light changed and we walked, hurrying away from everyone staring at us. I had to stop myself from touching the cuts I knew were there.

"My car's parked on View," he said, looking all around and over his shoulder. "I owe you barbeque pork and you—"

We stepped around a large mud puddle. I thought about my barbecue pork and shoulder bag with the second bottle of wine left in the alley. Thank God I had left my wallet and ID at home. At any rate, some mice would be getting wasted tonight.

"—and you, counsellor—" he slid me a critical gaze as he stepped away from me and up to the door of his Jeep "—you can tell me why the hell you're trying to get yourself killed."

12

Member

"Jade, you're dealing with an invisible enemy disguised as a colleague, a best friend, maybe even a lover."

"EXCUSE ME? Get myself killed?"

"Jesus, Jade—" Osmond glanced at the passersby looking and listening to our conversation. "Will you get in the Jeep?"

"I wasn't out to get myself killed! I went to find Norman."

"Jade."

I sat in. Osmond slammed the door and climbed in on the other side, filling the Jeep with his presence. "The Railyards?"

I stared. "How do you know where I live?"

"I know everything." He paused, scanning the people walking past the Jeep. "So, The Railyards? That new development?"

"Yes."

He turned the key in the ignition, dropped the clutch and screeched out onto the road. Horns blared, tires squealed. A white fender skimmed past my vision. Osmond swerved. I was thrown to the right, my arm and shoulder hitting the car door. I grabbed my seat belt and clicked it in. "Seriously? We have to go this fast?"

Osmond shifted gears and lanes while wrestling with his own

seat belt. I finally grabbed it from him and jammed it in.

The concern on his face and his constant checking of the rearview mirror bothered me. I wasn't used to him acting this way, especially when I was the object of his concern. I pressed the lock down on my door and leaned forward in my seat to check the side-view mirror. No one seemed to be following us. That's what I hoped. Outside, people walked and jostled each other, dashing across the street, waving cars down. I cringed at the sight of any man with black hair and blonde tips.

Seventy-two hours . . . and a second attempt on my life. I wasn't Chin Chin. I didn't have nine lives.

I checked the side-view mirror again. No one. It took Osmond driving around a few blocks before I finally released my grip on the seat and armrest and allowed myself to relax, but that didn't relieve the throbbing in my lower back. Where was my Vicodin? Ripped jeans, scraped skin and soiled shirt were evidence that I wasn't safe and I wasn't alone. Somebody, hiding under the robes of the Society, was too aware of my motives and my actions.

I shivered and groaned.

Osmond fired me a quick glance but I pretended not to notice. He placed his hand on my knee. "Are you all right?"

"Yes." I looked out the side window. So much for playing amateur detective and finding Norman. I had stupidly walked into Chinatown, flashing bread and wine at street people, hoping to get answers. I, who garnered unwanted attention because I had a white skunk curl.

Osmond gave my knee a squeeze before placing his hand back on the steering wheel. He turned off Douglas and onto Belleville Street, dodging cabbies and pushing between double-decker buses.

"We're being followed," he said.

"What?" I turned in my seat, not really knowing what vehicle to be on the look out for.

"Whoever it is, they're not a big person." Osmond made another turn.

I looked again at the vehicles in my side-view mirror. "Which car?"

"Not a car. The Harley."

And then I saw the Harley pass a car and was now two cars behind us.

"What colour is the gas tank?"

Osmond looked at me. "You want to know the colour of the gas tank?"

"Is it rose-coloured?"

"Rose-coloured? You mean, pink?"

"Yes. A dark pink?"

"Yeah."

"Pull over."

"What?"

The Harley was now behind us. "Pull over. I'd recognize that riding-bitch face anywhere."

Osmond frowned and pulled to the side of the road. "Who is it?"

I had the passenger door open.

The Harley pulled into a parking space a car ahead of us. The rider removed her helmet, and, dressed in leather pants and a leather jacket, she swung her leg over her bike and walked towards me. Long red hair, tall and slim build, she walked with a purpose.

"Jade. What the hell are you doing?"

Sage. My sister. The last time I had spoken to her was at our mother's funeral. "Nice to see you too."

"Why are you pissing off Ziggy Pop's boys?"

Gang leader Ziggy Pop had his posse chasing me? Crap.

Sage looked over at Osmond's Jeep. "Is he cool?"

"He's a cop. Got any unpaid traffic tickets?"

"No."

"Then you're good."

"I don't know what you've gotten yourself into, but you're attracting the wrong type of attention."

Wrong type of attention? My sister stood in front of me all of five minutes and a dozen guys had already checked her out. "I'll be more careful next time."

Sage looked at her bike helmet in her hand. "I heard what happened to Jules. I, I should have been at his funeral, but, I couldn't do it. You holding up okay?"

"How did you know where I was?"

"Ever since you put Dolly's bastard husband behind bars for pounding on her, she's been keeping an eye out for you. She heard that someone had your number. The girls and I have been looking for you. You should check your text messages, Jade."

"Thank the girls."

"I will. We should go for a ride sometime. You still riding the rebel?"

"No. I ride a Triumph Bonneville."

"Cool. Be safe."

I nodded. "Safe travels."

Sage nodded as she took a few steps back, then turned and walked back to her bike.

I sat back in Osmond's Jeep.

"That's your sister?" he asked.

My younger sister was everything I wasn't. Tough, slick, statuesque, and beautiful. When we'd go to a party, everyone gravitated towards her. I was the reserved one. Sage spoke her mind, was a member of the MotoCityDolls motorcycle gang and vegan.

I smiled. "Yes, Osmond, that's my sister."

Osmond turned the key in the Jeep and pulled into the traffic. Sage was long gone.

We cruised past the Legislature Building with the gold statue of Captain Cook—polished and glittering from the rain—on the domed roof. The front lawn littered with protesters waving placards. On my right, the Port Angeles ferry unloaded a stream of American vehicles. Canada's dollar at one point was worth more than the American, but it now lagged, making Canadian cities and wilderness parks popular tourist attractions for our neighbours south.

Osmond turned onto the street leading to The Railyards, then he made another turn into the parking lot in front of my building. He pulled into a guest parking spot, killed the engine and sat. A few long seconds ticked past.

He finally looked at me. "Are you going to be okay?"

Mr. Black-hair-with-blonde-tips, shoulder to shoulder with his buddies, jumped into my mind. "Sage told me Ziggy Pop's boys were after me."

Osmond eyed the Mercedes pulling out of the parking lot and then turned to look at me, his mouth a flat, grim line. "For a mere ten grand, they were going to take you out."

I swallowed hard. "Ten grand, hey? How do you know this?"

"An informant did me a favour. Do you want to file a report with the police? I can take you to the department."

"No."

Osmond tapped the steering wheel with his finger. "Do you want me to go to the police?"

"No."

A few more long seconds passed.

"Do you want me to come up?"

Simple words loaded with conflicted meaning.

I looked at Osmond. In the close confines of his Jeep he seemed huskier, built. He had a scar on his cheek that I didn't remember from before, tiny lines around his eyes. Long hair, wavy, his roguish demeanour I found incredibly attractive. He offered safety.

During our early university years, when I had worked part-time with him in his aunt's bookstore, he didn't have the long hair but he still had the unrefined intensity, like raw sugar. At night after we'd close down the bookstore, he and I would sneak into the back room and make out. I had abandoned my inhibitions and let his hands explore my body—parts of which, according to my mother, good girls didn't discuss, let alone brazenly display for members of the opposite sex. Osmond had always shown me respect during our steamy forays and never forced himself on me. I had never felt at risk and I had always been a willing participant. But now sitting beside him, thirteen years later, I felt awkward. Times had changed and I felt stuck in a time warp. Did Osmond remember our passionate encounters, tripping over boxes, knocking books from their shelves? Or had more adventurous excursions with other women, experienced women, pale our little affair?

"Jade."

I smiled. "I'm sure you could do with a coffee."

He looked at me with the most attractive green eyes I had ever seen, then opened his door and stepped out.

I scrambled out my door, putting on a brave face of nonchalance but my heart pounded and my knees felt unsteady. Maybe he did remember. I led him through the front garden and past Jabba Java. We caught the elevator up to the eighteenth floor, making small talk about the weather and if our favourite hockey teams would make it to the Stanley Cup playoffs. I, all the while, was too aware of how close he stood, and the graze of his hand on my arm. With keys clutched in hand, I unlocked the front door and invited Osmond in.

Standing in the middle of my living room, he returned a number of calls while I quickly showered, washing away dirt and any remnants of fear. Smelling of soap, I embraced my new calm with a pair of black jeans and a black sweater.

I pulled open the bathroom door and returned to the living room just as Osmond tucked his cell into an inner coat pocket, exposing his gun and shoulder holster. He stood out, dark and dangerous, amongst the cream leather furniture and vintage prints in my coffee-coloured living room. It had been awhile since a man visited my home. No wonder Chin Chin conducted her own surveillance of him from under the sofa.

Osmond looked up. An appreciative expression passed over his face and a butterfly fluttered in my stomach. "You clean up well, Jade."

"Considering what I've been through, I'll take the compliment. Would you like anything? I'm starving."

"You said coffee."

I walked into my kitchen relieved to be redirecting my attention on something besides Osmond.

I grabbed the Vicodin and shook two pills into my hand. I walked around the island and filled a glass with water. What I really needed was vodka. But not with these drugs.

Osmond slid onto a wooden stool on the other side of the island. "So, Jade, who are you looking for?"

I choked on my water. Coughing and sputtering, I hit my chest and gulped another mouthful, trying to dislodge the Vicodin stuck in my windpipe. I cleared my throat again and through teary eyes looked at Osmond. "How do you know?"

"I was following the guys following you."

He'd been trailing my assassins.

"You've never seen them before?"

"No. I've heard of them. Seen them in passing at the courthouse." I walked over to the refrigerator and took out a head of broccoli, a block of Monterey Jack cheese, and deli meat coated in peppers. "And I'm rather insulted that my life is only worth ten grand."

"Do you know who wants you dead?"

"No."

"Then what the hell are you doing?"

"I was looking for Norman Bastine."

"The firm's missing law partner."

"Yes."

"Why?"

I glanced from the broccoli to him. "I think he knows who killed Jules and Anna. My father's implicated for both murders—" I slid a large knife out from the butcher's block "—and despite what Stone says, Dad didn't do it, and neither did I." I swung the knife swift and hard, chopping off broccoli florets. Osmond pulled his arm back.

"Stone's trying to carve out a career," he said, warily watching me swing the knife. "Norman's been missing for over a year and is presumed dead. His biker client was found not guilty of murder, and then a week later he's found beheaded at the gravel pit, the same time Norman disappears. All leads suggest a rival gang taking out Norman's client, but do you think we can get anyone to provide a statement? Christ, Jade!"

I looked up.

"You're going to chop off a finger doing that."

I stopped chopping. "That's what everybody wants to believe."

"That you're going to chop off a finger?"

I put the knife down. "No. Norman. I don't think it was the rival gang." I picked up the Monterey Jack and began unwrapping it.

"Who do you suspect?"

"The Society."

Osmond gave me a sharp look, and I could picture him—the detective hammering out a confession from a reluctant accused. "I wouldn't be saying that too loud, Jade."

"Jesus, Osmond. I'm in my own home." I picked up the knife again and shaved off slices.

"Yeah, but next time you may not be."

"I know the Society's involved in my car accident."

"How?"

"To prove my accident was a hit and run I need a police report. Something on paper to satisfy my insurance company that another vehicle was involved. My word's not good enough." The knife slipped, scraping the granite cutting board. I repositioned the block and continued cutting. "I've been on the phone with the police, but they have no paperwork of my accident happening even though an anonymous tip called it in. The ambulance attendant at the scene, his CREW report suggests all my injuries were due to a single car accident." I picked up the cheese slices and placed them on the platter.

"How did you find out about the anonymous tip?"

"That was by fluke. A file clerk happened to pick up my call when I was transferred to the traffic section. She accidentally blurted it out."

Osmond looked over at the French doors just as Chin Chin made a dash from under the sofa to under the armchair. He looked back at me. "I'm your anonymous tip."

I dropped the knife. It clattered on the ceramic tile, missing my foot by a couple of inches. "You!" I retrieved the knife. "What were you doing out there?"

"Undercover surveillance. Three cops cooped up in a van for thirty-six hours, head phones plugged into our ears, only to have our drug deal go down and our suspect start beating the crap out of his old lady."

I placed the knife in the sink. "So what did you do?"

"We abandoned the operation and arrested Johnny Bee for assault with a weapon. While I'm reading this asshole his rights, your car whips through the red light. We heard the crash but at that point Bee's old lady goes psycho, probably coming down off of something, because she starts hitting me. I saved her life and she's hitting and spitting on me. We subdued her, got her handcuffed, and then I called in the accident. The ambulance arrived just as we were about to head down to the detachment. There should be an Occurrence Report."

"You saw the black Corvette, then?"

"Yes."

I took vegetable dip out of the refrigerator. "You're my only witness. Somebody at the detachment is in on this, or connected to the Society."

Osmond drummed his fingers on the counter. "I'll look into it. Not you. Maybe one of the other guys made a note of your accident in their CAD report, or mentioned it in their notes."

I popped the lid off the dip, stared at the green goop inside, and sniffed. Dill and chives. I looked at Osmond.

"Science project?"

"No. It's fine." I placed the dip on the platter then stepped back, bracing my hands on the counter. It was all getting to me. The fatigue, angst . . . fear—not knowing who I should trust. Bianca had been right. I should have left well enough alone but did I really have a choice? I pinched the inner corners of my eyes, then rolled my neck from side to side. "It's a conspiracy, isn't it?"

Osmond remained silent.

I had been the one giving up all the information. "Jules and I were going to talk. He wanted to give me a thumb drive. He warned me that I'd be in danger. But instead, someone beheaded him."

"And you think Norman knows what Jules was going to tell you?"

"Yes."

"And that's what you were doing in Chinatown?"

"Correct."

"How did you know Norman was there?"

"A reliable source. But obviously someone doesn't want me asking questions, or finding Norman, which means he's still alive."

"Jade, you're dealing with an invisible enemy disguised as a colleague, a best friend, maybe even a lover. Don't trust anybody. The Society thrives on secrecy and intimidation. That's what gives them power, and the fact they kill people and get away with it. Don't take them on, because they will kill you."

I bit off a broccoli floret and resisted the urge to tell Osmond that I had no lovers to stab me in the back, so I had nothing to worry about. "So—" I took another bite "—can I trust you?"

Those damn green eyes looked at me long and hard. Osmond reached forward, tilting my chin, turning my head from side to side. "Those cuts aren't from me, Jade Thyme, and I'm the one who could have killed you in that alley before Ziggy Pop's boys arrived." His finger trailed under my jaw. "Real easy." He leaned back. "I'm the only one you can trust."

I swallowed the broccoli floret—whole. Once again Detective

Osmond Reeves made me feel protected and vulnerable at the same time, just as he had thirteen years ago. My face grew warm. "So," I croaked, "you're—" I cleared my throat "—you're telling me that the Society killed Jules."

"I didn't say that."

"But they could have?" I slid the platter toward him.

"Yes. The Society could have murdered Jules, but I have no proof. You and I know the cops and the Crown need evidence. They need witnesses, names. No one is willing to testify against them."

"I am."

"Don't make promises you can't keep."

"What is that supposed to mean?"

"The Society has been around for twenty years, Jade. Think about it."

"There has to be some sort of trail." I grabbed the Keurig's plastic water reservoir and held it under the tap. "Ledger sheets, membership lists, dues—" I looked at Osmond.

"—What?"

"The thumb drive. The thumb drive Jules wanted to give me. That's our proof."

"Jules never gave it to you?"

"No."

"The Society's the goddamn mafia with a law degree. Don't, because of some guilt-ridden motivation, think you can go farther than cops who have years of experience. Or, that you have an edge because you once dated a member!"

I turned sharply. Cold water sloshed out of the reservoir, spilling over my hand. "Jules was a member."

Osmond leaned forward and picked up a broccoli stem.

"Osmond?" I slid the water reservoir onto the Keurig and turned it on. "Jules was a member?"

Osmond swirled the broccoli floret in the dip.

I pulled the platter away. He looked at me with an indignant expression on his face. "Was Jules a member of the Society?"

"Yes. Jules was a member. Explains how he got the thumb drive and why he was killed. He was going to expose them. Can I have the dip now?"

I placed the platter back on the counter.

Osmond dunked his broccoli and popped it into his mouth.

I stared at him. His profile gave nothing away, but his revelation explained everything. My invisible protection. Why jealous or disgruntled colleagues never messed with me while I dated Jules. Who in their right mind would screw around with a Society member's ex-wife?

Osmond took another piece of broccoli, twirled the floret between his fingers then looked at me. "Jules was responsible for many undercover agents losing their cover. We still don't know how he did it. He must have had inside help." Osmond resumed the cold cop façade. "We figured he was involved in a double cross. The Society found out. They didn't kill him right away. They used him to weed out our undercover agents."

"But when he threatened to expose the Society—"

"—They set him up to take the fall for Anna's murder and to destroy his reputation or anything he might say. They didn't anticipate you defending him, or electing trial by judge and jury. They have no influence over which jurors were selected."

I rubbed my hands over my cheek, feeling the roughness of the tiny cuts. I had only been doing my job—proving Jules's innocence. I hoped to God that Osmond didn't consider me Jules's 'inside help'. And if Jules had been trying to expose the Society, then what had Anna been trying to do?

"So, Jade, who's your source?"

"I can't say."

"Can't say!"

"She's scared."

"She?" He looked at me. "Scared of what?"

"Retaliation."

"You should be, too. At least if I knew her name, I could keep an eye on her."

Did I dare divulge Bianca's name? "You can't tell any one."

He glared.

"Bianca."

"The Crown prosecutor?"

I nodded, feeling incredibly guilty, wondering if I had just turned on a friend. "Norman was her principal while she was articling." I should just shut up. "They were good friends, but you can't say anything."

"Bianca told you he was in Chinatown?"

"Yes."

"And you're looking for him because you figure he knows who killed Jules?"

"Yes. And Anna. I don't know why Anna was murdered. Norman's alive, Osmond. He has answers. That's why he's hiding."

"Anna was an aspiring actress. How could she be a threat to the Society?"

"Are you interrogating me?"

Osmond smiled. "I'd rather be doing other things that could get me in trouble."

I smiled.

"Anna was involved with Jules and my father. Maybe she found out something, and the Society got rid of her. I've tried talking to my father but—" I thought of my father's backhanded response "—he's uncooperative. Norman's the key. He's the one I need to find."

"Not necessarily."

"What do you mean?"

"Who else is central to both investigations?"

I scratched my head and slid onto a stool. I tried to conjure a mental list of names but I couldn't think of any one else involved with Anna.

"Olive," Osmond said.

The photo from the birthday party when Anna gave Olive a playful kiss on the cheek flashed before my eyes.

"Jules was involved with Anna. Anna and Olive were good

friends. You've got a threesome, Jade. One man involved with two women. That's asking for trouble."

"You think Olive's involved with this?"

"Big time. Who found Jules's body?"

"Olive. She was a hostile witness during Jules's trial, and from what I understand, during the entire investigation. Her best friend is killed yet she didn't want to cooperate."

Osmond picked up a napkin. "Does she still work for that theatre company?"

"The Animal Crackers Theatre Group. The same one Anna worked for. Why?"

"I'm going to pay Olive a visit. Find out what her friendship was like with Anna."

"I'm coming too."

"Like hell you are."

"I don't have to be back at work until the day after tomorrow. I'm available."

He looked at me. A smile tugged on his lips. "No."

"Why?"

"Christ, Jade, you were shot at today. You are not going to be the Society's next victim."

"Osmond—" I looked over at the French doors and the sparkling view of the Gorge Waterway. I knew what I had to say but I was scared to say it, as if verbalizing my fears would make them come true. "—I have no choice."

His expression hardened.

"Even if I hadn't started asking questions, the Society knows about me. I defended Jules. Guilty by association." My eyes glazed over. I looked toward the window again. "They're not going to take a chance on what I know, or don't know. I either do nothing and hope I don't get killed, or I try to figure out what's going on and maybe save myself. Either way my life's at stake. My only hope is that the next contract killer—" I looked at the platter "—the next one doesn't know what the hell he's doing."

Osmond scrunched up his napkin and dropped it on the

counter. "I wish you had never defended Jules."

"Don't say that."

"No, Jade," Osmond said, his voice rising. "Jules knew the danger he was putting you in asking you to defend him. You just said it, guilty by association. He couldn't think of any other lawyer to go to? No. He chose you."

That hadn't crossed my mind.

Osmond reached across the counter and covered my hand with his. "We'll visit Olive. Go back to the beginning. Figure out why Anna was killed."

13

Animal Crackers

She tossed her head back and with arms outstretched shook the tassels that surrounded the sequin hearts on her breasts.

I PARKED MY TRIUMPH motorcycle in the parking lot and walked past a nautical sign welcoming visitors to the Arbutus Bay Marina. After a night of heavy rain, the sun had finally made an appearance, and the waves in the harbour glittered like diamonds. The unexpected warmth eased the stress in my knees. Years of running were taking their toll, and I wondered if I would have any knees left when I was a little old lady with more than a skunk white streak. The Vicodin worked wonders on my back. I had run out and needed to renew my prescription. I stopped at the ramp leading down to dock "D" and breathed in the smell of salt water, a smell I very much missed when I traveled to the Prairies.

I shielded my eyes from the sun and gazed over the large and small boats, wondering which one was Osmond's. The gurgle of a motor caught my attention. I looked over to my left and saw a teenage boy push *Reckless Dream* away from the dock and jump onto her stern. Like a swan the boat glided out of the harbour taking my hopes with her.

After a lengthy discussion the day before, Osmond and I had come to a compromise: I had agreed to stay away from dark alleys and people of disrepute as long as he agreed to take me to the theatre. We agreed that Olive knew something and it was high time she did some talking. We agreed to meet at the marina and head to the theatre.

I leaned my forearms against the rail, squinting at the brightness. Now where was Osmond?

"So who's the idiot who stood you up?"

I spun around.

Osmond stood, dressed in his customary leather jacket and jeans, a cardboard cup in each hand.

I placed my hand over my chest. "Jesus, Osmond."

"Sneaking up on you is not the smartest thing to do."

"No, Detective Reeves, it is not."

He smiled, his green eyes dazzling, and held out one of the cardboard cups. "Raspberry truffle mocha."

"Yes," I said, taking the cup. The mingling smell of raspberry syrup and coffee was heavenly. I took a scorching sip. "Perfect. Thank you. I can't teach a seagull to fly before a coffee, and seriously, they should have that shit figured out, unless they're a chicken."

Osmond frowned. "You're calling me a chicken?"

"No, no."

"So, I'm a seagull?"

"No, no. Never mind. Too much Vicodin."

"So I'm forgiven?"

"Yes. Tell me—" I looked over the harbour "—which boat is yours?"

Osmond stepped close. "See dock 'D'?"

"Yes."

"Two down from *Lady Mistress*. You can just see the bow. I'll take you out one day. Come on. I'm parked over here."

I scooped up my bike helmet, and we walked through the parking lot and climbed into Osmond's Jeep. Soon we were cruising out of the marina and down the Patricia Bay Highway. Today's trip was easier and more relaxed than the day before. In fact, yesterday's chase seemed surreal as we sped past a blur of peaches and cream stuccoed homes. Smurfville. But it wasn't blue cartoon characters with white hats bouncing down the sidewalk, instead it was a group of teenage boys on skateboards. Osmond slowed to a stop at an intersection and my eyes drifted over to a placard in the middle of a farmer's field.

JULES FOR MAYOR was written in bold black letters, but Jules's handsome face had been desecrated with black spray paint. I closed my eyes.

"Idiots," Osmond grumbled.

I looked at him. "He—" I looked down at the cup in my hands "—there wasn't much left of him when I last saw him."

"I read the report and saw the pictures. You shouldn't have witnessed that, Jade. Why'd you go running into the study?"

"I couldn't believe larger-than-life Jules was dead. That's what Olive had said. 'He's dead,' not 'he's been murdered.'"

Osmond frowned. The light turned green. He shifted into first and we lurched through the intersection. "In the glove box there's an envelope. Take a look at the pictures inside."

I reached forward and opened the glove box and removed the envelope. "Are the pictures gruesome?"

"Quite the contrary."

"Not more pictures of Anna and my father?"

"Just take a look at them."

I shook out three photographs. Each one depicted a man of Asian decent. I looked at Osmond. "Who are they?"

"You don't recognize them?"

"No."

"They're the three chefs who worked at the Aubischon dinner party on the night Jules was killed. The guy in the middle is Aubischon senior's personal chef. The other two have their own restaurants in Vancouver and were hired for the evening."

I looked back at the photographs. "Where's the fourth guy?"

"Fourth guy?"

"Yeah, the fourth chef. At first there were three, then there were four. The fourth guy tossed me the washcloth."

Osmond's face paled. "According to the police report, there were only three chefs scheduled to work that night. Do you remember what this other guy looked like?"

"Hell no. Keith had just hauled me away from—" seeing my ex-husband's decapitated head "—from the crime scene. I wasn't in the right frame of mind to remember any of these men, but there were definitely four. Do you think this fourth chef is the murderer?"

"An accomplice. Someone had steady access to the study; someone knew the layout of the house, the comings and goings of the guests. There were over two hundred people at that party, yet no one saw a thing." He glanced at me. "You don't find that odd?"

"Very."

"So how do you behead a man and place his head on a dinner table, without anyone noticing?"

"Have someone standing guard?"

"Exactly." Osmond made a right turn.

"So two people were involved with his murder. Olive was the first to discover Jules. She did have blood on her dress and she left a bloody handprint on the doorframe leading outside. Maybe she was the guard?"

"That's a possibility, but—" Osmond glanced at me again "—I don't think she'd have the stomach to stand guard and watch. But this fourth chef—"

"—He could very well have been a Society member disguised as a chef."

"You're getting pretty good at this, Jade."

"Have you heard if the police have found Jules's body?"

"You know I can't divulge that information."

"Stone mentioned his cell phone was found."

"Stone's an idiot."

I slid the pictures into the envelope and placed the envelope back into the glove box. I looked out at the buildings and cars whipping by. "Jules bought a lot of things, a lot of people, but he couldn't buy his mortality. The one thing that gets us all whether you're rich or poor, young or old—death. You can be a terrorist, or the woman who's about to get in her vehicle and be killed by a drunk driver. Sooner or later your number is up."

Osmond geared down. "You're not talking about Jules now, are you?"

No. I was thinking about my mother. I was supposed to die at birth—that's what usually happens when one has the umbilical cord wrapped around one's neck but instead, I lived. "You forgot your signal light."

He glanced at me, a twist to his smile. "I am a trained professional driver."

"Really." I smiled and looked out at row upon row of grey, blue, beige and white vinyl siding houses. *We have Vinyl Village on our left, folks.*

Osmond glanced out his rearview mirror. He abruptly shifted into third, grinding the gears. "Jules the reason why you never re-married?"

"Jules the reason why I never remarried?" I repeated. "Hmmm. Most likely."

"Any prospects?"

I thought about Osmond, the feeling of security whenever I was with him, like now. "No."

The street light turned red. Osmond braked and maneuvered the gear shift back into first. His eyes followed a black Porsche crossing the intersection. I didn't know whether he was intrigued by the car or its blonde female driver, or both. The light changed and Osmond pressed on the gas and swung the Jeep into the left-hand lane. A horn blasted and a souped up blue truck with fat wheels and low body sped up beside us. The driver made a rude gesture and then cut into our lane.

"Asshole," Osmond said.

I cleared my throat.

"Look at him." Osmond pointed at the truck that had now cut

into the right-hand lane before a yellow cab, and then back into our lane.

I brought my cup to my lips. "Where's a cop when you need one?"

Osmond glared. "Watch it, counsellor."

I smiled.

We crossed the Franklyn Street Bridge and I immediately spotted the tin roof of the Animal Crackers Theatre Group. We drove into the parking lot. Unable to find a parking space, Osmond pulled up beside the curb.

I took one last sip of my coffee, then put the cup in its holder and stepped out. We walked to the front of the theatre and entered into a lobby featuring hardwood floors, red plush carpets and red comfy sofas.

Osmond sidled up to the counter, flashed his badge at the young female receptionist and asked to speak to Olive Aubischon. The receptionist smiled and pointed at two closed doors on our right. Osmond thanked the lady, and we walked to the doors where a billboard propped on an easel advertised the theatre's latest production, *Kiss of the Moon*, starring Victoria's own critically-acclaimed actress Olive Aubischon as Gypsy Margarite. Underneath the title was a picture of Olive dressed in a spaghetti strap pink bodysuit with tassels covering her breasts. She knelt on a man's lap and clenched his necktie between her teeth.

Osmond pulled the door open and we were transposed into a dark tomb of magic and make-believe. The seats were empty except for the front row. I felt the excitement of past performances and smelled the anticipation of future ones. We slipped into two back row seats.

On stage a piano player belted out a vaudeville tune on an upright piano, as Olive, dressed in the pink bodysuit and fishnet stockings, clicked and tapped, a large circular spotlight following her like an obedient puppy. Eight dancers dressed in tuxedos and top hats formed a chorus line on either side of her, tapping in sequence. Olive flipped her mane of black hair over her shoulder, firing the audience a brilliant smile, then she jammed her hands on her hips and kicked out a long leg, while falling backwards into the arms of male dancers.

"My God," I whispered. Not the frantic woman screaming her fiancé was dead.

Osmond and I sat mesmerized as Olive kicked and leapt across the stage, at times being carried in the arms of her fellow dancers.

"She's good," Osmond said.

She tossed her head back and, with arms outstretched, shook the tassels that surrounded the sequin hearts on her breasts.

"Cut! Cut! Cut!" shouted one of the audience members in the front row.

The piano keys trickled. The dancers stumbled. Olive pulled herself to her full height and sauntered to the front of the stage. "What now?"

A short man with Einstein hair, smacked his hand against a script as he lumbered out of his chair. A squabble erupted between Einstein and Olive, which resulted in Olive flipping her hair over her shoulder and prancing off the stage. Einstein marched up the centre aisle and his mismatched entourage scrambled behind him.

"I guess that's it for the dress rehearsal," I said. Osmond opened his mouth to speak when the young clerk who had let us in tapped him on the shoulder. Osmond had parked in a tow away zone and if he didn't move his Jeep, it would be towed.

"I'll go find Olive." I nodded to the stage. "Meet me back there."

Osmond disappeared with the young clerk.

After making a few enquiries of the piano player, who fired me hurried instructions as he gathered up his sheet music, I made my way through the cement maze of backstage. I stepped around stage props and broken pot lamps, flattening myself against the wall as one of the dancers flew past, fanning the schedules on the opposite wall. I came to two sets of stairs. Right or left? To heaven or to hell? I took the stairway to the right which led up, paused, then turned left. I walked up four steps and found myself in the wings. I stepped onto the deserted lit stage and looked out at dark rows of seats that climbed all the way to the far balcony. Just me and my shadow. A door closed, echoing throughout the small theatre. I looked behind. No one.

I glanced at the catwalks and rows of pot lights and pulleys—the ribs of backstage, and I had been swallowed whole. Failures and successes, my misdemeanours were on trial. Did I have a defence? A breath brushed my ear. I flicked my hair and turned. The sweet scent of lavender. I stepped to the edge of the stage and looked down—way down. A cymbal crashed. I jumped. A violin string plucked. But only black and dusty music stands occupied the orchestra pit.

I stepped again to centre stage. Another breath. I whipped around, my hand pressed over my chest, feeling the heavy beat of my heart. "Osmond?"

No one. Yet . . . yes, there was someone. I reached a trembling hand for a presence.

Who watched me from behind dark curtains?

A ghost?

An apparition?

My conscience?

My brain creaked as the curtains of my mind opened. Anna stepped out in a rhinestone pink bodysuit and a pink boa draped around her neck. Blood dripped from the hole in her head. I stepped back.

She looked all around, then at me, her eyes petrified. *Are they here*?

I swallowed and took another step back. *Who*?

Something red and sticky slid down the side of her head and plopped onto the floor. *All of them*.

No. Just me.

Her lips didn't move. She moved toward me.

I moved back.

Find them.

Find whom?

She patted a clump of stiff sticky hair in a futile attempt to hide the hole in her head. *They'll kill you. They killed me. Find them.*

A hand clutched my arm.

I screamed and whipped around, my fingers clenched in a fist. A strong hand grabbed my wrist in a paralyzing grip.

"Let go!" I tugged on my wrist.

"Jade, stop."

"Let—"

"—Stop!"

The voice. Rough. Deep. His voice. I stopping fighting and blinked once then twice and stared at the dark figure taking shape before me. Not Anna. Osmond.

Relief flooded through my limbs, my knees wobbled, then the anger. "Goddammit Osmond!" I yanked my wrist from his grip. "You said you wouldn't sneak up on me anymore!"

"I called your name. Twice! What the hell were you doing?"

"Nothing."

"Who were you talking to?"

The dead.

I dragged my hand through my hair. "No one."

He shifted his stance, bracing his hands on his hips. "Christ, Jade. And you think you can work tomorrow?"

At that moment I didn't think I could do much of anything. I had lost my mind on centre stage. I looked at my feet, then to the back curtain. Anna was gone.

"How much Vicodin are you taking?"

My face damp with perspiration, I pulled my hair back and looked at him. "What?"

He looked over at the wings. "You heard me. How much Vicodin are you taking?"

"My doctor prescribed that Vicodin—" for a childhood injury "—for my back spasms as a result of the accident. I'm not an addict."

Osmond leveled a stare that made me shiver and raised the hackles on my back. "I never said you were," he said, voice calm.

I hugged my elbows. I didn't have a drug problem.

Osmond's expression softened. He stepped forward and slung his arm around my shoulders. "Come on." He gave my shoulders a little squeeze. "I found Olive."

He guided me off the stage and down a labyrinth of hallways where I heard the murmurs and laughter of the crew and actors. It was as if I was his little sister and had been caught doing something wrong, and big brother Osmond was going to keep me out of trouble. A feeling I hated. I stepped around store fronts and potted trees—they looked so real but were only props for Olive's burlesque show. I nodded at a few performers whose faces were still covered with that ghastly white make-up. Had they heard Anna? Had they heard me? 'Turn that frown upside down,' Mom used to tell me. I couldn't shake the feeling that I was being watched.

Osmond knocked at a dressing room door.

"Come in," a female voice commanded.

He turned the knob and pushed the door open. Immediately I was aware of the smell of percolating coffee and *lavender*. Christ. I stepped in and there she sat—legs crossed, dressed in the pink bodysuit and fishnet stockings, dabbing at her make-up encrusted face before an illuminated mirror. I hardly recognized her except for her hard eyes that cast me a long scathing look in the mirror—Olive.

"What the hell is she doing here?"

"Olive. Nice to see you too," I said. We sized each other up and drew invisible swords.

Osmond closed the door.

"You didn't mention her, Reeves."

"Olive," Osmond said.

"I'm not talking to her." She nodded my way. Rubbing the tip of a cloth into a clear liquid in a jar, she scrubbed her cheek. Pink flesh peeked through the white smear. "I said I'd talk to you."

"I only have a few questions." Osmond said, as if placating a temperamental child.

I edged my way around a coffee table covered with entertainment magazines and discarded water bottles and sunk into a red armchair. Across from me a pink sparkling bodysuit and a pink boa had been thrown over the sofa. I shivered. Had Anna shed her skin after her little appearance, or was she still with us but in a different form?

"If you want a lawyer, one can be provided," Osmond offered.

"I'm sick of fucking lawyers." She glanced my way. "I told everything to the police. Even gave them a statement."

And this fine specimen of a woman was Keith's sister.

Osmond pivoted a director's chair around and sat. "Right. A statement littered with inconsistencies."

Disgust lined Olive's face, which she tried to hide with sharp dabs from a make-up sponge.

Osmond leaned forward, his head level with Olive's shoulder. "Be straight with me, Olive."

She pushed the jar aside and grabbed another small cream jar, her movements jerky. She unscrewed the lid. "I'm not talking to her, Reeves."

Osmond sat back, pulled out his notebook and clicked a pen. "Then talk to me. I'll start with you and Jules." He flipped the notebook open and scribbled the date in the margin. "When did you two get engaged?"

"Just over a year and a half ago. Around August."

"In your statement you said June."

"I had just seen my fiancé's head on our Louis the XIV buffet table, give me a break."

"So you got engaged three months before Anna was killed."

"Yes."

"Was Anna happy about your engagement?"

"Yes."

Osmond turned a page and continued scribbling Olive's

responses. "When did you find out that Jules was having an affair with Anna?"

The jar lid slipped from Olive's fingers and spun on the make-up table. She slammed her hand over it. "Affair? With Anna? Anna hated Jules. She wouldn't cheat—" she bit her lip.

"Cheat?" Osmond looked at her. "Cheat on whom, Olive?"

"No one." She grabbed another small sponge.

I maneuvered my way to the edge of the sofa. "Was Anna seeing my father?"

A slick smile cracked Olive's face but she remained silent.

"If Anna hated Jules," Osmond said, tapping his pen against his knee, "why would she be happy about your engagement?"

"She was happy *for* me."

Osmond arched an eyebrow. "There's a difference?"

Olive swallowed. "Yes."

"Were you and Anna seeing each other?"

Her forehead wrinkled. "No. What the hell made you think that?"

I stood and gave Osmond the photo of Anna and Olive.

He held up the photo. "Supposedly you and Anna were an item before you hooked up with Jules."

Olive stared at Osmond.

"Where do you get this shit, Reeves?"

"Were you two involved?" he asked.

"No!" She smeared cream over her cheeks, stripping away more make-up.

"So you and Anna were never involved?"

"No."

"Anna and Jules were the hot couple?"

"No! *I was engaged to him*!"

"So how could Anna hate Jules if she never knew him?"

Olive glumly dabbed the other cheek. "She knew *of* him."

"Just like she was happy *for* you."

Olive's face turned red.

"When did you and Anna break off your relationship?"

Olive teetered. "We never had a *relationship*."

Osmond sat back, stretching out his leg. "I have an informant who says you two were lovers."

He had never told me this.

Olive wiped her face harder. Her pretence now foundation smears in a pile of discarded sponges.

I wondered how many layers she'd wipe off before she'd tell Osmond the truth, because God he was setting her up.

Olive stretched her neck, dabbing cream under her chin.

"Anna dumped you for Jules."

Olive wiped her face even harder. "That's not true."

"You and Anna were lovers."

"No we weren't! I'm not a dyke."

"Must be a bitch," he said, leaning forward, rubbing his jaw, "having, Jules, your fiancé, sleeping with the only person you love."

The jar slipped from Olive's hands, rolled off the desk, and crashed onto the floor, a puddle of white cream and broken glass. A black mascara tear trickled down her cheek. She clenched the sponge in her hand and pressed it to her lips.

Osmond nodded at me.

Oh yeah. Now that he had gotten her pissed off, I was supposed to take over? She didn't want to talk to me. I cleared my throat. "We're not blaming or judging you, Olive. We just want the truth. We're trying to solve Anna's murder."

Olive dabbed the corners of her eyes with the sponge. "Shit." She leaned her forehead against her fist and released an unsteady breath. She sniffed, dropped the sponge on the dressing table, and crossed her arms over her tasseled chest. In the mirror's reflection, she glared at Osmond. "You're an asshole, Reeves."

"And you're lying to me, Olive."

She sniffed again. "Jules—" she slid a brush across the makeup table "—was a fraud." She swiped at a tear. "He didn't have relationships, he had possessions. A wife for Jules is a woman who puts out on demand, looks great in a cocktail dress, and lets him do the talking at social engagements. A life-size Barbie." She looked at me, eyes now blood shot, and I remembered that same pained look on my own face. "You should know."

I did know.

"Why the hell did you get him off?"

I wasn't going to defend my decision again.

Olive looked at the picture of Anna tucked in the corner of her mirror. "Anna was one of Jules's possessions, and Anna—" Olive sniffed again, then with trembling fingers reached for a pack of cigarettes. After a few attempts with a lighter, she managed to light one. She tilted her head and blew a stream of smoke. "Anna—" Olive scratched her temple with a long fingernail "—loved to be his play thing." She hooked her arm over the back of the chair and took another long drag from her cigarette. "She was supposed to be my play thing."

"How did they meet?" I asked.

"At my birthday party."

"Which was?"

"In July. A month before Jules and my engagement. That's where the picture was taken." Olive tapped the cigarette over an ashtray. "Anna wanted advice about this studio we were going to buy in Sweden.

"And Jules gave it to her?"

Olive again tapped the cigarette. "Yeah. And so did your father." She flicked a strand of hair over her shoulder. "Anna and your father became friends."

"Why Sweden? Why did she want to leave the country?"

"That's where she grew up. You know that. She wanted to act and direct her own musical. She knew people who could help her. I, I was going with her. I had the lead."

"But you were engaged to Jules?"

"For appearance-sake only. The plan had always been to take off to Sweden with Anna."

"But then she got killed and you still stayed with Jules? The man who stole her away from you?"

"I was scared."

"Of what?"

Olive remained silent.

"Or should I ask, of whom?"

She took another long drag from her cigarette.

Osmond leaned forward. "Jules was a member of the Society. You figured he'd protect you."

Like he had protected me.

Olive blew more smoke.

"Olive?"

"I don't know what you're talking about, Reeves."

"Anna was not happy about your engagement, was she?"

Olive jammed the cigarette butt in the ashtray.

"What did Jules find out about the Society, Olive?" I asked.

"I don't know."

"He didn't tell you while you were with him?"

"No."

"You're lying."

Olive glared. "Screw you, Jade. You don't know shit. Surprised they haven't nailed your ass."

"Olive!" Osmond shouted.

"I told you, I didn't want to talk to her. I don't want to see—"

"—Somebody already tried to kill her!" Osmond pointed at me. "Do you want another death on your conscience? Or maybe you know who tried to knock her off?"

She sat back, eyes wide.

"Now," Osmond said, rotating his shoulders. "Your lover is killed, you're setting a wedding date with the man who cheated on you with the dead victim. You're a suspect in both homicides."

Olive swallowed.

"The truth, Olive," Osmond said. "What was Jules up to?"

"Jules was a Society member, and the Society's mandate is to uphold the law and protect man, woman and child," Olive said, as if reciting from rote. "Those who break the law shall be punished. Those who protect those who break the law, shall be punished."

"This is bullshit." Osmond snapped his notebook shut.

Apprehensive, Olive looked at Osmond, then at me. "Okay, wait. Jade proved Jules not guilty of second-degree murder and the Society decided to issue sentence."

"But Jules wasn't guilty!" I said.

"The Society believed he was."

I remembered how Justice DeWitt had looked at me and shook his head after the verdict had been read. Did he know what was coming?

Osmond tapped his notebook against his thigh as he stared at Olive. "Why was he charged in the first place?"

"They . . . they knew he wanted to expose them. He had names."

The thumb drive. "So they pinned Anna's murder on him? Did Anna know he wanted to expose them?"

"Yes," Olive said. "She shouldn't have gotten tangled up with Jules. Anyone associated with him winds up dead."

I thought of myself.

Olive brushed a tear on her cheek. "Everything went to hell as soon as Jules showed up. Anna knew she had screwed up getting involved with him. She begged forgiveness. Hey, we all screw up, but we still couldn't have each other." Olive tapped out another cigarette. She flicked her lighter twice.

"Why couldn't you and Anna be together?"

Olive's lips trembled. "Because of my homophobic father. My engagement to Jules was for appearances only. I continued to secretly see Anna. Our move to Sweden was our way out. Same sex marriage has been legal in Sweden since 2009."

I felt sorry for her.

Osmond cleared his throat. "What about Troy?"

"Anna wasn't involved with Troy. Jules was her last before she realized who she loved." The look of supremacy returned to Olive's face. "Then she only comed for me."

Olive studied me through the smoke of her cigarette that curled as if performing a striptease. "If you really want the truth,

Jade, speak to your father. Nobody's killed him, yet everyone dies around him. You should ask him about the recruitment. They try to get them when they're young. All those eager new lawyers who have just been called to the bar."

From the corner of my eye I could see Osmond watching me. I told myself to stay calm. Don't bite at Olive's bait. Olive was hurting. Anna, her love, had been murdered. I was bent and angry because of Mom's death and Jules's murder. "Thank you, Olive. Two more questions. Why did you break off the engagement on the morning of Jules's verdict?"

She looked tired and pale. "I was fed up being the dutiful fiancée."

"Last question. Who gave Anna the money?"

Olive smirked. "Your father."

14

Partnership

Jean-Claude Van Damme and the mini-marshmallow army would bust him out.

WIND SLAMMED INTO the side of my office building causing the windowpane to quiver and scatter rain. I caught my reflection in the pane and felt protected from the storm that raged and scarred Victoria. A few of the taller skyscrapers poked out of the clouds in stark determination not to be covered. A lone seaplane, motor grinding, rose from the water and braved the grey horizon.

I tossed a Vicodin into my mouth and chased it with my mocha. I leaned against the window casing. As heavenly was the blend of chocolate, raspberry, and coffee, the exotic flavours couldn't melt my anxiety.

Olive had seemed so sad, so angry, so exposed. With her true sexual preference no longer a secret, and the games Jules had played at her expense, I wondered if she had become so vengeful to kill him? She obviously had forgiven Anna for her forays, but what about Jules?

Another shattering of rain washed the window. I checked my watch. Five fifteen. My first day back had been a long one. Throughout the day lawyers had trickled into my office, seeing how I was doing. Secretaries had also slipped in offering me friendly smiles and inquiring about my health. Kate, bless her soul, had an extra large raspberry truffle mocha waiting on my desk along with a cranberry raspberry muffin—my favourite. She had also left detailed notes about the outcomes of my trials, what matters the Crown Counsel Office still wanted to make deals on, and a list of files that Keith had reassigned to Troy.

Reassigned.

I glanced at my desk and the stack of files underneath that list. I appreciated Keith's thoughtfulness, but I questioned his motives. I had been in a motor vehicle accident, I was not suffering an emotional breakdown. I hoped this reassignment was not a reflection of his confidence in my abilities. With that in mind, I pushed myself away from the windowsill and pulled out the police report I had been working on the other night.

Since the Crown Counsel had an employee who was related to the accused, they wanted me to approve a charge of first degree murder on one of Victoria's most notorious drug dealers, Romeo, who had pumped eight rounds into Colton Yorke, the son of an influential restaurateur and businessman. There was no evidence that the shooting had been planned or deliberate. Colton had agreed to meet Romeo that night to buy fentanyl, the drug that was killing its users and was laced in every street drug. It was common knowledge that Romeo was Colton's steady supplier, and the two men had been childhood friends since their days at private school. It was also common knowledge that Colton had a bad habit of being late in payment.

As much as I wanted to charge Romeo with first degree, and as much as first degree would appease the public and the father of the victim, who had witnessed his son's brutal death, Romeo had not planned the killing. And to make matters worse, the police had witnesses that would testify that Colton had acted like an ass in his dealing with Romeo, flinging hundred-dollar bills across the table, even going so far as to grab Romeo by the necktie and hold a fork to his throat.

Provocation. So to hell with second degree, Romeo could only be charged with manslaughter. I couldn't charge anyone with anything if there was *no substantial likelihood of a conviction.* The six-word mantra engrained in every prosecutor. I swallowed another gulp of my mocha.

There'd be hell to pay. The father of the victim would flip. He'd deny that his son had a drug problem. He would sue everyone, including me. My decision would be appealed to the Deputy Regional Crown Counsel, then to the Regional Crown Counsel, and finally to the Assistant Deputy Attorney General. Hopefully, the Assistant Deputy wouldn't succumb to pressure. He might see that justice would be better served if Romeo was convicted of manslaughter, rather than walked on second or first. I turned a page and looked at the crime scene photos of Colton's bullet-ridden body. God help us if Romeo only received the minimum four year sentence.

"Goodnight, Jade."

I looked over at the door. Kate stood, tying the belt on her shiny yellow raincoat.

"Goodnight, Kate."

"Don't stay too long."

I smiled. "Is Keith back from court? I need to talk to him."

"You mean that drowned rat in a suit who just walked in? Yes." Kate turned to leave but then stopped. "Oh, Sergeant Stone called for you yesterday."

My heart dropped. "Oh."

"He mentioned something about getting back a list. That you would know what he was talking about."

The list I had given to Keith. "Yes. Right. Have a good weekend and I'll see you Monday."

Kate waved, then disappeared from sight.

I stepped out of my office and walked down the hall. I passed another secretary in a black tailored suit carrying an empty coffee urn and a plate of leftover danishes. Today had been the accountant's last day, and the social committee had organized the customary morning tea, a farewell gesture for any departing staff member whether the poor sod wanted it or not.

I walked past the photocopy room. The photocopier groaned as it shot out volumes of paper. Around the corner I came across Keith's secretary's workstation that looked more like a jungle with thick ferns and wicker furniture than it did an office. A number of the partners, plus the office interior designer, had abolished Cheris's choice of decorating. But Keith had stood up for his secretary, telling the partners that as long as Cheris's father, an African diplomat, referred work to the firm, he didn't care if Cheris turned the place into the Amazon.

I spotted Cheris holding a brass watering can, kneeling before a fig tree. With dark, smooth skin, high cheekbones, long black hair and a bone-skinny frame, I often wondered why she worked as a legal assistant, when she could be strutting her stuff down Toronto's catwalks.

She straightened, revealing a cream-coloured suit with gold buttons. "Jade."

Her deep voice made me think of the maple syrup I had once tasted at the orchards in Québec.

"I thought I'd catch Keith before he went home." I nodded to the closed door. "But it looks as if someone beat me to it."

Cheris rolled her eyes and placed the watering can on a bookshelf. She walked around her desk and with long fingers spun her daybook around and pointed at a name. "Yesterday—" she tapped her finger against the page— "Troy, determined to speak with Keith, paced up and down on my carpet, mumbling obscenities, while waiting for Keith to come back from court. Finally, he makes me put his name in the book. Keith does not want to see him. He has the Walker trial today."

Troy wanted to see Keith? About what? I parked my hip on the corner of Cheris's desk near an exotic plant which would be dead if I had to look after it. "Any idea what about?"

Cheris glanced over her shoulder then leaned forward. "The partnership," she whispered.

My throat went dry, and a sticky uneasiness pricked my skin. Stress sweat, according to the latest deodorant commercial. I looked at the closed door, which reverberated from the raised voices inside.

"Congratulations," Cheris said. She winked, then flipped her appointment book around. "If you want, I can tell—"

Keith's door flew open. Troy marched out, saw me, and stopped. His face contorted into a number of frowns. He opened his mouth, saw Cheris, then stepped forward and in a low whisper so only I could hear, said, "You *bitch*," then marched off.

Cheris stared after him, then looked at me and nodded at Keith's door.

I stepped up to it, placing my hands on the frame. Keith paced behind his desk. "Hey—"

He whipped around, grabbed a file folder and flung it across the room. "Fucking asshole!" His facial expression dropped. "Jade."

"I'll come back."

"No! Jade. Come in." He lunged around his desk, kicking through the papers, and grabbed my arm. "Come in." He pulled me forward and closed the door. "I'm sorry." He dragged his hands over his face, then released a deep breath. "Mr. Pothead—" he held his hand out to the door "—now knows he's not getting the partnership."

"He didn't take it well."

Keith arched one eyebrow. "Understatement."

"Should I be concerned?"

"Not one bit." He placed his hand on my shoulder. "You're our star. Have a seat." He indicated a chair. "The guy's an asshole," he continued, kicking through the papers on the floor.

"So my partnership is now common knowledge? No secrets?"

Keith sat down, tilting his chair back. "Not yet. Give me a few weeks. Give Troy a few weeks. Tell me if he gives you any grief."

Keith rubbed the side of his face again. His hair stood up in chunks and looked as if he had run his hands through it one too many times. The top button of his shirt undone, his black tie hung loose around his neck. Knowing I had the partnership, I felt silly complaining about the reassignment of my files. Maybe Keith was lightening my load for bigger cases? He had also been focused on an ad hoc prosecution for the Crown. "You look wiped. How's your trial?"

He groaned.

"That bad?"

"Like shit down a pipe."

I sat back. "What's happened?"

Keith leaned forward, his elbows propped on his desk. "The mother of the victim is recanting her statement. She says the sex assault on her boy never took place. She said she lied to the police because of pressure from the investigator and the victim services worker. I now have to call the cop and the victim services worker as witnesses."

"This is the case the Crown didn't want to conduct because the mother is an ex-employee?"

"Right."

"The mother's trying to protect the accused."

"Exactly."

"Do you think he threatened her?"

"No need to." Keith reached for a brown paper bag and pulled out a muffin and a plastic knife. "She doesn't want to admit the sex assault happened, and she doesn't want to lose the creep even though he's messing with her son. I wanted to run her statement by you this morning but then remembered you wouldn't be in until the afternoon. How are you doing?"

"Not bad. Taking it slow." *Questioned your sister yesterday afternoon.* "Actually, I wanted to ask you about Norman."

Keith froze, the knife half way through the muffin. "The man was a nut, Jade. Rumour had it that he rode around the city on a bicycle buck naked."

"Norman. The partner who used to work in this firm?"

"That's right. Black mark on this organization," Keith said, as he hacked the muffin in half. "I don't think Queen had him in mind when they wrote the song, *Bicycle*. He'd still be riding his bike if my father hadn't let him go."

I thought of the psych ward on the fifth floor of the hospital. "Your father had him committed?"

Keith eyed me, the knife still in his hand. "No, but he should have. According to Norman, Elvis had given him orders to blow up the local grocery store, and it didn't matter where the cops locked him up, because Jean-Claude Van Damme and the mini-marshmallow army would bust him out." Keith reached for a butter portion and ripped it open.

Mini-marshmallow army. Elvis. Jean-Claude Van Damme. Great. "How come I had never heard about this?"

"Only a select few employees knew. We kept it very quiet. We didn't want the firm being sued because of his lack of representation. Father had Norman let go before he became a judge." Keith frowned as he buttered half the muffin. "Norman never showed up for his last day of work. The motorcycle gang probably got him. He was defending their ringleader when he vanished. He thought government spies, politicians, lawyers—" Keith pointed the knife toward me "—and your father were after him."

"My father! Why my father?"

"Because your father was the first to notice him falling apart."

I dropped back in my chair. My father's involvement always became an issue. I looked over at the large framed picture on the wall of Keith and his father dressed in their robes. Respectable. A Supreme Court Justice, Keith's father didn't look anything like the drunk I had seen on the night of Jules's murder. At least he talked to his children. My father ignored his.

"Norman caused a lot of problems." Keith crumpled up the muffin bag and like a star basketball player preparing for a lay-up, he tossed the crumpled bag into a waste paper basket. "He should have been more concerned about the motorcycle gang going after him, not his own colleagues."

Maybe his own colleagues posed the real threat? "The police didn't find it odd? His disappearance?"

Keith stared. "No. They figured it was self-induced."

"Self-induced?"

"That Norman wanted to disappear."

"Why would he want to do that?"

"Maybe he knew he was losing it."

"Did he believe anyone else was after him?"

"The Premier, the Attorney General, a couple of local MLAs and a few judges. Why? You're going to haul their asses in for questioning?"

"No. It's just odd. The man defending the ringleader of a motorcycle gang disappears. The police didn't find that suspicious? More likely they're too damn scared to investigate."

The hardness in Keith's eyes told me I had gone too far. He stood and walked to the front of his desk, sitting on the edge. "What's this about, Jade?"

I looked over at the globe by the bookshelf, then back at Keith. "Norman was not crazy. He needed help. He was going up against the Society."

Keith's eye twitched. "Jade, I know you liked Norman, but remember what these mental cases are like," his voice softened, "you've defended enough of them to know they'll give any bullshit story as long as you save their ass. The cops could have done a better job investigating his disappearance, but you can't change that. You also—" he lowered his voice "—can't throw around accusations about the Society if you don't want to wind up dead."

Wind up dead?

"You can't change the past, Jade."

Rain slammed against the windowpane. I shivered. Something seemed *off*. I didn't know if it was Keith, or his story. "You're right." *Play along.* "It's been a long day. I've been sleeping and eating the Vandenberg search warrant hearing. Now the Romeo charge approval." I stood. "I'll let you get back to it."

"My trial will be over in two days, then we can hash out Vandenberg."

"I'll be ready." I walked to the door.

"Are the cops any closer to finding the jerk who hit you?" Keith asked, following me.

"No, but at least they're now considering that another vehicle was involved."

"You're lucky you're still alive."

Again, a hint of my mortality. Images of the black Corvette speeding towards me and the rip of metal against rock flashed through my mind. "I had my guardian angel with me."

Keith stepped closer and cupped my cheek with his hand. A gesture so intimate I was scared to move. Scared that his touch would crack the splinter that kept my mind and body together. I had been so accustomed to being alone, to handling situations on my own, that Keith's small gesture rattled me. It was inappropriate yet I didn't stop him. I released an unsteady breath, then felt his hand around my waist and his lips pressed against mine. I placed my hands on his shoulders.

He stepped back just as fast as he had kissed me."Sorry. I shouldn't have done that. If anything happened to you," he whispered, "I could never live with myself. I'm acting like an idiot."

I cleared my throat. "I better go."

"If you need help on anything—" he pulled open the door "—I can get an articling student to help you."

"Thank you." I glanced at Keith as he stood in the open doorway, and in the glow of the hall light, I noticed the dark smudges under his eyes. He stared at me, before shifting his gaze to the carpet. "It's Friday night prawn night at the Blue Oyster." He shoved his hands into his pockets and looked at me. "A group of us are going down there. Come along."

I had no interest in socializing with my fellow lawyers. I wanted to talk to someone more important. Edith. "I better not, maybe another night. I'm tired and I still need to write up my charge recommendation on the Romeo file, but thank you."

He nodded and toyed with the change in his pocket. "Be careful, Jade."

15

Sister Act

They would be eaten by the lake monster.

WHEN I GOT HOME, I changed into my motorcycle gear, fed Chin Chin and got on my Triumph and headed towards Pearl Drive, the perfect cruising road.

One fact bothered me about Stone's investigation, or lack of investigation, and I was tired of waking at 3:00 am thinking about it. Had anyone interviewed Edith? Were the only witnesses questioned those at James party? The Aubischon house was next door to my father's house. There had been little reported in the paper about Jules's murder.

I made a right turn onto Pearl Drive towards my father's house. Father would be at a board meeting. I could have a friendly visit with Edith.

I geared down and made a right turn into the driveway. I drove around the circular garden and parked. More tulips flowered and a squirrel zig-zagged across the lawn. I swung my leg over my bike seat. The squirrel darted in front of my bike and disappeared into the shrubs. I unfastened my motorcycle helmet and put it on the seat. I climbed the stone steps. Before I could press the doorbell, the door opened and Edith stood in her black uniform.

"Edith, hi. You must have seen me arrive."

She wrung her hands. "Your father's not here."

"That's alright. I came to see you."

"Now is not good. You better go."

"Oh. Are you expecting someone? I can come back—"

"—No. You need to go."

What was going on? Edith wouldn't look me in the eye. "Edith, are you in danger?"

"No. You better go."

"I want to talk to you."

"Your father's in a meeting. He's not here," she said, using the short, no-nonsense tone she had used on Sage and I when we were kids. But I wasn't ten, and I wasn't moving.

Her facade faltered. "Please, Jade." She swallowed. "Good night." She closed the door.

I was stunned. I wasn't allowed in my own house. I stepped back and surveyed the pillars and tall hedge on the left. I walked down the cobblestone steps to my bike. The Aubischon residence was to my left. The third-floor windows and the tile roof were visible over our tall hedge.

Well. So much for talking to Edith. I looked again at the Aubischon residence. Was Jules killed there? In this neighbourhood each home was a minimum 3000 square feet and each lot two-acre parcels. Jules's body would have been heavy to carry and hard to hide. I didn't want to think about the mess. Jules could have been killed elsewhere and only his head displayed. As gruesome as it may be, it was much easier to pack around a man's head than his body.

Time to get out of here. I put on my helmet, looking at the back yard through the wrought iron fence. Trimmed lawns. Manicured gardens. I felt dejected, like a child not invited to a birthday party. The cobblestone paths twisted between the blossoming cherry trees, one eventually stopping at a bench, the other at the Koi pond. The twisting paths were supposed to ward off evil spirits. The Japanese garden was on the other side of the stone Moon Gate where Sage and I had played.

I glanced at my father's castle. Screw it. No one was around. I unclasped the gate latch and walked into the backyard, removing my helmet. I passed the trickling water fountain and for the first time in a while I felt peace. Mom used to sit on the bench under the cherry tree and keep an eye on us as she read a book or tried to do violin practice, depending on how well Sage and I behaved. The wine-coloured Japanese maples waved their pointed leaves, welcoming me home. I walked through the Moon Gate and saw the pagoda, which extended over the lake and was supported by stilts.

I shoulder-checked the house. The arbutus and evergreen trees had grown since I had left, concealing it. No lights. No one was home except Edith and she didn't want to talk to me. All I wanted was a few peaceful moments to remember a better time playing with Sage, and remember Mom.

I ducked maple tree branches. The pink Azaleas had bloomed and bees buzzed from one flowering shrub to the next. A leaf fluttered to the ground by the closed in pagoda. Weeds choked out the Japanese Anemone. I think that's what they were called. Sage knew all the names of the flowers. She used to help Mom in the garden. The pagoda was a great play area. Many times Mom warned Sage and I not to fall into the lake or we would be in serious trouble. Not that we'd drown, but that we'd be in trouble. When my parents had garden parties, they'd opened the pagoda and served food and drinks inside.

I kneeled, placing my helmet on the ground. I plucked weeds, freeing up the iris bulbs. I miss you, Mom. I looked at the lake. One summer Sage had thrown all my Barbies into the lake, telling me they would be eaten by the lake monster, all because I wouldn't let her play with Astronaut Barbie. I had been so mad at her and swore I would never ever play with her again.

I chuckled. I tugged at a dandelion and something shiny flashed. What was that? I pulled out more weeds and that's when I saw it.

A signet ring.

I picked it up. Too big for my fingers. A man's ring size. I brushed away the dirt and saw the letter "J".

Oh shit.

Jules's signet ring.

He had been here on the night he had been murdered. Had he visited my father? I had last seen him getting into James's Mercedes.

I stood and looked at the pagoda. I walked to the door. The latch was fastened with a new lock. I stepped back. Had this peaceful building been used as an execution chamber? I walked slowly around the balcony. Were those drops of blood? Or was that dirt and nature's age spots?

Father's motor boat was tied up to the side of the pagoda. I walked over to it. The blue tarp flapped. I kneeled, grabbed the corner of the tarp and looked under. Nothing. Clean. Very very clean. I stood and stepped onto the grass and walked along the side, trying to find something, anything. I grabbed my motorcycle helmet and crouched on the rock embankment and looked under at the stilts. Grunge, mold, spider webs and more weeds. My gaze shifted to the lake. Was Jules killed in the pagoda and his body, weighted down, tossed into the lake like Astronaut Barbie?

I stared at the water ripples. Saw a frog spring from a rock into the water. He wasn't giving anything up. Insects fluttered from lily pad to lily pad. Pink Japanese Bottlebrush grew in patches around the lake. *Not here. Please.* This had been Sage's and my refuge. Yet, the logistics made sense and the shiny new lock on the pagoda door. Had the murderer removed Jules's ring, keeping it as a trophy but accidentally dropped it? Oh, Jules. I placed his ring in my coat pocket and zipped it up. That's when I noticed the shape reflected in the water.

The reflection gradually grew bigger as the man snuck up behind me.

The pointed light grey tip of a hoodie, its strings pulled tight, hiding most of the man's face.

I gripped the chin guard of my motorcycle helmet.

My pulse pounded.

Stay . . . calm. Move now and he'll push you in and drown you. *Wait.*

The man leaned forward. His hand reached out.

I swung around and smacked my motorcycle helmet into his nose. My helmet flew from my hand.

The man screamed, stumbling back, covering his nose with his hands.

I took off. The trees. I knew this garden. He didn't. It would take too long to get to my bike and he could catch up or there could be more men waiting. I could hear him, chasing me, cursing.

I ran up the wide cement steps, batting at the maple branches. I burst into the treed area. Twigs snapped under my feet. Uneven ground. I splashed through mud puddles, looked back and my foot caught on a tree root. I was airborne. I landed hard on my chest. I couldn't breathe. I slid my hands through leaves, trying to push myself up. I wheezed. Air. I needed air. Move. I stumbled forward. Stinging nettles clawed my skin. I looked back.

He was close. Too close.

Get up.

An evergreen branch swung above my head and smacked the man in the face, knocking him off his feet onto his back.

I heard a groan.

Mom's ghost grabbed the branch as it swung back in my direction. She looked at me. Terror in her eyes. "*Run!*"

I took off, careening into a stump. I lurched around it.

Up ahead was the path. Further ahead the road. Traffic. People.

I heard cars. Saw the embankment. I clambered up it. The man was coming, not moving as fast but closing in. My feet gave way to pebbles. I clambered up the side of the road, my fingers scraped raw against stones.

Not one single car.

I hobbled in the direction of the city. My ankle gave out and I fell.

The man clambered up and stood at the side of the road, panting, his face and hoodie covered in dirt and blood.

I tried to put pressure on my foot and fell again.

"It's over," he shouted, his voice hoarse. He walked toward me.

I scrambled back along the side of the road.

Then I heard it.

The throttle . . . of a Harley.

I looked behind.

A single headlight came over the hill, then a lone rider on a motorcycle. The rider flashed her headlight and behind her four more motorcycles fanned out forming a "V" taking up both lanes.

Sage.

And the MotoCityDolls.

Five dark silhouettes in the lilac sunset.

Sage cranked the throttle and accelerated. The MotoCityDolls did the same.

The man looked at me. Looked at them. Cursed and slid down the embankment and stumbled into the forest.

I stood.

They formed a 'U' around me.

Sage flipped up her visor. "You all right?" she shouted.

I hobbled toward her. "How'd you find me?"

"Edith called. Get on."

"My bike."

"You're not going back there. Roza, Gabrielle."

Roza cruised forward. Gabrielle sat behind her in the two-seater.

"Can you get Jade's bike? You'll need to be fast."

"On it."

I gave Gabrielle the keys.

"Meet back at the clubhouse."

Roza and Gabrielle circled around us then took off towards the house.

"I found Jules's signet ring by the lake."

"You think they dumped him in the lake?"

I nodded.

"*Fuck*." She shook her head. "C'mon, we gotta get outta here."

I swung my leg over the seat. "I don't have a helmet."

Sage revved the engine. "Where is it?"

"In the lake. With Astronaut Barbie."

I thought I saw my sister smile before we took off.

16

Norman

The body moved and a hooded creature slid across the ground into the centre of the alley.

THE MOTOCITYDOLLS didn't have an ordinary clubhouse. Sage inherited the shop from a mechanic who had once built custom cars. She had saved the mechanic's life one night when she worked part-time as a server at a local pub. The mechanic had screamed and leapt from his chair—the Vancouver Canucks had won the Stanley Cup—when he choked on a nacho chip. His drunk friends didn't know what to do. Sage, knowing CPR because of being a personal trainer, bent the guy over his chair and, positioning her hands a little higher than normal, pressed hard into his chest with quick thrusts. She later told him and his buddies that she wasn't demonstrating a sexual position, but had performed a version of the Heimlich maneuvre to be used on large people. He left her a great tip and in exchange got her phone number.

She and the mechanic dated a few months until he wanted her to move in. Sage broke up with him. But the mechanic never forgot about her, and when he was diagnosed with throat cancer, he left his shop to her in his will, now the MotoCityDolls clubhouse.

On the outside the clubhouse was a boring white cement building with a double wide garage. Sage had a security alarm installed and then there was Lizzy, the German Shepherd, a rescue.

Inside the clubhouse the girls worked on their bikes, socialized, or relaxed. Upstairs, Sage lived with Lizzy in a closed-off area.

We were 20 minutes outside Victoria. We should be close to the clubhouse now. Sage and the rest of the dolls geared down and we made a right turn onto the clubhouse driveway. One woman was outside cleaning the chain on her bike. The garage doors opened and another doll waved from inside. The idling of motorcycle engines amplified in the garage until each one was turned off.

Bike helmets removed, the members talked amongst themselves as if my rescue was just an everyday task, while Lenny Kravitz's *Are You Gonna Go My Way* played in the background.

Sage made coffee as I sat at the kitchen table, resting my leg and throbbing ankle on a chair. I told Sage about finding Jules's ring by the pagoda and my suspicion that he had been dumped into the lake. She told me Edith had called, having seen me wander into the backyard and a man follow.

"The little boat, Sage. I think whoever killed Jules used it to dump his body."

She pushed a cup of coffee towards me. She sat down and sipped her own. Lizzy lay on the floor, resting her head on Sage's foot. "Father couldn't have done it. He's not strong enough. Maybe the guy chasing you?"

"Maybe."

"Do you know who was chasing you?"

"No. He had his hood pulled tight around his face and hardly spoke. Which tells me, it's somebody I know. If it wasn't . . . if it wasn't for Mom's ghost whacking the guy with a tree branch, he would have caught me."

Sage stood and walked to the cupboard. She returned, dropping Lizzy a dog treat and placing a bottle of rum on the table. She unscrewed the lid. "Want some?"

I pushed my coffee mug towards the bottle.

Sage poured rum into my mug and then into hers. She replaced the cap and took a long swallow of her coffee. "I should have offered you this earlier . . . I've been seeing her too."

"Thank God."

Sage stared into her coffee mug. "I can go for months and be okay. Then there are days when I miss her so bad, and I realize I'm not the victim in a cruel joke. She is never coming back." She took a swig of her coffee. "Three months ago, I thought I saw Mom on the handlebars of my bike." Sage chuckled. "Then just after her funeral, I dreamt she was sitting in the motorcycle's sidecar. We were having an argument, as usual, because she wouldn't wear a helmet. It would mess up her hair."

I laughed. "She was in the forest with me."

Sage smiled but her eyes misted over. "According to Edith, Dad hardly stays in the house anymore. He thinks it's haunted."

"Good."

"Edith said Dad's thinking of selling it."

"We should buy it."

Sage looked at me from the corner of her eye. "Are you telling Osmond about the ring?" She took another sip of her coffee. Lizzy had now made herself comfortable resting her head on Sage's lap.

"I don't know. I don't know who to trust. I'm supposed to meet Osmond tomorrow. We're looking for Norman in Fan Tan Alley."

"If Osmond's nose is two sizes too big, you know he's the one who tried to kill you."

~

I limped down Wharf Street. I checked my watch. Two-thirty. I was late. I continuously found myself going over what Olive had told Osmond and I, coming to the conclusion that several people had either the opportunity, or the motive, for murder. Troy, a brilliant lawyer, smarter than Jules, but not as powerful, could easily have cut off his head. He had the physical strength. Maybe Jules had prevented Troy from getting the partnership.

Olive on the other hand had not only found the body, but she also had plenty of motive. Had Jules threatened to expose her relationship with Anna to her father? Why? He didn't need her to secure his future. Why did he want Olive? Just because? Also, if Anna had dropped Olive for Jules, Olive could have shot Anna out of jealousy, and then placed blame on Jules. But I couldn't see her doing that. Olive loved Anna. She was still mourning Anna's death. It was Jules she didn't give a damn about.

Then there was James. He had drunkenly mumbled to Bianca and me that he wanted his future son-in-law dead, but he had been in no condition to swing an axe, nor could I see him putting a gun to Anna's head. And what possible motive would he have for killing Anna? Or did he get someone to do it for him?

And then my father. Jules had something on him. The reason for my father's secrecy. But what? Information about his dealings with Anna? Why my father gave her money? What was the real reason for paying her to leave the country?

Finally, Keith. What could Jules have had on him? Keith loved being a lawyer. He was proud of the firm. He hadn't blackmailed or screwed anyone over. If anything, he was always rescuing someone from some snag or crisis. Hell, he had rescued me from the crime scene before I destroyed any further evidence. Keith. A man who had kissed me at work and whom I liked a lot. The kiss at work was inappropriate. Anywhere else, would he have pulled away? Would I have kissed him back? We had history. We were best buddies when we were kids, but I did not need a romance right now.

So which one of them belonged to the Society? Or did they all? And whom did Jules threaten to expose?

I shook my head. I couldn't think about this any more. Too many unanswered questions for a Saturday afternoon.

Osmond and I had agreed to meet in Victoria's very chic Trounce Alley, where Gaultier and Versace clothing boutiques rubbed elbows with art galleries and beauty salons. Our plan was to branch down Government Street in an attempt to find

Norman Bastine, otherwise known as Noxzema Man. For some bizarre reason, one of Victoria's richest areas was near one of the poorest—Piccadilly. So the most likely place for a street person to beg money for food was Government Street especially during tourist season.

Osmond and I hoped that besides the murderer and my dead ex, Noxzema Man might know what Jules and Anna had been up to. Someone had to know. And maybe he could enlighten us about the Society.

The sun shone but low hanging clouds caused a sultry humidity, making me feel as if I were in a Brazilian rainforest. Japanese tourists swarmed the sea wall.

"Ocean? Ocean?" asked one tourist as she pointed to the harbour.

Not quite.

Black Clydesdale horses pulling white carriages adorned with flowers clomped amidst Mercedes, Hondas, and SUVs. I turned up the street that connected with Government. A mime clutching a saxophone and dressed in black pants, a white shirt and a red bow tie, stood motionless. A saxophone's case lay open at his feet. A blonde in a leather mini-skirt dropped an American bill into the case, and as if winding up a music box, the mime played, *It's a Wonderful Life*. More tourists gathered and watched. After a few bars the mime stopped, his body leaning back, the saxophone held out before him.

I fished two loonies from my pocket and dropped them in his case. The mime continued playing.

I smiled, turned, and walked along Government Street. Taxis and cars drove cautiously as pedestrians darted back and forth. A young woman leaned against a turn-of-the-century lamp post and seductively smiled at a man walking toward her, a Starbucks cup in each of his hands.

I turned right at the green wrought iron gates and stepped underneath the lilac flower-painted Trounce Alley sign. The romantic words of a Latin love song floated from a restaurant's patio. The house special of roasted lamb smelled heavenly. I strolled over to my favourite clothing shop and eyed the black Versace t-shirt, black knee-high suede boots and black Capri pants displayed in the window. Next to the Versace boutique a large jewel-encrusted elephant winked at me from inside a Middle Eastern art gallery.

I looked over my shoulder. No sign of Osmond, but a black Pickwick from the time of Charles Dickens caught my attention. In Dickens's time the adorable contraption with its rectangular body, wooden wheels and wooden handles had been used to bake bread while the top half warmed soups. Now it was a hotdog stand. I forgot about the designer clothes and walked over to it.

"What'll it be, ma'am?"

I eyed the menu written in gold letters on the side: jumbo dog, regular dog, veggie dog. I looked at the giant pretzels hanging from a separate wire rack. "A jumbo dog, please."

"Brown or white bun?" the hotdog vendor asked.

"Brown."

The vendor unwrapped a plastic bag of brown hotdog buns. His biceps twitched under the short sleeves of his black t-shirt. A plaid cap on his head, and dark jeans and apron, he could have stepped out of an Al Capone movie.

He pulled open the little black drawer at the top. Onions sizzled. "Onions?"

"Yes," a male voice said from behind my shoulder. "She hates sauerkraut, loves ketchup and God forbid if you put mustard on that dog."

I turned.

Osmond stood. Narrow gold-tinted sunglasses reflected my image and made his smile even more wicked. His grey ribbed shirt looked good against his olive skin and black leather jacket. Faded jeans and shoulder length hair, that was my Osmond. And his nose . . . looked normal. "You remembered?!"

"Jady," he said, using the nickname he had given me during our university days, "you'll never change. I'll have the jumbo, loaded, and a root beer." He took my hot dog from the vendor's hand and gave it to me.

"What else do you remember?"

"That you love lemon meringue pie but only after you've scraped off the meringue."

I laughed as I spooned condiments onto my hot dog.

Osmond took his hotdog and Barq's soda and gave the vendor a five dollar bill and a toonie. He turned to me. "How have you been?"

"Rough night."

Osmond stepped away from the pickwick and out of a rollerblader's path. His arm rubbed mine and for a brief moment I warmed at his touch. "Really. How so?"

"A man tried to drown me in Pearl Lake."

Osmond stopped. "No."

"Yes. Pearl Lake, back yard of my father's house." I moved closer to him as a stream of buses roared past. Somewhere along the street, Caribbean drums battled it out with a twelve-string guitar. Conversation fragments mingled with a variety of dialects. "I whacked the guy with my motorcycle helmet and got away. Thank goodness Sage showed up when she did or we may not be having this conversation."

"Whoa. Hold on. Back up. Details."

I reiterated, this time to Osmond, how I had gone to my father's house to question Edith, but she didn't want to talk to me. How I strolled into the back yard and found Jules's ring by the pagoda, then the man in the grey hoodie sneaking up behind me.

"Was your father there?" Osmond asked.

"According to Edith, no," I said, raising my voice so to be heard over a FedEx truck.

Osmond took a bite of his hotdog and looked at me. "The man could have been there already."

"Yes."

"Or followed you."

I stopped at the intersection and pressed the button so the

light would change. "That too."

"Jade, I need Jules's ring. I could get the dive team to look for Jules's body."

The light turned red. A grey and white Rolls Royce, its white flags flapping over its headlights, slowed.

Osmond stepped across.

A dozen giggling school girls dressed in blue pleated skirts and matching blazers darted across the street. Escapees from St. Mary's Academy.

I bit my hotdog and chewed it for a long time, debating whether I should hand the ring over. I had it on me, tucked in my purse. I looked over at the Ralph Lauren shop, a Gothic building, and bit again into my hotdog, chewing but not tasting, swallowing more big chunks.

Osmond walked a little slower, and I stepped in beside him. Memories of better times, walking side by side, casting flirtatious glances taunted my mind. "So, how's the investigation going?"

"The shits."

"Oh."

"We can't find the revolver used to kill Anna. Whenever we try to obtain a search warrant for the Aubischon residence, some judge denies our application. That's why finding Jules's body in the lake would give us the break we need, turn this investigation around."

We stepped apart to accommodate a small group of tourists.

Osmond crumpled his napkin into a ball and tossed it into a garbage can. "I'd like to ask your law partner, Mr. Keith Aubischon a few questions, but he never returns my calls," Osmond said, a shade of bitterness in his voice.

"But Keith's not involved in this."

Osmond eyed me. "That's what you think."

"You don't honestly believe—"

At that moment the blonde in the leather mini-skirt stepped up to Osmond.

"Sir," she said with a European accent, holding open a map and giving Osmond Bambi eyes. "I look for Royal British Columbia Museum."

Osmond pointed at her map as he gave instructions.

I looked down the street, my attention diverted to the mime. He again stood motionless, saxophone in hand, eyes staring at me. Jesus. Somebody drop him a quarter.

I looked back at Osmond. He and the blonde had moved closer to the street.

"Dis vay?" the blonde asked, pointing.

"No, straight—"

"—Straight," the blonde said.

I glanced over at the pickwick. The hotdog vendor watched us. I rubbed my hands. The blonde attracted too much damn attention. I wished she would leave.

"Yes—" Osmond turned and pointed to the map "—this way. Straight then left."

"Left?"

"Right. I mean yes."

"Right?"

"No left, *Jade*!"

There was a loud bang followed by Osmond lunging at me. My arms flung out and my half-eaten hotdog popped from my hand. Palms scraped brick. My jaw hit a window ledge, snapping my teeth together and my head back. The brick wall angled and loomed. I hit pavement. Flat on my stomach, gasping, panic closed in and dark splotches spotted the outer edges of my vision.

"*Get up*!" Osmond shouted.

Another bang. He pushed me back down, shielding me with his body.

"Gun!"

Screams.

"*Fuck*!" Osmond grabbed my arm and hauled me to my feet. Flicks of light darted before my eyes.

"Get her out of here!" the hotdog vendor shouted, running across the street, a gun in his hand.

Osmond hauled me, limping, down the sidewalk. People scurried in every direction. Blood trickled down my stinging chin. Osmond pulled me around a corner, and the grey and white Rolls with its flapping flags screeched to a stop. The passenger doors flew open and men in suits jumped out.

Osmond yanked me back and dragged me down another street, weaving between tourists. My breath came out in chunks and I clasped one hand to my ribcage. We dashed through an intersection. Horns blared, brakes squealed. We careened into Bastion Square where Victoria's artisans had set up kiosks.

A mother pushing a stroller stepped in front of us. The woman screamed. Osmond dodged her, pulling me with him. My foot caught on an artist's stool, and my ankle buckled and I fell again.

"Get up!" Osmond yanked on my arm. He kicked the stool down the hill. It hit a man before spinning and crashing into a stained glass mirror. I lurched to my feet. Pain shot from my ankle to my stomach.

Osmond dragged me, half running, half limping. Tourists and tables bobbed and blurred. I collided with a soap vendor dressed in a tropical print shirt, sending him head first into a steel bowl of avocado face cream. He stumbled around, green muck on his sunglasses and cheeks.

Another shot rang out, hitting the bowl, spinning it into the air.

More people screamed.

Osmond yanked me back from the kiosk. He pushed between two teenage boys, sprawling both of them into a perfume table. A child wailed. Table umbrellas collapsed. Wire display racks folded. Osmond took a set of stairs two at a time, and dragged me down an alley under a brick buttress-like arch. Liquor bottles rolled at my feet. A crow took off in a flap of black wings. Hell. I was going to Hell for all the criminals I had defended.

Osmond turned a corner and halted. "Shit."

Dead end.

He turned and dragged me back when the mime ran into the

other end of the alley. Osmond shoved me behind a garbage bin and crouched. He reached for his gun.

The mime's feet slapped on the pavement, his breath fast short gasps. I sucked in my breath, straightening my leg, trying to ease the pain. I pushed back against the dumpster when a leg slid out from the other side of the darkened alley. Osmond and I were not alone. The mime tripped on the leg and launched into the air like Superman, landing face first with a sickening thud.

Osmond catapulted to his feet, gun pointed. "Don't move!"

The mime looked up, his face a mess of black and white paint and blood.

"Arms out!"

The mime spat out a gob of blood and stretched his arms out.

Osmond stepped toward him as he reached with one hand to grab his handcuffs from his belt. "Who are—"

"Osmond." I croaked.

"Jade, not now."

"But there's—"

The body from the other side of the alley moved again. Osmond pivoted, pointing his gun at it.

The mime bolted.

"Fuck!" Osmond pointed his gun first at the mime, then at the body in the corner. "You! Out!"

"Can't," replied a worn voice. "Have to shoot me."

"Don't tempt me. Get out!"

The body moved and a hooded creature slid across the ground into the centre of the alley.

I slid further along the wall, my back bumping over black bars.

"Remove the hood."

Gnarled fingers reached up and the hood dropped to a man's shoulders, exposing a wrinkled face surrounded by shoulder length grey hair and a grey beard. Watery eyes squinted through dusty John Lennon glasses. An elf.

"Do you know what the hell you just did?"

"Prevented the arrest of a wanted accused?"

I straightened. Accused? That was prosecutor's jargon.

Osmond's arm wavered. "Who are you?"

The elf looked at me. "I thought you would have known, Jade."

And that's when I noticed the stained tabs hanging from around the elf's wrinkled neck.

"Osmond."

He must have seen them too because he lowered his gun. "Jesus Christ."

"No, Norman. Norman Bastine. But the locals call me Noxzema Man."

17

Questioning

If I don't figure out what's going on, they're going to kill me.

"OR Nox," Noxzema Man said, wiping his glasses with the edge of his blanket. He slipped his glasses back onto his face and squinted at me, one eye looking fractured behind a cracked lens. "Like the Fort, but without the 'K.'"

Osmond glanced at me as he tucked his gun back into his shoulder holster. The brightness from the entrance a few yards back caused me to squint. It clouded the dark corners of the alley and cast Osmond in a grey-green hue. At some point, he had lost his sunglasses and his shirt got untucked from his waistband.

The undercover officer from the pickwick had come charging around the corner. Osmond spoke to him privately, before the undercover officer took off in the direction of the mime.

"Nox," Osmond repeated, shifting his weight from one foot to the next. "Well, Nox, you damn well just about got yourself killed. Not smart startling a man pointing a loaded gun."

"You would have missed. Besides, it was the mime you were after. You got something against mimes, Detective Reeves?"

Osmond stiffened.

"I know everything," Nox grumbled, as if reading Osmond's mind.

At that moment, a furry body with a naked tail scurried past Osmond's feet. I grabbed for the bars behind me. My hands slipped and I grabbed the bars again. Something small with many legs dashed over my skin. I hauled myself to a vertical position and swiped my hands against my jeans.

"Then you know—" Osmond pointed at me.

"—Jade." Nox nodded.

"Hello Norman." I offered a tentative smile as I continued to wipe my hand on my pant legs. What did one say to a legal genius who once commanded the respect and admiration from Supreme Court Justices, but now only walked one step ahead of insanity? Who sought sanctuary not in an oak-paneled office with mini bar and pool table, but in a damp, stinking dark alley with flea-infested rodents? "We've missed you at the firm."

Norman grunted. "Like hell." His fractured eye stared at me. "So, did they kill him?"

I slid closer to Osmond. "Kill whom?"

"The man you defended."

"Jules?"

"Yeah."

"Yes. They did." I stared at his scraggly grey hair and the cutting wrinkles on his face. Did he really care about Jules? He hardly cared about himself.

"Bullet?" Norman asked. "Execution style?"

So blunt. So blasé. "No, Norman. . . they cut off his head." I swallowed. "And put it on a silver platter."

Norman's expression softened. "Jesus," he whispered.

And that's what unhinged me. A tear leaked over my cheek and I quickly wiped it away.

Norman leaned forward bringing his knees to his chest. "He was an example."

"Who's example, Nox?" Osmond asked, pulling his notebook out of an inner coat pocket and flipping it open.

"Nobody I know."

"I thought you knew everything, Nox?" Osmond clicked the

tip of a pen.

Nox grumbled again and shifted his body so his back was to Osmond.

"Who's in the Society, Nox?" Osmond persisted.

Norman shook his head, not looking at Osmond. "Nobody. Now leave me alone." He yanked his blanket closer to his body, hugging it to his chest. A bottle rolled across the cobblestones. I stopped it with my foot. Shame passed over Norman's face.

"Come on, Norman." I rolled the bottle with my foot. A brown liquid trickled out.

"If . . . if I told you—" he eyed the bottle then me "—you couldn't handle them. Jules . . . Jules thought he could—" his hand snaked from under the blanket and he snatched the bottle, spilling the brown liquid on his blanket "—and they served him as the main course. Don't mess with the Society, Jade. Now, go away. Go away."

"Norman."

He looked at me through his cracked lens. "I said go away."

"It's too late, Norman. They're messing with me. If I don't figure out what's going on, they're going to kill me. So far I've only been run off the road, shot at, third time . . . third time I might not be so lucky."

Nox, or Norman, was silent and watched me with the sharp-eyed look I remembered from his days in court. "Free legal advice, Jade. Leave the bastards alone and get the hell out of Dodge."

"Did Anna know about the Society?" Osmond asked.

"Eventually." Nox glanced over his shoulder. "Anna thought Jules could protect her from them. But he couldn't. You can't beat them. That's why I repeat: leave the Society alone."

I shifted position, alleviating the throbbing in my ankle. "Why did she need protection?"

"I can't remember." Nox tugged the blanket over an exposed part of his leg.

The pain was not letting up. I moved again. "We know she was in love with Olive. That she cheated on Olive."

Nox shrugged. "I don't know."

Osmond groaned. He rubbed the back of his neck then leaned against the dumpster. It may have been dim in the alley, but I could sense his exasperation for I felt it too. We were tired, cold, and marinating in the stench of rotting food, urine and God knows what else. My knees ached from the dampness in the alley, my ankle throbbed, and the dripping water echoed the desperation I felt. If Nox would cooperate, being shot at would seem worth my while.

"Nox. You're a good man."

He grunted again. "Word has it you give people wine and bread."

Crap. "I know you still hunger for the law."

"No. Sardines."

Osmond flung his arm out to his side, exasperated.

"You risked your life being seen at the courthouse. You were there. I spoke to you the day Jules was found not guilty."

Nox pulled his blanket around him as if to shield himself from my inquiries. "He didn't kill her." He pulled a Noxzema jar out from under his blanket. "Any fool could see he was innocent." He unscrewed the lid on the jar. It slipped from his fingers and splattered into a puddle. A horrible fish smell rose into the air.

"Why did Anna need protection?"

Norman plucked out a sardine and slipped it into his mouth, slurping the oily juice from his dirty fingers and thumb. "You know why they call me Noxzema Man?"

Like a cat tormenting a mouse, my old colleague wanted to play. "Because you eat sardines out of a Noxzema jar."

Nox stopped eating. Sardine juice glistened on his chin. "Always told Charles you were smart."

Osmond stopped taking notes and dropped his arm to his side. Legs apart, leaning against the dumpster, his body vibrated from a controlled exasperation. I had to get Nox to talk. If I could make a drug dealer rat out his suppliers, Noxzema Man should be easy to tap into. It wasn't his fault that the horrors of his occupation had finally driven him underground.

I hobbled across the alley. "Nox—" I knelt down in front of him "—why did Anna need protection?" I reached over and picked out a cold squishy sardine from the jar. I shivered. What the hell? I popped the sardine into my mouth. I gagged as the slimy fish stuck in my throat and fish oil coated my lips. All I could smell was fish.

"Shit," Osmond said.

I closed my eyes and swallowed hard, feeling the disgusting thing slide down my throat and into my stomach. I shook. When I opened my eyes, Nox stared, open-mouthed. He swallowed and held his Noxzema jar closer to his body. "They didn't want Anna seeing Olive. They warned her."

"The Society?" I croaked, shaking my head.

"Yes." He picked out another sardine and sucked it into his mouth. He covered the jar with his hand as he chewed.

A crow cawed and landed at the entrance. Norman flinched. "Out of here." With a pathetic effort, he threw pebbles at the bird, which cawed again and flew out into the daylight.

"Did James not want Anna seeing Olive?" I wanted specifics and I wanted collaboration.

"Correct."

"Why?" Osmond asked.

Nox glared at him. "Why do you think? He was mortified. If people found out that Justice James Aubischon had a daughter who was lesbian . . . the damage to his career would be inconceivable. That's why he approved Olive marrying Jules."

Anything to protect his reputation. "Did James threaten Anna at any time?"

"Not in public. James gave her money to go away."

I looked at Osmond. So my father hadn't given Anna the money, Olive had just said that to make me angry. "But she didn't leave," I said.

"Correct."

"She took the money and instead went to Jules, hoping for

protection? James's future son-in-law?"

"Yes. You do not make a fool of the Society. If Olive and Jules still married, she would secretly see Olive."

"What did James do?"

"Had her killed."

I looked over at Osmond. He briefly stopped writing then continued. "James belongs to the Society?"

Sadness passed over Nox's face.

"James belongs to the Society?" Osmond repeated.

"Yes." Nox slurped up another sardine. "Jules was livid especially given they stuck him with the murder rap."

"Jules knew who murdered Anna?" Osmond asked, still writing.

"Jules had his theories."

"How do you know this?"

"He visited me." Nox shifted his gaze from Osmond to me. "He said you were working your ass off on his case but the police—" Nox glanced at Osmond and lowered his voice "—had only disclosed a third of the evidence. He said you were the only lawyer he could trust in a city full of dirty lawyers and dirty cops. If you wanted to screw him over, you would have done so when you divorced him."

I pressed my fist to my lips, smelled sardines, and dropped my hand to my side. So true. When we had divorced, I had only wanted what I had brought into the marriage. Maybe that's why Jules wanted to know why I had taken on his case. It still mattered to him if I thought him guilty or innocent.

"You are the only one, Jade, the Society hasn't sunk its claws into."

Osmond straightened. "You said Jules had a theory?"

"Theory. Speculation."

"What was it?"

"He believed he had uncovered the Society assassin ordered to kill Anna, but he couldn't prove it."

"Society assassin?"

Nox looked at me. "Yes."

"Who?"

"It was a theory, Jade. Einstein had theories."

"Who?"

"Jules wouldn't tell me until he had gathered enough evidence."

"He must have been right," Osmond mumbled, "because whoever it was eliminated him."

"And before he could give me the thumb drive. That's the evidence," I said. "Who determines the Society assassin?"

"A panel."

"A panel?"

"Of three."

I dropped my head forward. "Like the Court of Appeal."

"The panel of three selects who will be the Society assassin. The assassin can commit the crime himself, and increase his standing, or hire someone. The selection is done on a revolving basis and in complete secrecy. Only the assassin and the panel are aware of the task at hand."

"And what happens if the assassin selected refuses to complete the task?"

"They are abolished from the Society. Then a few months down the road he'll find himself unemployable, chasing accident victims or stuffing his business card in the pockets of dead men."

"Is that what happened to you?" Osmond asked.

Nox glared. "We're not talking about me, Detective Reeves." Nox looked at me. "I don't like him."

"He saved my life, Nox."

Nox grumbled. He unscrewed the Noxzema lid and sucked back another sardine. He replaced the lid, thank God. I could still taste salt and oil and fish, and I was damned if I was going to choke down another one.

"The lawyers actually commit these crimes?"

"You don't understand, Jade," he said, sighing. "Only a select few are chosen. The avenging of a criminal to that degree is not often done. First there are threats, blackmail, assaults."

"And the Society does all of this?"

"Yes. Do unto others as you would have them do unto you. If you are an accused found not guilty of an assault, be guaranteed the Society will review your file and determine if appropriate action should be taken."

"Such as?"

"A beating. Depends on the circumstances of the case. Each member brings his or her case that he or she would like avenged. The panel decides which case shall be acted upon."

"My God, a twisted Court of Appeal."

"Or a dignified vigilantism," Osmond mumbled.

"And when it comes to murder?" I asked.

"Then only the ones with undisputed loyalty are privy to conduct such acts. Once the deed is done, the lawyer rises in standing and cannot be touched. Why do you think in court some lawyers get away with what they do?" Norman reached up a dirty finger and tapped his temple.

I rubbed the back of my neck, staring at the rippling circles water droplets created in a puddle. I remembered the atrocious rulings I had endured, wondering what had possessed the judge to make the decision he did. Now I knew. "How does one become a member?"

"It's not something you join, Jade. You are recruited by a Recruiter. The Society has two Recruiters. No member associates with any other lawyer except if he or she is a fellow member. It's a huge organization, a prestigious one, and the members know it."

"Find the Recruiters and you crack the Society," Osmond said. He had stopped writing.

Noxzema Man nodded, his glasses reflecting the light from the entrance.

I thought about Jules and his bulging eyes and the prawn whiskers adorning his cheeks. What prestige was there in the taking of another man's life? Who was the sick individual who felt compelled to cut off his head and drop it on a buffet table?

"It's a very tight system. Excellent benefits. Vacation and

retirement packages. Ran smoothly, that is, until Jules came along. The Recruiter who recruited him is still paying the price."

"Enough to kill him?"

"I don't know."

"Who recruited Jules?"

"I *don't know*. But his murder—" Nox rubbed his eyes "—that was a clear message. A member does not turn on its members."

"How do you know all this information?"

"Jade, I want to keep my head."

I stared at Norman. He was a brilliant lawyer. He didn't belong here and he didn't deserve this. Twenty years from now if I stayed in this occupation, would the same happen to me? I was already haunted by crime victims and cavorting with ghosts about verdicts. Would I become a ranting bag lady? Scrounging for pennies and discarded gum wrappers while pushing a baby carriage with a mannequin in it? The tragic lawyer my colleagues referred to at parties as 'the lawyer they knew when.'

"You were a member."

Norman looked down, squirmed beneath his blanket, then finally looked at me with his fractured eye.

"That's why you're hiding. What did you do?"

"I successfully defended the biker gang. I was supposed to lose."

"Like throw a trial," Osmond said, "like throwing a game."

"Yes."

"And as soon as the gang leader's decapitated head was found, you disappeared," I said.

Norman looked ashamed.

"I am so sorry, Norman."

He shrugged his fallen shoulders. I stood. Pins and needles pricked my joints. I hobbled back to the bars and leaned against them. "Tell me Norman, has my father ever—" I couldn't ask. I couldn't ask if my father had taken another man's life.

"You must ask him, Jade." Nox hunkered down in the folds of the blanket. He knew so much more than he was willing to tell.

I dragged my hand through my hair and looked at Osmond. "That's why he wanted to meet me, Osmond. On the night he was murdered. Jules knew. He had finally found his evidence." I closed my eyes and pressed my fist to my lips. "But I was too late."

"Jade."

If I had been a little more punctual instead of bad-mouthing him with Bianca could I have prevented his murder?

"Jade."

I sniffed. Dabbed my cheeks with the palm of my hand and looked at Osmond.

"I'll take you home."

I took a step forward as Osmond came around to my right side, his arm around my shoulders.

"Be careful Jade," Nox said, crouching down into his blanket.

"You be careful, Nox. They will just as soon kill you as they will me."

18

Addiction

The water bottle slipped from my hand and I saw myself, on my knees, hands bound behind my back, head hung in shame.

"Jade," Kate said, following me into my office with a bundle of papers in her hands. "You look like—"

"—Shit." I slapped my briefcase on my desk and pressed my fingertips to my temples. "Rough night. Is Keith in?"

"Boardroom." Kate arched her eyebrows. "Emergency meeting."

"Now?" I looked at my watch. "We have the search warrant hearing! Who called the meeting?"

"Aubischon senior. Keith told me to give you his notes and authorities—" Kate placed the bundle of papers in my hands "—and he would meet you at the courthouse."

I dumped the papers on my desk. "Keith's going to be there?"

"He doesn't know for sure."

"What?"

"He said it's a big agenda."

Agenda? What agenda? The pounding in my head dropped to bass tones. I reached down and yanked open my desk drawer, pushing aside Post It notes, pencils and pens. Where the hell was my Vicodin? "Any idea what the meeting's about?"

"The only thing I got out of Keith's secretary is that it had to do with restructuring."

"Restructuring?"

"Yeah." Kate raised her eyebrows and attempted a smile. "Whatever that means." She threw her arms out to her sides. "Maybe they're going to buy us another photocopier."

Yeah, right. I sat down in my chair and stared at the pile of papers. Restructuring. Who was getting the boot?

"You all right, Jade?"

"Yes." I tapped my heel against the floor. I didn't feel good at all. I felt like I was going to throw up. "Who's all in the meeting?"

"All the partners and Troy."

"Troy! He's not a partner." I grabbed the water bottle on my desk, unscrewed the cap and sloshed back a gulp.

Kate tucked a short blonde strand of hair behind her ear. "Keith called him in."

What was so bloody important to cause Aubischon senior to cancel his Thursday morning golf game so he could have a meeting with the partners?

"Is my father in there?"

Kate's cheeks grew a faint shade of pink, matching the colour of her suit. She looked down at her feet and readjusted her stance. "I'm not a hundred percent sure but I think so."

"Dammit." I fell back in my chair. The joke around the office, albeit true, was better to be included than excluded. I glanced from the books on my desk to the photocopied cases and Keith's notes. I was buried under the legalities of a search warrant hearing while the rest of the firm, including Troy, discussed my conduct. I picked up my pen and clicked and unclicked. What the hell was Troy doing? He wasn't the new partner, I was. Click, unclick. How could my father discuss my conduct with him? As if there was anything wrong with my conduct! Dammit! I tossed the pen onto Keith's argument. I did not have time for this. I was expected in court. Vandenberg's future now rested solely on my shoulders. I sat forward and grabbed Keith's notes. "When's the hearing supposed to begin?"

"Nine-thirty."

"Which courtroom?"

"Three-twenty-three."

I checked my watch again. "I have forty-five minutes."

"I'll hold your calls," Kate said, walking back to the door. "Ah, Jade."

"Yeah."

"It's going to be okay."

Kate had such an encouraging smile. I wasn't in the mood for her Mary Poppins attitude. I flicked on my computer. "I don't want to be disturbed."

"Want a coffee?"

"No." I wanted Vicodin. I whipped the briefcase around and pressed the catch. Still Troy's briefcase. I wanted mine back.

"If you need anything—"

"— I'm fine. Thank you."

She closed the door.

I slipped my finger under my glasses and rubbed my eyelid. I should have known today was going to be a bad day, considering it had taken me two hours to notice that I had put my nylons on backwards after my shower that morning. I stared at the closed door. They were deciding my future. Analyzing my conduct. What had I done wrong? I had back-to-back wins. Hadn't bullied any staff as some lawyers do. I was always bringing in doughnuts and flowers for the secretaries. This meeting had nothing to do with my work and everything to do with Jules and Norman and me. Is this how the Society conducted its business? I broke into a sweat. My stomach churned. I grabbed my recycle bin and threw up. *Shit.* I fumbled for a tissue, wiping my mouth. I pulled open my desk drawer and found gum. I straightened and sat in my chair. With trembling fingers I pulled the cases toward me. I had a more pressing problem. Trying to convince The Honourable Crotchety O.G. Sullivan that the RCMP had conducted an illegal search when they searched my client's law office.

I quickly read my notes and highlighted portions of texts in my first book of authorities. I then flipped through the second book of cases. The law was currently in a state of flux when it came to searching law offices, making my job that much more difficult. All I knew is that the Crown could not have access to the note seized during the search. A note currently sealed in an envelope. That note could kill our case. But if the worst happened, I could always discredit Mr. Beattie, the Crown's key witness. At eighty-six, I doubt if the old man could recall what brand of oatmeal he ate this morning, let alone what his wife had written eight months ago while she was in the throes of radiation treatment.

I checked my watch. 8:45. I looked at Keith's notes and the books he had prepared. If I hadn't known better, I would have thought he had given his argument a bare bones attempt. A pivotal precedent-setting decision was absent from his argument and case book. I swiveled around in my chair and clicked the mouse on my computer. After a flash of numbers and the gold letters of the office logo shooting to the centre of the screen, I logged onto the legal research program.

Emergency meeting. What the hell for?

After a few more beeps, I clicked onto the Court of Appeal decisions.

Whom had I pissed off?

I scrolled down the list of cases and found the identical one to Vandenberg's where the judge had ruled in the defence's favour. I printed three copies—one for the judge, Crown and myself—and then logged out of the program. I stood and gathered my notes, Keith's books, and my books.

Emergency meeting.

I looked up. A dizziness overcame me and my antique bookshelves seemed to slant and slide to the left. I braced my hand on the desk. The bookshelves then tilted to the right and slid back in place. What was happening to me? A little light-headedness, that's all. Food poisoning. Yes. Norman's sardines. Overtired, over-stressed and under-sexed. I unscrewed the cap of my bottled water and threw back a slosh. I gulped another mouthful as colour splotches flashed before my eyes, then a foggy image of mud and boot prints.

The water bottle slipped from my hand and I saw myself, on my knees, hands bound behind my back, head hung in shame. Rag-tag children rose from the fog, jeering and pointing. A man dressed in lawyer robes, his face hidden by a black hood with eye cut-outs, laughed at my kneeling figure. The material over his mouth sucked into the shape of an 'O'. With both hands, the man raised an axe above his head, then swung.

"Jade!"

I screamed and fell back, landing in my chair. "What?"

"You haven't heard a word I've said." Kate stepped in from the doorway. "The hearing. It's time."

My heart pounded. I must have still looked stunned for Kate tapped her watch. "The search warrant hearing. You've got to go."

I looked at my wrists, unbound and free of rope burn. I slid my fingers around my neck. What crime had I been found guilty of?

"Jade, you don't look well."

An opportunity. "I've been so busy with work that I forgot to renew my prescription. My back is killing me and I think I'm suffering from food poisoning. Ate some bad fish yesterday."

"I have some prescription Tylenol 3s. Will that hold you over?"

Bless you, Kate. "Yes. Please. You're an angel."

Kate dashed to her desk and brought me back Tylenol 3s.

"So, Jade."

"Yes."

"Is it true? Are you leaving?"

"Leaving?" I stared at her. "No. Who says I'm leaving?" I stuffed the Vandenberg file into my briefcase.

"There's a rumour going around that you're leaving."

I stared. *What the hell?* "No, Kate. The rumour is crap. I'm not going anywhere except court."

"Good." Kate smiled. "Text me if you need anything." She stepped out of my office, closing the door behind her.

I looked over at the picture above the bookshelf of my father wearing his black robes.

Judge, jury or executioner. Which one? I tossed back the Tylenol 3s. Leaving.

~

Mr. Justice O.G. Sullivan stared down his nose through his bifocals at Bianca as he read his reasons as if it was the Magna Carta. There are lawyers and judges who love the sound of their own voice. Crotchety O.G. Sullivan is one of them.

I sat, with pulp for brains, trying not to fall asleep during Sullivan's dissertation. Bianca had put up one hell of a fight, and I was sure I had lost this battle. Fortunately, Justice Sullivan hadn't seen it that way. The most damning piece of evidence crucial to the Crown's case—Mrs. Beattie's letter—would remain sealed. The contents of the sealed envelope seized during the RCMP's search, which I argued was an illegal search, would not be revealed. Searching a law office is a little more difficult than searching the home of Joe Public.

Bianca would most likely appeal Sullivan's decision, but I was ready for her.

Garlic-breathing Vandenberg sat beside me, snorting and clearing his throat. I erratically clicked the end of my pen with my thumb. At any minute the spring would bust, and the pen would become a messy projectile—something out of a Bond film. Wouldn't Sullivan be impressed. I tossed the pen onto my notepad and sat back in my chair. I was being paid well for this. That's all that mattered.

Sullivan placed his reasons on his desk then began his hemorrhoidal tirade about Bianca's lack of legal expertise. Even though she was a seasoned veteran, the experience of being publicly humiliated by Sullivan before a gallery of fellow counsel, the accused, members of the press and the spectators in the courtroom is not a pleasant one. I know. Last month it had been me.

I rubbed my hands over my face and glanced up at the rafters. At the start of Bianca's argument I had heard the hanging ghosts, laughing and rattling their chains. Crazy that I hadn't heard them on the day Jules was acquitted. They should have laughed. It was as if they had known something the rest of us didn't. I stopped rubbing my cheeks. Goosebumps prickled all over my skin. Jules had been acquitted. Could the ghosts have known that Jules was a dead man?

I shifted on my chair. Vandenberg eyed me, then turned his attention back to Sullivan. Folklore. That's all the ghosts were. Not one ounce of truth to their myth. Yet a clammy dread soaked through my clothes and into my skin and I glanced at the worn crisscrossing beams.

"Ms. Thyme!"

I jumped.

"Are you with us, Ms. Thyme, or have you taken counsel with some other entity?"

There was a murmur of laughter. I straightened and shuffled my notes. "No. My Lord. I am here."

"Good. I do not appreciate my time being wasted by counsel's lack of attention. Maybe you and Ms. Taylor might learn something about practising law if you'd pay more attention. Now, this hearing is adjourned."

"All rise," bellowed the sheriff.

I clambered to my feet, gripping onto the edge of the table.

With his flailing robes, O.G. Sullivan descended the bench and disappeared into his chamber. The final thud of his chamber door reverberated through my heart. I exhaled a long slow breath.

"Wonderful job, Jade." Clive Vandenberg flashed me a row of tobacco-stained teeth and pulled me in for a suffocating hug. "Don't ever embarrass me like that again."

I pulled back and opened my mouth but Clive had turned and

was now shaking the hand of another politician.

How the hell had I embarrassed him? He embarrassed me. I pressed the catch on my briefcase and tossed in his disgusting file. What had propelled me to represent this asshole? The partnership? I looked at Vandenberg, all yellow smiles and fumes as he leered over the daughter of a fellow politician. Lecher.

I heard the protestations of Mr. Beattie from the corner.

Clive still nodded and smiled at the members of the press, punching the shoulders of his fellow colleagues. I tossed my *Criminal Code* into my briefcase and glanced to my left. Bianca spoke with the investigating officer while pushing through the throng of people. Peggy, the Crown Victim Services worker, tried consoling Mr. Beattie. Dressed in a beige suit and matching beige hat, Mr. Beattie clutched a cane as he tried one last time to plead his deceased wife's case. "He stole Jeannie's money."

God. I looked down at my briefcase. Nothing like a little guilt worming its way into one's conscience.

I slammed my briefcase shut, snatched it and the one on the floor, and jostled my way through the spectators. A half-dozen reporters in raincoats clenching notepads descended upon Bianca. Her attractive face couldn't mask the burden Sullivan's ruling had dropped on her shoulders. The RCMP would be outraged. There'd be another enquiry into her conduct. That's all she needed. Hopefully she wouldn't be pulled from the file. A bad sign when another lawyer is ordered to take over. Bianca fed the hungry pack the standard bait about having a strong case with reliable witnesses, and the search warrant hearing being only one hurdle on the road to justice. Little did the reporters know that the sheriff had slipped me her note suggesting a deal.

I squeezed between sheriffs and past a group of teenagers, all interspersed amongst the various suits crowding the courthouse hallways. A three-year old boy with a soggy diaper and stained shirt let loose a deafening scream as his gum-popping teenage mother dragged him down the hall. I walked through the metal detector, nodding at the two sheriffs on either side.

I pushed through the outside glass doors, inhaling the muggy moisture of a fresh rain shower, trying to clear my mind from the stench of despair. I nodded to the lawyers dashing up the outside steps and marched past a half dozen bikers leaning against the metal rail. Drug bust the night before at the ferry terminal. Supposedly a local produce distributor decided to ship a little fentanyl with his skids of corn and radicchio lettuce. His buddies must be putting up his bail. I stepped around a disheveled man only to come face-to-face with Sergeant Stone.

"Jade," he said. "You're still here."

I stared at his face. His nose looked all right, not like it had a close encounters with a motorcycle helmet. "Tell me, Sergeant Stone, where did you expect to see me? At the bottom of a lake?" I had it with niceties and Stone's cave-man mentality.

"You were always the dramatic one of the two sisters. Tell me, Sage still hanging with that dyke motorcycle gang?"

"Ah, is my sister still hanging with the all–female motorcycle group. Yes, she is."

"From what I understand, she's their ringleader."

I knew he was fishing.

"And from what I understand some of these idiots—" he nodded at the bikers "—have ties with the MotoCityDolls, and for some reason, whenever we execute a raid and think we've found their cook house, we find an empty warehouse."

I glared. "Goodbye Sergeant."

"Tell Sage to drive safely on that Harley. Crazy drivers out there. Wouldn't want her to get hurt."

Do not give that asshole a reaction. I tried to catch up to the suits walking ahead of me. My heels clicked a staccato rhythm and my sprained ankle, reeking of Absorbine Junior and swathed in a gauze bandage, throbbed. I stopped at the crosswalk and waited for the light to change. Cars and trucks streamed past.

A horn blared.

I jumped.

A biker, straddled on a Harley, revved his engine. "Hey."

I looked at him.

"You're Sage's sister. Tell her Meatloaf says hi and thanks."

"Meatloaf," I repeated.

"Yeah. That's me. She's a doll."

I smiled and quickly hobbled across the crosswalk. Good grief. The biker revved his engine again. I stepped up onto the sidewalk on the other side of the street just as a Molson brewery van barreled around the corner. I released a deep breath and slowed my pace.

For the first time in my life, I tasted the fear and despair of my client's victims. A vile taste. By representing accused, I shared their guilt. I readjusted my grip on my briefcases and flipped my hair back over my shoulders, catching my reflection in the glass window of our building. Shoulders stooped, hands laden with briefcases, I was the crumpled figure in designer clothes staring back at me. I slowed my step and stopped. The gold letters of Aubischon, Thyme and Bastine painted on the glass distorted my face.

When had I become this caricature? I squinted as I looked up at the floors of black windows towering to the sky. I made my wages from the pain and suffering of others. Shielding those whom should be held responsible. Getting the accused off on technical issues and charter breaches regardless of the circumstances of the case, or whether the victim lay hospitalized, or worse—dead. A raindrop splattered my forehead. I looked down at the concrete.

The wind tugged on my hair and apple blossoms swirled around my ankles. A man bumped my shoulder. I slowly stepped forward, my fingers stiff and cramped. I pushed through the building's glass carousel doors. Had the practices of my occupation eaten my soul?

The security guard smiled and nodded. I nodded back. Along with a handful of business people, I merged into the mirrored elevator. The numbers of the passing floors flashed and after a dozen stops, the elevator doors opened at my floor. I hesitated. One of the law students pushed out of the crowded elevator and lunged for the beveled glass office door, pulling it open.

"Ms. Thyme."

He had the innocent and eager enthusiasm of all first-year law students who vowed to "make a difference." I wanted to tell him to get out. Now. While he still had a chance.

I stepped out, thanked the student, then affixed my smile and walked in.

Secretaries offered me congratulations and lawyers waved to me from their desks. Kate sat at her desk with her phone to her ear while weaving a pencil between her fingers. Eyebrows furrowed, she gnawed on her lip. I walked into my office, dumped my briefcases on the floor, and kicked the door shut.

I slipped my arms from the sleeves of my leather suit, dropping the coat on the back of my chair. I strolled over to the mini-refrigerator and opened it. I needed alcohol. Something to deaden the cheap sleazy feeling. Instead, I grabbed a bottle of Evian, twisted off the cap, and hip-checked the fridge door closed. I strolled over to the window, drinking a mouthful of cold water. I leaned my head back against one of my bookshelves and stared at the sail boats that streamed across the water, their snail bodies secreting a white foamy discharge. I drank another mouthful of water and rotated my head from shoulder to shoulder.

My time would come when I would have to account for all the criminals I have defended. Or had it already? I glanced over the roofs of buildings, seeing the Yates Street Tower at the far end of the city, and the anthill of vehicles streaming over the streets and bridges.

My time would come. I could feel it, sense it, taste it. My gig would be up and I would stand exposed. I sucked back another mouthful of water. A knock rattled my door. "Come in?"

Kate stepped in, her eyebrows still furrowed.

"What is it, Kate?"

"Keith would like to see you."

"Okay."

She wrung her hands together. "He said, now."

19

Leaving

His mission—to enforce Society justice.

"There you are," Keith said as he hung up his phone.

I stepped into his office. "You wanted to see me."

"Yes. Close the door behind you." He slid from behind his desk. "You made Vandenberg a happy man."

I limped over to a black armchair. "Please—" I dropped into it, smelling the distinct scent of leather "—I don't need the mental picture. You're never doing that to me again, are you Aubischon?"

"You won, Jade," Keith said, walking over to a water cooler "—and as I understand it—" he pulled down a cup "—Crotchety Sullivan tore a few strips off Bianca."

"Yeah, but Bianca's tough—" I unscrewed the cap on my water bottle "—she can take it. Granted, she's probably down at the tavern knocking back a few Jack Daniels." I wished I was with her. I straightened my leg, trying to relax my ankle and took a drink of water. "Where were you?"

Keith moved over to the window. The brightness from outside cast his profile in shadow. "First, thank you."

I straightened. "I'm pleased with the outcome. But I feel there's more to my being here?"

Keith smiled and drank from the paper cup. "A crazy business we're in, Jade. Work your ass off getting your client off just to have the miserable fucker turn around and hire new counsel."

I stared. "Is that what Vandenberg's doing?"

"Hell no. Although—" Keith straightened and pointed the paper cup in my direction "—he did threaten to take his business elsewhere."

"Let him. The guy's slime. We don't need him."

Keith smiled his crooked smile. "He pays our bills, Jade."

"So do a lot of other wealthy clients. Besides, what does Vandenberg have to be concerned about? We won."

Keith tipped the paper cup and looked into its depths before shifting his scrutiny my way. "He mentioned you blacked out in court."

"I did not!"

"Sullivan didn't reprimand you?"

"Sullivan reprimands everyone in his courtroom, from lawyers to spectators. You know that. It's no big deal."

"To you, no, but to Vandenberg—" he stepped away from the window "—image is everything."

I leaned forward. "Let's get one thing straight, I am not a part of Vandenberg's image. And if Vandenberg is so concerned about *his* image, then tell him to buy some breath mints! And a little deodorant would help."

Keith sat on the edge of his desk. "The man has power and connections."

"Doesn't mean we have to kiss up."

Keith sloshed back a mouthful of water then looked at a framed portrait of his great-grandfather wearing his robes and the traditional white curly wig. "No, but we can't antagonize our own clients, Jade."

"I didn't antagonize Vandenberg. I was his lawyer, acted on his behalf, nothing else. He didn't buy my soul when he paid my retainer, and I'm shocked that we're having this conversation. What brought this on?"

Keith looked down at the paper cup before finishing the last drops. He crumpled the cup and fired it into the waste paper basket by the cooler. "He complained to my father."

"When?"

"Last night. He made a number of complaints about your handling of the case."

"We both worked on his case."

"I know. Father spoke to me also."

"And?"

Keith stepped away from his desk. "Father wants you on leave starting immediately."

"What?" I crawled out of the armchair and stood, tenderly placing my weight on my ankle. "I've done nothing wrong."

Keith looked out the window, his back slightly turned.

"Keith, I've done nothing wrong. You know that. Is this what your emergency meeting was all about?"

He stepped back, his eyes following the route of a wailing fire truck. "The guys feel you need a break."

"The guys?! Which guys? Troy? My father? You? Well, you're wrong. I won't do it, and I don't need—"

"—Jade, when a client raises concerns—"

"Vandenberg is a liar! I successfully defended that jerk on Crown's application. If it wasn't for me his ass—"

"—Sergeant Stone wrote a complaint letter to the Assistant Deputy Attorney General regarding your involvement in Jules's murder and how you're jeopardizing the investigation."

"I'm jeopardizing the investigation! If Sergeant Stone knew how to conduct an investigation—"

"—Jade!"

"—I wouldn't be involved! And since when have you been concerned about Stone?" I clutched my water bottle and hobbled over to the window.

"You should have taken leave the day after Jules was killed."

"Yeah, right. I know how the gossip flies around this place." I dumped my water over Keith's umbrella plant. "This has nothing to do with Vandenberg or Stone or my mental health. Who have I pissed off, Keith?" I twisted the cap back on the bottle and placed it on the window ledge. "Or is someone after my job?"

"Jade, you're blowing this—"

"—You guys call this meeting and I'm not invited!"

"You had court!"

"Defending our client!"

"And I was defending you!"

"Fine job you did!"

The colour drained from Keith's face and a muscle twitched in his jaw. I shouldn't have said that, but what did he expect? My work was all I had, and now he was taking that away. I tapped the water bottle against the window ledge. "You've got to understand where I'm coming from. You guys went behind my back, passed judgment on my behaviour, without giving me the chance to defend myself."

"Father called the meeting as soon as he found out what Stone was up to. Someone needed to appear with Vandenberg. We weren't going to send him up there on his own!"

"You could have gone and I could have at least addressed the firm's concerns."

"Jade, you're blacking out in court—"

"—I am not!"

"Seeing things that aren't there!"

I spun around. "What did you say?"

Keith looked down at the floor, then leveled dark cold eyes at me. "Seeing things."

How could he know? *Kate*. She could have inadvertently said something, not meaning any harm, but not knowing that her comments would be used against me. How long had the firm known? And if they were concerned about my mental health, why assign me such huge cases in the first place? Unless they were hoping I would fail? The last two months flashed like a deck of cards in a magician's hand. "*Why did you do it, Jade*?" Jules had asked me, his cigar smoke curling. He had wanted to know the real reason why I took on his case. Why? Did he suspect I was being set up? With only half a police report and no cooperation from the authorities?

My pulse pounded in my neck. I thought of my executioner with his axe. All I had ever worked for was slipping from my grasp. Years of education, hard work and political two-stepping in order to succeed in a field where the old boy's network determined one's success or failure.

Old boy's network.

The Society.

My knee joints softened and I sat on the window ledge. "I am not—" I swallowed, trying not to lose it "—seeing things."

Keith walked over to me. His hand lifted my jaw. "Jade, the staff are starting to notice."

I closed my eyes and turned my face away from his touch.

"Jade. I don't like doing this. You're my best lawyer and I don't want to lose you, but—"

"—but what?"

"I have to do what's best for the firm."

I inhaled a deep breath as I watched the steady flow of cars below. The Society was trying to get rid of me. If I didn't comply, would I be their next casualty? My existence determined by a panel of three? "How long am I supposed to be away?"

"According to company policy you're entitled to three weeks bereavement. You've been pushing yourself too hard, and it's affecting your work, the people around you, your clients. The Crown's not happy about the Romeo charge approval. Vandenberg is keeping his business here but he wants to deal with a man. I managed to soothe Stone. He's ripped up the complaint letter, but on the condition—"

"—that I go on leave." The window ledge blurred and I blinked back tears. *Do not cry.*

"Take the time, Jade. Get some rest. When was your last vacation? I heard there are cheap flights to Paris. Hell, that's where I'd be—on a French vineyard."

I tucked a strand of hair behind my ear and crossed my arms. "So three weeks?"

Keith straightened. "Actually . . . five months."

My hands dropped to my sides. "Five months!? What happened to three weeks?"

"Jade, three weeks isn't—"

"—and there goes my partnership. Troy will get it!"

"He already has it!"

I froze.

Keith's face paled. "*Shit.*" He walked over to the bookshelf.

"Troy—" my voice faltered "—Mr. Pothead *Troy* has my partnership and my briefcase!"

Keith's shoulders tensed, the back of his suit tightened across his shoulder blades.

"When did you plan to tell me? Or did I miss that office memo?"

Keith picked up a limestone statue of a Buddha, weighing it in his hand, then placed it back on the shelf. "It'll be official at the end of the week."

"*Tomorrow!*" I turned around and braced my hands on either side of the window. Every loser I had defended, every scum sucking snitch I had been civil to, every victim who had sat in the witness stand and looked at me with hate, or lay silent on a coroner's slab, all rose up and laughed in my face.

"What have I done, Keith?"

He looked down at his desk, then over at the picture of him holding a rifle and his father standing proudly beside him holding a dead duck.

"Who have I pissed off? You?"

He dragged his hand through his hair. "Jade—"

"Your father?"

"I don't have time for this." He stepped behind his desk. "I expect summaries of all your files on my desk by the end of tomorrow." He picked up a file.

"The Society has spoken and its faithful members have complied."

Keith dropped the file and glared. "Don't ever mention that

organization again."

I walked towards his desk. "I know about the Society and how it exercises a vigilante justice system. How it has Recruiters to solicit new members. Jules and Anna found out about the Society and they were killed. Am I next, Keith?"

"Do you want to be next?"

I gulped.

"Then leave." He picked up another file. "You think you know what's going on? You know only what Detective Reeves wants to tell you. He's a member, Jade. Did you know that? His mission—to enforce Society justice. Hell, he's got the badge. Ever wonder why something always happens to you when he's around?"

My knees bowed. I clutched the back of the leather armchair. "That's not true."

"Oh, no? Think about it. He was with you when you were shot. How about the gang in the alley? You told me he was with you then. Have you ever asked him if he belonged?"

No.

"The next time you talk to him, ask. Cops are also a part of the Society—the front men, the pawns."

"That's not true."

"Ask him!"

"You're lying. You're a member and you're scared."

"I am not a member! But your father is, and so is mine! There's upheaval in the Society. The younger generation wants to oust the old. Jules started it and Reeves is following through. Why the hell do you think he showed up in your courtroom when Jules was acquitted? He wants an inside track to your father and he's using you to get it."

"You're lying."

"I'm sure that's what Osmond will tell you. But then again, just like in law, it's a matter of which truth you choose to believe."

I kneaded my fingers into the leather cushion. The emotion I had choked back for so long slipped. I swiped my hand over my cheeks and pushed out my chin. "I'll have the summaries for you by tomorrow evening." I turned and hobbled to the door.

"Oh, and Jade, Troy will be moving into your office while you're gone. Make sure your stuff is out and don't forget to give the secretarial student your leave form."

20

Secrets

A breeze flapped at the tails of his leather coat, and the smoke from his cigarette trailed from his hand.

With one arm overburdened with legal texts, and a raspberry truffle mocha clutched in my other hand, I stumbled down the cement steps leading out of my office building. In the illumination of the street lamps the darkened sidewalks glistened, and the musky scent of heat and moisture rose in swirling clouds. I half expected Sherlock Holmes to walk around the corner, smoking his pipe, in search of Watson.

I blew a strand of hair away from my face and heaved the sliding books, trying to get a better grip. I spotted my rented Volkswagen parked under a street lamp up ahead. A wannabe gang of teenagers with toques pulled down over their ears, baggy sweaters and loose jeans, strutted toward me. Foul words spewed from their mouths, and I found it hard to believe that these individuals had at one time spoken the cooing words of babes. I placed my coffee on the roof of my car and fished the keys out of my pocket.

"Repent!"

I jumped, dropping my keys and almost losing my books. I looked over the roof of my vehicle. Across the street, looking like a poor imitation of Moses, thumping his fist on a bible, stood

Noxzema Man. My Lord. Something more than religion had brought Nox out of his alley.

Nox nodded and banged his fist again on the bible. "Repent! Repent! All false Messiahs, all creatures of Satan."

A reassurance overcame me as I watched Nox. When it came down to it, he was the only person I trusted. If Nox was my Guardian Angel, then the Lord definitely worketh in mysterious ways.

I crouched down, not losing hold of my books, and snatched my keys from a puddle. I found the right one and shoved it into the back passenger door.

"Death and damnation befall those unbelievers!" Nox's voice rang out.

I turned the key in the lock.

"Save yourselves from the raging fires of hell!"

The lock clicked.

"Go fuck yourself, old man!" One of the gang members shouted.

I couldn't help but smile, as I rested my chin on the top book, and slowly pulled the car door open.

"Thou speakeths in Satan's tongue. Save yourself!"

They're beyond saving, Nox.

The middle book in my stack began to slide. "Shit." I grabbed for it, missed. It splashed into the puddle, spraying my leg. The second and third books slipped. I lunged for them. My heel splattered in the puddle. Another book dropped, its sharp corner jabbed my foot. Then my entire pile collapsed. Two large hands clamped onto the sliding books, stopping any further catastrophes.

I looked up to express my thanks.

Osmond.

"Are you aiming for the puddle, Jade? I can let go."

"The backseat. Please."

A hint of a smile dimpled Osmond's face. He took the books from my hands and tossed them onto the back seat. He knelt down and picked up the other books. "What are you preparing, counsellor?" He held one book up and water trailed from its spine. "A parole hearing?"

"No. I'm cleaning out my office," I said, shaking water from my leg.

Osmond glanced at me as he tossed more books in. He reached down and picked up three more. "Cleaning out your office?"

"You haven't heard?" I watched for his reaction.

He stood, dropped the remaining three books on the floor of the Volkswagen, then slammed the door. "Heard what?"

I rubbed my arms, trying to ease the stiffness from clutching all the books. I didn't want to admit what had happened. "I've been forced to take a five-month leave of absence." There. I said it.

Osmond leaned his arm against the hood. "Why?"

I stepped from one foot to the other, feeling the squish of mud between my toes. "The Society is trying to get rid of me, Osmond."

At that moment Nox broke out into a full-blown sermon.

Osmond fired him an irritated look before stepping closer. "When did all this happen?"

"This morning. After winning Vandenberg, Keith called me into his office. He told me my poor judgment is affecting my work. If you call four back-to-back wins poor judgment . . . and according to Sergeant Stone, I'm hindering the investigation into Jules's murder. Stone tell you anything like that?"

Osmond scratched the bristle on his face. "Jesus." He reached into his coat pocket and pulled out a cigarette pack and a lighter. He placed the cigarette between his lips, flicked the lighter, cupping the flame, then turned his head and blew smoke. "I haven't heard a damn thing, Jade. Aubischon is full of shit."

I looked over Osmond's shoulder at the tall black shape of the office building which I had just come from. On the top floor a few lights were still on. "Before Jules's second-degree murder charge I could understand if the firm had concerns, but since that win, I've been crushing it in court."

Osmond took another drag of his cigarette. "All of this started with Jules." He blew smoke away from me. "If Jules had been convicted—"

"—You mean if I had lost?"

Osmond nodded. "If you had lost he'd have gone to jail, and in the Society's eyes—"

"Justice served."

Osmond inhaled again from his cigarette.

"But being in jail wouldn't have stopped Jules. He would have appealed."

Osmond scratched his forehead with his thumb. "Unless someone was waiting for him inside."

An assassin. The realization must have shown on my face.

"You know as well as I do that undercover officers are planted in cells all the time in the hope of extracting a confession out of an inmate. It wasn't a cop waiting for Jules."

Jules had hand-picked me as his defence counsel because he didn't trust anyone else to fairly represent him. We had won. The firm had seemed pleased with our success. Or were they? With Jules being acquitted, that left Anna's murder open for further investigation, and Jules a free man. So how did the Society exact justice? They killed Jules at Justice Aubischon's dinner party. "I spoiled their plans," I whispered.

"Look, Jade—" Osmond stepped away from the car "—this is not the place to be discussing this." He glanced over his shoulder. "You look like you could use something stronger than a mocha."

I stared at Osmond. Who the hell did I trust? With Jules dead, was Osmond trying to oust the older generation in the Society? Was he friend or foe? He couldn't really be involved with the Society, could he? Keith must be wrong. The only way I'd find out was to ask. On our third date, Osmond had told me, 'I'm the guy your mother, your grandmother, your great uncle and your sister warned you about.' Then he kissed me on the lips, very slow.

"What'll it be, Jade?"

A proposition like many I had received before, and I responded as I had done before. "All right. Jabba Java."

"Sure." With the hand holding the cigarette, Osmond passed me my coffee. "I'm parked to your left, by the bank."

I took my coffee, unlocked the driver's door and sat in. "Meet you there."

Osmond closed the door after me. He stepped in front of the Volkswagen with the same ease and confidence I had found incredibly attractive at university, then he strolled across the street. A breeze flapped at the tails of his leather coat, and the smoke from his cigarette trailed from his hand. I was struck by his gangster's aura. Could he really be a member? God help me if he was.

Osmond flicked his cigarette to the ground, stepped on it. He looked back, nodded, then swung open the door of his Jeep.

I cranked the key. The Volkswagen purred to life and I was soon turning out onto the rain-slicked street, following the tail lights of Osmond's jeep.

After a quick drive over the Bay Street bridge, Osmond pulled into the guest parking of my building, and I pulled into the underground parking lot. My mind reeled with thoughts of Osmond's possible motives for joining the Society. Could he be involved in a deep undercover operation? Was he a true member, hence his lack of denial when asked? Had the callousness of the criminal justice system finally blistered his soul? Or had he given in to the temptations of a life of crime? He wouldn't be the first police officer to do so.

Could he be responsible for the foiled attempts on my life?

Damn it! I hit the steering wheel with my fist, tooting the horn. I'd be scared to go anywhere if I let my thoughts slide that way.

I grabbed my purse, opened the door and stepped out. I walked up to Osmond as he stood, hands in his coat pockets, waiting by the outside water fountain. The doorman nodded to us as we walked past the lobby. Osmond held the café door open and we walked into a room of lime green walls, tangerine tables and stainless steel lamps. I loved this place.

The warmth generated by the Jabba Java's patrons and the smell of freshly ground coffee beans eased the tension between my shoulder blades. Classic rock melodies drifted from the overhead speakers. I was immediately taken back to the mischievous days of my youth, when all my frustrations could be resolved in a song. Unfortunately, that wasn't the case now. I unbuttoned my business suit, squeezed between the tables and made my way to the two vacant stools by the wooden counter overlooking the front window.

Vampire Red sidled up to us. "What'll it be?"

"A Tazo Chai tea." I draped my coat on the back of the high-back stool then sat, pulling on the hem of my short skirt.

"That's not your usual."

I looked at Vampire Red.

"Okay, then," she said, rolling her eyes.

"A medium of your house blend. Black." Osmond slid onto the stool facing me.

Vampire Red scribbled down our orders. "The kitchen's closed. What's left is what you see behind the glass." She pointed to a case displaying a few baked goods before sashaying over to a nearby table.

Osmond pulled out his cigarette pack, then stopped and frowned.

I nodded at the pack in his hand. "I thought you gave those up?"

"I did."

"What happened?"

"This case happened." He rubbed his hand over his mouth and scratched the bristle on his chin. "Going to drive me to drink like my old man."

"No it won't. You're a lot better person than him." And once again I had stepped into the shoes of a defence lawyer, defending a man whose integrity I questioned.

"What did Aubischon say to you?" He tapped the pack against the counter.

I reiterated my conversation with Keith, omitting Keith's accusation of Osmond being a Society member and my hallucinations. Patrons squeezed past causing Osmond to lean in towards me, pressing his knees against mine. His strong body overwhelmed the tiny space, and I resisted the urge to place my hand on his knee.

"So you've heard nothing at the detachment?" I asked, sitting back as Vampire Red shoved my mug across the counter, spilling my tea. She put her hand on Osmond's shoulder as she leaned in and placed his coffee in front of him.

"What did you say?" he asked, peering around her.

"You heard nothing at the detachment?" I repeated, glad that Vampire Red had moved on to another table.

"Nothing. But consider yourself lucky."

"Meaning?"

He eyed me. "You're not dead." He ripped open the packet and emptied white powder into his mug. "Someone's watching out for you, Thyme."

I leaned my elbow against the wood counter and looked out the window at the passing headlights. Was he watching over me? Was that the reason for his appearance tonight? Or was he trying to kill me? I rubbed my forehead. Two men walked arm in arm before the window.

Osmond sipped his coffee, grimaced, and reached for another sweetener. "So what are you not telling me, Thyme?"

My cheeks grew warm and I had a strong feeling they were turning red. I looked at my lime green mug as I twirled the end of the spoon between my fingers. "Are you a member of the Society?"

Osmond didn't answer.

My heart pounded. I breathed shallow breaths.

"Keith Aubischon say I was?"

"No." My voice sounded weak. I was a pathetic liar.

Osmond sat back and picked up his mug. "Why are you asking me this, Jade?"

"I need to know. A lot has happened in the last seventy-two hours, and I don't know who I can trust." With a shaky hand I brought my mug to my lips. Tea splashed over the rim. I swallowed a scorching mouthful which burned all the way down my throat.

Osmond placed his mug on his saucer. "I have acted," he said, his voice rough, "only to protect you."

"Well that's not answering my question now, is it?" My cup scraped the saucer. "Seems everybody's trying to protect me but nobody will tell me a damn thing, and I'm still getting shot at. Are you, or are you not, a member?"

His face paled. Lines of anger creased his forehead.

At that moment the click of heels across hardwood and a flash of black stockings distracted Osmond and the university guys. Conversations hung suspended as the males checked out the stockinged legs and where they led.

"Osmond!"

He looked at me. "I'm not a member."

Time to re-word the questions. "Are you involved with the Society?"

He placed his mug down, hard.

"Come on, Osmond. Answer me."

He glared. "Yes."

My fingers trembled. I placed one hand flat on the counter and the other on my leg. "Why?"

"It's complicated."

"That's a Facebook relationship status."

"I can't say."

"*What?*"

A man and woman turned and looked.

"You're a member," I whispered.

"I didn't say that."

"But you're involved?"

"Yes."

"Why?"

"I can't say."

"With whom?"

"I can't—"

"For Christ's sake, Osmond!"

The university guys looked at me. I leaned forward and pressed my fingers to my temples. "How the hell am I supposed to trust you? How the hell—" *am I supposed to survive?*

"Trust me like you always have. Stop listening to Aubischon who's feeding you this shit! If I tell you who I'm involved with I risk your life and the life of my informant. I'm not about to do that. Aubischon tell you I was a member?"

I didn't want to bring Keith into this. I needed to see if Osmond—with the history we shared—could be straight with me. No outside influence to place blame, no convenient scapegoat. "That's confidential."

"Bullshit. You expect me to spill my guts to you, but you can't do the same? Who's the one with something to hide?"

"Since you've come back into my life I've been run off the road, chased by a gang and shot at!"

"And you think I'm responsible?"

"Are you?"

Osmond's face turned grey. He stood abruptly, the legs of the stool grated on the floor. He placed a crumpled five-dollar bill on the counter. "No. I'm not. Enjoy your coffee." He marched out the door.

Who else could I tick off tonight?

21

Warning

You stay in this city for another twenty-four hours, and I guarantee you an assassin will be waiting for you with orders to kill.

Many times, while standing at my office window, I had felt that the sun had deliberately picked out my window from the checkerboard of windowpanes that made up the building, and with its rays, God, or some higher being, was trying to tell me that I would escape from my glass prison. I just needed strength, time and most of all patience.

Well, the sun was shining on my windowpane but because I was being forced to leave, I didn't want to go.

The thud of a box being placed on my desk broke my reverie. I shifted my weight from one foot to the other and leaned against the windowsill. I gazed across the glistening ocean to the Olympic Mountains. I would miss this view of Victoria. "I saw a red sky last night," I said, looking over my shoulder at Kate.

"You mean pink," she said, stuffing my *Criminal Code* into a box with my other legal books.

"No. Red. Poppy red. I've never seen a sky like that before, red where the sun sets. It was beautiful—mesmerizing, almost prophesizing."

Kate brushed her hands over her skirt. "So what do you think it was prophesizing?"

I looked back out at the water. A harbour plane choked to life, propellers whirling. A man clutching a suitcase teetered down the dock towards it.

"Jade."

"Yeah?"

"What do you think it was prophesizing?"

The end.

I tapped my pen against the ledge. "I don't know. I never really believed in that sort of stuff."

"Maybe it means better things to come."

For some reason, I didn't believe her.

Kate brushed her hands once more over her skirt. "Well . . . we're all done here and—" she looked at her watch "—it's time."

That's what I feared. I glanced around my barren office. Wasn't there one more item that needed to be packed? As a rule, I disliked office socials, and especially this one—I was the star attraction. The last procedure: cakes, cookies, a card and refreshments to celebrate a legal career that had become nothing more than ashes to sweep into an urn. I kicked through the charred embers, trying to find something to feel proud about.

I should have known something was up when I walked past the deserted workstations this morning, but I blamed my lack of attention on my upset stomach. After my fight with Osmond, I had gone home and wallowed in self-pity—Chin Chin and a new Vicodin prescription eased the edge. It didn't help that I had forgotten to set my alarm, so I had begun my day with a thump when I'd rolled off the living room sofa and banged my head on the coffee table leg.

Kate cleared her throat. "Jade."

"Yes?"

"Ah, Troy—" she tucked a strand of hair behind her ear "—wanted to know if you were taking—"

"—the microwave," Troy interrupted.

Kate took a few steps back. "Jade, I'm going to check on the arrangements." And closing the door behind her, she abandoned me.

I stared at his nose which looked a little wider, like it had been broken. "What happened to your nose?"

The glare he gave me. "Racquetball accident."

"Bugger when that happens. I understand the YMCA offers lessons."

"I don't need lessons."

"What do you want?"

"The microwave."

I rolled my eyes.

"And to give you this." Troy placed my briefcase on my desk. He looked around my office—correction, his office.

"Amuse me, Troy. Did you see Jules on the night he was murdered?"

"You really want to get into this now?"

"It's not like we're playing racquetball or anything."

He looked like he was about to explode, and I wanted to keep jabbing.

"I looked up to Jules. I wanted to be just like him, as powerful, connected."

Was that it? Really? Could Jules have been Troy's first assignment? Like with some gangs, in order to earn a full patch, Troy had to kill a fellow lawyer. Jules was no fool. He would have figured Troy out. "People are just human rungs for you to step on. So you didn't send him a text on the night he was killed?"

"Yes, I did. I saw him arrive with James after the courthouse centennial. I wanted him to introduce me to his inner circle."

The Society. I thought Troy was already involved with The Society? The reason for trying to drown me. Troy was obviously lying. "Jules's inner circle took him out."

"Advice coming from a pill-popping disgruntled lawyer. Enjoy your time away, Jade."

Troy gave me a mock salute. He walked to the door and stopped. "I have movers coming tomorrow morning at eight.

Make sure your shit's gone." He closed the door.

I turned, bracing my hands on my desk. *Come on. Pull it together.* I looked at the rectangular outlines decorating my walls where pictures had once hung. Bookshelves usually overburdened with volumes of law books stood vacant and streaked with dust. After this afternoon's sentencing, it would be over.

I stole one more glance at the harbour plane as it magically lifted from the water. They were waiting. I closed the file on my desk. "Get this over with."

"Not yet," a male voice said.

That voice. A voice I recognized that caused shivers down my spine. My pen dropped from my hand. I slowly looked up. In the doorway stood my father.

"Christ," I whispered. He was the last person I wanted to see today.

"That's how you greet the man who raised you?"

He hadn't raised me, but I wasn't getting into that now. I leaned against my desk, my fingers pressed against its surface. What did he want?

My father sauntered into my office. He looked skinnier than usual; cheekbones more pronounced. Grey hair spiked, sharp double-breasted suit. Some people in life have to work for power, others, like my father, always had it.

"Tell me you're not here for the tea and scones," I blurted, hoping my voice didn't sound as squeaky as it did in my head.

"No." My father stepped around a box. His small dark eyes assessed me. I must have passed inspection for he shifted his gaze to the cardboard mayhem that had overtaken my office. "I heard about your departure."

"Should come as no surprise. You were involved with the decision."

"Involved? What the hell are you talking about?"

"Oh, please, Father—" I picked up my sentencing books and tossed them into the briefcase "—yesterday morning, partners's meeting."

"Yesterday morning I was teeing off at the Douglas Springs Golf and Country Club. You know I always have a Thursday morning game."

He was right. Nothing had ever distracted my father from his Thursday game—not school assemblies, award presentations or court dates. "So you weren't at the meeting?"

"No. Played the worst game in my life. Lost fifty dollars to Lewis on the eleventh hole and double-bogied on eight all because of you."

"Me."

He pushed out his chest and leveled me a hard look. "Do not come to the house unless you've made an appointment. You upset Edith terribly. As well, you need to leave Jules's case alone."

Not, *'I'm sorry. I didn't mean to slap you when you had visited.'* "Well that's not going to happen."

"The Society will destroy you, Jade," he said, anger slipping into his tone. "This leave of absence is just the beginning. In five months, if you live that long, your caseload will have been diminished; you'll be out the door, chasing ambulances. No one, and I mean no one, on the island, on the mainland, in the province, in this country will hire you."

The bikers probably would. Sage would put in a good word. I closed my briefcase. "I have no choice."

"Bullshit."

There was a knock on the door. Kate poked her head in. She looked warily from me to my father then back to me. "I'll tell them a few more minutes."

"Thank you, Kate."

She nodded and closed the door.

"Look, Father—" I swung my head around, angry that he was making a difficult morning much more difficult "—there have been three attempts on my life. One in your back yard. When did the door on the pagoda need to be locked? You see, I can't stop. The Society has no idea what Jules may have told me. I am too much of a risk. My survival depends on my finding who killed him before he or she kills me."

"Don't fool yourself, Jade. You'll never get the truth."

"I have to!"

"They will kill you!"

"And you're still protecting them!"

His face flushed and a vein in his temple bulged. He stepped around my desk and stood looking outside the window. Didn't he have a lecture to go to, or somewhere else he'd rather be?

"Did you ever think," he said, his tone crisp, "that I was trying to protect you?"

"Protect me! Trying to keep me quiet. Let's be honest here, Father, the only person you're protecting is yourself."

A muscle twitched in his jaw and for a moment the fierceness I remembered as a child flashed in his eyes. "If I tell you why Anna and Jules were killed, will you back off?"

I stared at him. "I already know, but I'm curious about your take on what happened." I sat, realizing how much I didn't want to go to my social thing.

He looked away from me and out over the harbour. "I knew Anna quite well. Met her at an office barbecue. She wanted to produce her own play in Sweden. I gave her legal advice."

"When did entertainment law become your forté?" I asked, my tone dry.

"Contracts, Jade."

"Right. As in money, or as in killers?"

"Jesus. Jade!" Again, the sharp look. "I had nothing to do with that young woman's death."

"You haven't been forthcoming with the police either."

"And I'm trying to explain why!"

I told myself to let my father speak. His visits were few and far between, and God knows what had propelled him to show up today.

"Anna and Olive were lovers."

I nodded.

"James couldn't understand. He couldn't accept that his

daughter favoured women. Overcome with shame, he decided to eliminate the problem."

"James killed Anna to eliminate that problem?"

"No. I have known James since law school. He is not a murderer."

"Right. So who do you think he got to do it?"

"No one! James is not a murderer. You think I'm lying?"

"You haven't told me anything convincing."

"James funded Anna's production to get her out of the country."

"But she wouldn't go. She wouldn't leave without Olive."

"Correct."

"James must have been outraged."

"He was."

"And he didn't kill her?"

"No."

"Then who did?"

"For God's sake, Jade, I am not a suspect, I'm your father! Stop treating me as if I'm a criminal!"

"Well, Father—" I whipped a stubborn strand of hair back from my face "—I think you're lying. I think you're caught in the middle, torn between your loyalty to the Society and your duties as a parent."

My father's face paled.

"I've seen the pictures. All of them. Don't tell me you two were just friends."

My father teetered back on his heels as he slid his hands into his pockets. "Jules introduced us, and yes, we became friends."

"Right," I said, shoving a Post It pad across my desk with my pen.

"Jules believed I could help her."

"Really? How? Show her the heterosexual lifestyle? The error of her ways?"

"Jade! I never slept with the woman. She loved Olive. I was her best chance at pleading her case to James."

"Why?"

My father pulled a kerchief out of his pocket and rubbed his neck and forehead. "Because of your sister." He leaned his forearms against the windowpane. If the glass hadn't been there I swear he would have fallen to his death. He braced his hands on the windowsill. I wondered if he was going to pass out.

"Do you have any water?"

I stood and passed him my water bottle.

My father unscrewed the lid and with a trembling hand brought the bottle to his lips. One would think he was a recovering drug addict. He placed the bottle on the ledge.

"So because Sage is bisexual that makes you an expert. Seriously?"

"Jules thought James would listen to me—" he looked at me and in his eyes I saw trepidation.

I dropped into the chair for clients.

"Anna didn't want to leave Olive behind. They were in love. If I could convince James to accept Olive and Anna everything would be fine."

"Good convincing job, Dad."

My father's mouth contorted as if he were trying to hold something back. "Your mother gave me two beautiful daughters—"

"—You have to go."

"I will admit I was not a good father, but I always loved you, Jade, and your sister."

I stared at him. "Her name is Sage, Father. Sage. And her sexual preferences and Anna's and Olive's are nobody's business. Sage, Anna and Olive are all people. Human beings. Not individuals to be shunned or categorized or labelled." My voice broke. "I can't handle this now. I have a room full of people I'm supposed to see and you're just . . . go."

"I have no doubt that you'll expose the Society, Jade, but people—families, will be destroyed. It's not only the bad guys you'll be taking down, but husbands and wives, mothers and fathers, their children, innocent people who have nothing to do with the Society, but unbeknownst to them are married to a member, or born to one. Is it worth it?"

"Do not try to shift guilt of Society members onto me. Maybe those Society members should have thought about their families before they were recruited. Thought about what being caught and sent to jail would do to their children, their wives."

"The Society is crumbling. They have had their day. They will be exposed. Anna was killed because she was a lesbian in love with an ignorant man's daughter. You may not care about your own life but stop before they target your sister."

I stared at him. *Sage.*

"The Society knows how to get people to cooperate."

There was a tentative knock on the door. "I'm coming, Kate." I had heard enough. "Goodbye, Father."

My father stepped away from the window and walked towards the door. He stood there for a few moments, his hands clenching and unclenching as he stared at the floor. "I won't be there, at the tea, if that makes you feel better."

I wanted him out.

"What you do will affect us all, especially your sister."

~

I had never been so angry in my life. The thought of anyone harming Sage made me lose control of any reason. As soon as father had left, I called Sage and got her voicemail. I left her a brief message and asked her to call me back.

As soon as I stepped into the conference room, Kate placed a coffee in my hands, mumbling something about looking like death warmed over. The cup had immediately rattled on its saucer, so like a child I gripped the silly porcelain with both hands. Duchess Meghan Markle wouldn't be impressed. After the political niceties of a few partners, I clambered to Kate's side as she told me about her date from the night before with the office's hot new articling student. I faded in and out of her conversation, catching bits and pieces. When another lawyer cornered me and spoke about his two-year-old's latest exploits with the family dog, I forced a smile and nodded, making the appropriate responses when hearing the same baby story for the ninth time. Yet in the back of my mind, I kept thinking about my father's visit. Why Jules had been killed and what Jules had known about my father.

I gazed around the conference room. The happy new father had moved on and was now reciting his story to an expecting secretary, who rubbed her belly. I checked my cell. Nothing. No voicemail from Sage. No text message. I gazed at the conference table, now a buffet table laden with food. Three coffee urns and a pitcher of juice occupied the far end where I had spent many nights poring over case law, and where James Aubischon had supposedly gotten it on with a renowned Supreme Court Justice. A bouquet of calla lilies stuck out of a crystal vase in the centre, and I again thought of Jules and funerals. I took a scalding gulp of coffee, stepped out of my stupor, and made my way around the table. I deflected questions about what I planned to do during my five-month sentence. The firm may have called it leave, but I knew better. One lawyer patted me on the back and wished me good luck before she popped the last of a Nanaimo bar into her mouth and dashed off to court. As much as I loved sweets, I stayed away from the butter tarts and brownies. After seeing svelte Sage I was trying a no-sugar diet thing and failing miserably.

"I hope you like the flowers."

I turned. Kate stood, an eager smile on her face.

"They're beautiful. What a lovely idea."

"The least we could do. I've learned so much working for you, Jade. You got me re-classed as a paralegal."

I swallowed my sadness with a slosh of coffee and spotted Keith across the room speaking with his father, James. He had the audacity, Aubischon senior, showing up. As if sensing my gaze, Keith turned and proffered a hesitant smile.

I looked away.

"Jade?"

"Yes."

Kate twisted the napkin in her hand. "You are coming back, aren't you?"

Kate with her pixie-cut platinum blonde hair and big blue eyes, the uncertainty in her voice made my conscience do a three-sixty. This was not the screwdriver-wielding Kate I knew. I considered telling her the truth, but why involve her with the politics of my departure? She still had to work here.

"You will be the first to know of what I plan to do," I said, placing my hand on her shoulder. "Just don't take any shit from Troy. He's excellent in court but still an asshole."

"I won't. Besides Troy, I'm supposed to be helping Keith's paralegal. She'll probably give me all the Joe jobs. But—" she lowered her voice and stepped closer "—if you should strike out on your own and need an assistant, let me know."

"I'll do that," I whispered back.

A secretary pulled Kate aside, and I shuffled along the table, contemplating a blueberry square.

"Try not to have too much fun while you're gone."

I turned. Keith stood, a coffee cup in his hand, his lips forming a smile. His father was no where to be seen.

"Nice spread."

"Only the best for you, Jade. Maybe if you leave us on good terms, you'll want to come back."

My departure was now my idea? The spin doctor was working overtime. I picked up a knife and chopped a blueberry square in half. "You and I both know Mr. Pothead has made the kill and he's now picking apart the carcass." I put the knife down and picked up the square. "He probably has an interior designer scheduled to come in on Monday." I took a bite.

Keith placed his hand on my arm. "Jade—"

"You're going to tell me this wasn't your idea?" I said, mouth full. At the moment, I could care less about manners. "You were only following your father's orders." I took another bite.

He frowned and looked over my shoulder, scanning the conference room. "I don't want you leaving like this."

I popped the last of the square in my mouth. "Why?" I chewed, then swallowed. "So you don't feel guilty?"

He slipped his arm around my shoulders and guided me over to a corner by the bookshelves. "There's a lot more at stake. Yes, it's my father who's calling the shots."

I dabbed my lips with a scrunched-up napkin. "Yeah, but you're the one hanging me out to dry."

"Until the heat cools off, the best place for you is away from here." He leaned his arm against the bookshelf, cornering me. "A lot of shit is going down, Jade. I don't even want to be here. In three months when Olive and Troy are married—"

"Olive and Troy are getting married!"

Keith glanced over his shoulder. No one paid us any attention. Everyone was engrossed in their own conversations and stuffing their faces. "Yeah."

"Olive is marrying Troy?"

"Yes, about bloody time, but that's not important—" he leaned in so his lips were close to my ear "—when everything's settled down, call me. I'll get you back in."

Olive and Troy were getting married? It had been a month since Jules's murder. Whose idea was the marriage? Troy's? Or Daddy Aubischon's? Because it sure as hell wasn't Olive's.

Up to that moment I had held it together. Now, staring into Keith's dark eyes, searching for an integrity I doubted was there, my own insecurity and sadness leaked from my heart. Who was this man standing before me and where was my friend?

"I need another coffee." I pushed past him and marched over to the end of the table. Two lawyers broke into laughter. I would miss this. The legal stories. The humorous exploits in court. I fought with the large coffee urn, pumping the stupid black button on the top, trying to get the coffee to pour.

Keith stepped up behind me, his leg touching the back of mine. He leaned in and picked up another urn, poured coffee into a cup and held the cup and saucer out to me. I took it. The cup rattled again. I should just drop a few Vicodin in my coffee. I turned and stepped away from him, squeezing between staff. I walked into the private back meeting room, closing the door.

I veered around an abandoned desk and moved over to a dried-up plant on the windowsill. I placed the cup and saucer near the plant, then stood back and dragged my hands through my hair. I wouldn't make it through the day. Not at this rate. I had no use for last-minute-clear-my-conscience Hallmark emotions. Not from Keith. Not from my father. I was a threat to the Society so they were getting rid of me. End of story. I didn't need Keith or anyone else making my departure more than it was.

The meeting room door opened.

I looked over my shoulder.

Keith stepped in.

At that moment a flock of pigeons alighted from the roof of the building next door, swept down into the street, rose, circled another building before swooping down again.

He walked over. "Jade—" he looked at his feet "—there are things I want to tell you—" his gaze swung up to me "—but I can't."

My eyes glazed over and the building across the street blurred.

"Jules pissed off a lot of people, and you're doing the same. For every action there's a reaction."

I crossed my arms. "And you know who killed him, don't you?"

He shoved his hands into his pockets and glanced out the window. "So does your father."

"You keep deflecting."

"Did you ever think that I was trying to protect you?"

"That line is starting to wear a little thin."

"Don't let them destroy us, Jade."

"Us?"

"It's a temporary leave. You're coming back. I want you back."

"Am I coming back, Keith? Or does the Society have a Plan B

if I still don't behave?"

"Christ. Don't say that."

"Because it's true? I *wasn't* meant to win Jules's case, was I? You guys figured that with the amount of evidence he had stacked against him, there was no way in hell he'd walk. He threatened the Society and was the perfect scapegoat for Anna's murder. But what the Society hadn't anticipated was us electing trial by judge and jury, and miraculously, the jury saw the same thing I did, his *innocence*."

Keith jammed his hands deeper into his pockets and looked down at the floor.

"What I don't understand is why Anna? She was in love, she wasn't a threat!"

"Jade—"

"—Which one of you guys killed her?"

His face turned grey.

"I'm out of here." I stepped away from the window when Keith grabbed my arm and swung me around.

I tugged out of his grip. "Leave me—"

"You stay in this city for another twenty-four hours, and I guarantee you an assassin will be waiting for you with orders to kill. He's out there, Jade."

I stopped pulling out of his grip and stared.

"They don't give a shit about you!" He hauled me against him, smothering my head to his chest, his other arm wrapped around my back. "I can live with Jules's death but I can't live with yours. If firing you means saving your life then goddamn it I'll do it, because there is no fucking alternative!"

I pulled out of his grasp and lurched to the window. "Leave. I don't want to hear any more."

He reached out and turned my face toward him. "Don't leave tonight without me." He slid his hand over my cheek. "I'll escort you. Get you on a plane, on a ferry. Get you out of here." He leaned in and kissed my cheek, then ran his hand through my hair and kissed my forehead. "You'll wait for me?"

No bloody way. "Yes."

"Good." He turned and walked out of the meeting room. I stared at the closed door and shuddered. I reached for my steaming coffee cup and looked up.

Anna Von Altman's bloodied face glared at me from the window.

I screamed, dropping the cup and saucer. Coffee and jagged pieces of porcelain sprayed everywhere. I attempted to pick up the pieces and do something with the coffee trickling down the wall, but my eyes were riveted to Anna's angry face. A marble-cracked complexion, the whites of her eyes were grey with muddy blue centres. Blood from the wound on her head trickled down the side of her face, and once again, I could see where the bullet had ripped out half her brain.

I placed my hand over my heart and stepped back. "What? What do you want? I've been trying to figure out who—" I feebly pointed at the wound on her head, then cupped my hand over my mouth. I was defending myself to a ghost.

Anna released a breath which fogged a circle on the window, then like a bird hitting a windowpane, she slammed her hand against the glass and downwards, dragging a smear of blood.

22

Search Warrant

The revolver flew out of my hand and landed at a man's feet.

I HID IN MY office, jumping at every bump and thud, checking over my shoulder for any sign of Anna. All day I had tried to reach Osmond, but I was told he was in Vancouver at the RCMP Forensic Lab. Sage hadn't returned any of my messages.

Kate, seeing my distress, had brought in the plate of Nanaimo bars and brownies from earlier in the day so I wouldn't have to venture out. When I lost the will to write up any more files, I shredded a number of personal files. Around four-thirty the two female articling students, who had been present from the beginning of Jules's trial, stopped at my door to wish me good luck. Both of them had been hired by reputable law firms in London. Canadian lawyers were in hot demand on the other side of the Atlantic. Maybe that's where I should be.

I slipped on my suit coat that I had hung on the back of my chair, trying to ward off the cold that seeped from the window and settled on my skin. A relentless wind howling in from the harbour whipped the Canadian flag on the building next door and rattled the window. Raindrops veined across the pane. At that moment Kate hesitantly stepped into my office, her purse strung over her shoulder as she tied a knot in the belt of her yellow raincoat. "I thought you would have left by now."

I smiled and tossed my pen onto the Vandenberg file. "Unfortunately not." I sat back in my chair. "I'm just writing up Vandenberg in the event the Crown appeals, then I'll be off."

She nodded, eyed the box on my desk and the three boxes on the floor, one of which had the picture of my father sticking out of it. Her face crumpled and tears trickled down her cheeks.

"Hey."

She rifled a tissue from her purse.

I pushed back my chair, walked over to her and wrapped my arm around her shoulders. "You'll see me again."

She sniffed and blotted the tears from her cheeks.

"I promise."

She looked at me with her big blue eyes. "It doesn't make sense. You don't even practise criminal law anymore, yet you took Jules's file, which everyone thought you'd lose, and won! And now you're being punished."

I patted her on the back. "Kate, best not to say that to anyone, okay?"

She blew her nose, wrinkling her blonde eyebrows. "It's just not fair! You are coming back, aren't you?"

My heart twanged. "You'll be the first to know what I do, but in the meantime, play it safe. Expressing your opinions about my leaving isn't going to help you keep your job."

"Well if this is how the firm treats its employees—" she wiped her nose "—then maybe I don't want to work here."

I smiled at her feistiness. "Don't do anything drastic, yet. I'll let you know what I plan to do."

She sighed.

"So, are the computer guys coming to fix your motherboard?" I stepped toward my desk and picked up the plate of squares and offered it to her. Chocolate was always good for the soul.

"Yeah, but I also need new speakers, a new mouse, and maybe a new network card," she said, taking a Nanaimo bar.

"Why doesn't the firm just buy you a new computer?"

She took a bite and rolled her eyes. "That's too logical for this place."

"Right. I forgot."

She swallowed another bite and licked her fingers. "It's still not fair. You just did what Jules hired you to do."

"I know. But you can't say anything." I wanted to tell her that more than just her job was on the line if she made a fuss over my leaving, but giving out too much information could also be dangerous. The Society wouldn't hesitate to eliminate a little problem like Kate. They'd kill her. Pass her death off as an unfortunate accident. The less she knew, the better.

She brushed her hands over her coat. "I'll keep my mouth shut, or at least try."

I thought about Norman. I wanted to ask him more questions. I knew he had more to say. "Everyone's gone?"

"Yes. Keith's not back from court."

I arched an eyebrow.

"Justice Sullivan is giving him a hard time on the Thompson application. At three o'clock Keith had Cheris photocopying and binding a bunch of case law for some argument."

I hoped Justice Sullivan was chewing his ass off.

"You take care of yourself, Jade." She sniffed. "Keep in touch." She quickly waved, then spun around, head down, and marched out the door.

My heart pinched. She didn't let me say goodbye. I would miss her. Her jokes, the secret stash of M&Ms she kept in the bowl in the filing cabinet, her aunt's leftover Thursday night sticky buns. Most of all I would miss her companionship and hearing the continuing saga of her on-again-off-again relationship with the rich Texan she had met at the Calgary Stampede.

I looked over my office. Nothing but boxes and files to give me comfort. My phone buzzed. The symbol for message flashed.

Sage?

I checked my voicemail.

"Jade. It's Osmond. I was an A-1 asshole the other night. I have some news. Call me."

Crap. I called Sage again and waited. Voicemail. Crap.

I stepped over to the window and dialed Osmond's number. This time I got his voicemail. I left a message.

Across the street the black outline of the Commerce building loomed—uneven stripes of lit floors. Over by the harbour the domed Legislature Building with its dazzling strings of lights reminded me of a magical kingdom. Streetlights sparkled and car headlights formed a jeweled necklace across the bridge and along Douglas. I pressed my hand and cheek against the windowpane. The coldness soothed the turmoil pounding in my head. I closed my eyes. Osmond had news. Had the police found Jules's body?

I opened my eyes and took a deep breath. Against the outside of the window a bloody hand pressed palm-to-palm with mine. I slowly spread my fingers and the fingers on the other side did the same. I peeled my cheek away from the glass and as if it was my reflection, the cheek on the outside peeled away too. The window was all that separated a kiss from Anna Von Altman. The burlesque costume was gone and she was now dressed in a sharp tweed business suit and although I had become accustomed to her bloodied features, it was the sorrow on her face that got me. A tear trickled from my eye and I didn't know whether it was a tear, or rain, that trickled from hers.

"Hi," I whispered, touching her face through the glass.

Anna sniffed. She slid her hand up to mine, trailing a bloody smear.

"I don't know how to help you anymore. I've tried. I've really tried. I've been shot at. I've lost my job. I have nothing. I don't know what else to do."

With her finger, using her own blood as ink, she wrote 'T U O T E G.'

"Tuo teg?"

She shook her head. Something red dropped onto the pane and slid, leaving a gooey trail. She pointed at each letter.

"G-E-T, get."

She nodded.

"O-U-T. Out. Get out."

She nodded again.

"But my assassin's out there."

She wrote again.

"H-E. He."

She continued.

"C-O-M, coming. He coming. Who?"

Her eyebrows crossed and she fiercely wrote. *The man.* Then she slammed her hand against the windowpane. The blinds crashed down, nailing me on the head. I jumped, rubbing the sore spot. I grabbed the cord and yanked it up.

Anna was gone.

I slapped my hands against the glass. "Come back!" I stared at the Commerce building. The Canadian flag whipped and unfurled. I again slapped my hands on the glass. "Come back! Which man?"

I stepped back, stumbled, and grabbed onto my desk, knocking my phone and stapler to the floor. Bloody hell if I was going to stay here. I grabbed my purse and lurched around my desk, tripping over my feet.

The hallway walls leaned to the right then to the left. I crashed into one, smashing my sprained ankle on the door jamb. I hobbled to the front door, yanked it open and lunged for the elevator. My heart felt suspended as the elevator plummeted fifteen floors, taking me, I was sure, to Hell. The doors pinged open and I charged out into the familiar foyer with bubbling water fountain and marble floors, catching the smiling face of the security guard sitting behind his desk.

He nodded. "Good evening, Ms. Thyme."

I straightened, pulling at my sweater, hoping I didn't look as disheveled as I felt and that I didn't have Anna's blood on my cheek. I touched the skin under my left eye to double-check. "I'm getting a coffee," I announced with a forced cheerfulness. Was I? I guess I was.

He flipped a page of a magazine and nodded at my attire of

sweater and short skirt. "You'll catch your death going out like that."

If he only knew.

I looked back over my shoulder. The security guard flipped another page of his magazine. Could he be my assassin? Nah. I was being paranoid. My fear was making a fool of me.

I pulled open the outside door. The wind swept through my loose knit sweater and whipped the hair back from my face. Arms crossed, I huddled against the rain, stepping around puddles, staying clear of dark alleys and corners. I hobbled up the steps of the Mocha Cup and burst in.

The familiar roar of the espresso machine and the thump of hip hop music beat the frigid melancholy from my bones. I joined the line-up of coffee seekers as I had done many times before, letting the café's warmth coat my skin and evaporate my fear. The routine of what I was doing made me feel normal, safe.

Then Kate's words whispered in my ears. "*Everyone thought you'd lose.*"

Water from my rain-soaked hair dribbled down my face and neck. But I didn't lose. I had won. I stepped forward.

Justice Sullivan's arrogant voice cut into my brain. "*The documents in this sealed envelope seized in Mr. Vandenberg's office fall under the ruling of solicitor-client privilege and are not privy for inspection in these proceedings.*"

Yeah, I know. I did the argument.

"What would you like?" The young girl at the counter asked.

I ordered my usual and moved forward.

"*Seized in Mr. Vandenberg's office fall under the ruling of solicitor-client privilege.*" I massaged my temples trying to make the voices go away.

"*I can't get a warrant to search the Aubischon residence, Jade.*" Osmond had said after we bought hotdogs at the pickwick on Government Street just before someone had tried to shoot me.

"*Not privy for inspection in these proceedings.*"

"*Still can't find the murder weapon used to kill Anna, Jade.*"

"*Need a special warrant to search a law office*."

Get out!

"Christ!"

The Mocha Cup employee stared. "Ah, four-fifty," she said, wrinkling her pierced eyebrows.

"Sorry. I didn't—"

She crossed her arms above her studded navel and sighed.

Why even bother? I reached to pay using my phone app when I realized I didn't have my phone. I patted down my pockets. Crap. I had left it on my desk. "I have money upstairs. I come here all the time. I can go get it."

Miss Navel Ring slid me my mocha along with a glare, which I wondered was included in the price, or extra? I took several deep gulps of the hot coffee, savouring the flavour of chocolate and raspberry syrups, closing my mind to bloodied faces and suspicious law offices.

I stepped out of the coffee shop and stood under the awning, gazing at the building. My eyes followed the various lit floors. On the top floor were the offices of Aubischon, Thyme and Bastine. Get your phone then get out of there.

He coming.

I walked back. The damp weather and wearing high heels all day had caused my sprained ankle to ache. After a ride up the elevator, I pulled open the office door. It was unlocked. I couldn't remember if I had locked it on my way out, but it wasn't the unlocked door that bothered me . . . it was the silence, which breathed on the back of my neck and made me look over my shoulder. I dug my heels into the carpet, summoning my resolve as I walked down the hall. I stopped at my door. The blind hung crooked. I had pulled it up. Had it fallen down? Or had someone, or something, pulled it down? My phone lay on the floor. I had another message. I picked up my phone, tucking it into my pocket. Then I heard the muffled tick of my antique clock coming from one of the boxes. I looked around my empty office.

The Vandenberg file lay open on my desk. I thought I had

closed it. I had been writing up the file summary. Hard to believe that one case could cause me so much trouble. In the realm of things, my defence hadn't meant squat. Vandenberg had defrauded Mr. Beattie of money from Mrs. Beattie's will. What I had argued had to do with Vandenberg's rights as per the Charter of Rights and Freedoms. But Charter or not, Clive Vandenberg had still defrauded his client, and he had kept the incriminating evidence in his law office. He knew it would take a special warrant to get any of the evidence, thereby making it that much more difficult for the police. Foreboding stirred in my gut. *That much more difficult for the police.*

Who might have known? Someone besides me, who knew it took a special warrant to search a law office.

Keith.

The baseboard heater clicked and rattled. I jumped. With trembling fingers, I placed my hand to my throat, feeling the rapid beat of my pulse. Keith wouldn't. He couldn't. He was my friend. He had warned me. He wanted me out of the city, he wouldn't do such a thing.

This file offered both an answer and an excuse to go into Keith's office. Dear God. I was actually contemplating this. He wanted my notes. I had to give them to him. Put the file on his desk. That's where he'd expect it. I called Osmond. Voicemail. I texted him: *At office. Anna's murder weapon. Keith's office. Special warrant.* I slipped the phone back in my pocket, scooped up the file and hobbled out of my office and into the hallway.

The office was deserted. I turned to my right and walked toward Keith's office. I passed the conference room.

The fluorescent lights hummed. One set of tubes was burnt out. I walked around Cheris's tropical garden workstation and stopped. He had wanted my notes. I was returning a file. I knocked. Silence. I reached out a shaking hand and turned the knob, as I pushed the door open. I flicked the light switch. Keith's magnificent office flashed to life. A chill brushed over my skin. I was Dorothy standing at the edge of Oz, except I didn't have red slippers to take me home. I glanced over my shoulder to the hallway that led to safety and speculation. I looked back into Keith's office.

Images of him smiling, sitting with his heels crossed and propped on the edge of his desk reeled through my mind. His red felt-lined pool table stood ready, balls racked. Where were the lawyers and the cocktails? Pristine leather couch, the armchair with its thick wooden legs, the glass sculpture of the scales of justice, the lingering scent of Keith's cologne—success. I stepped in.

The plaques behind his desk honoured his excellent work on various trials and his commitment to redefining the criminal justice system. Judgeship material. The Buddha and other bulky statues reflected his strength. I walked around a stack of files on the floor, and the armchair where I had sat many times seeking his opinion. Keith always provided me with an angle I hadn't thought of. He was not a criminal. I was the one doing something criminal.

I stood beside his chair and looked across at the framed picture of his great grandfather, Judge Aubischon, in his wig and robes. He knew what I was doing. The loathing in his eyes mirrored what I felt inside.

I rubbed my cheek, dropped the file on Keith's desk and stepped back.

Why would he hide a murder weapon?

To protect someone.

Who?

The sleuths in movies always found what they were searching for, but the big screen didn't depict the guilt. I pulled my hair back from my face. The revolver used to kill Anna was still missing, and whoever killed her, had killed Jules.

Kate said Keith would be awhile.

Anna had written *he coming*.

Who? Keith? Or someone else?

I had to be quick.

I wiped sweating palms over my skirt and with shaking limbs, stepped over to his desk and pulled open the top desk drawer. A bottle of Tylenol rolled out and stopped against a bottle of Liquid

Paper and yellow Post It notes. Relief. Nothing incriminating. I closed the drawer and pulled open the second. Precedent files, case law. I closed it. I shouldn't be here.

My fingers trembled as I pulled open the third drawer. Ties, cuff links, Rolaids and Eno. A pharmacy. This was good. I closed that drawer. There was nothing of importance in the right bank of drawers. I eyed the cherrywood file cabinet to the left. The bottom drawer was ajar. I walked over to it, my limbs and joints wired from a potent mix of caffeine and nerves. I fanned my sweater from my body and pushed the sleeves up to my elbows. I leaned over and pulled open the drawer—file folders of sentencing cases. I closed it and rotated my shoulders. The second drawer rattled open on its own as if being pulled by an invisible hand.

"*Not* a good time, Anna." I flipped through the over-stuffed files. Law Society files, old issues of *Lawyers Weekly*, conference packages. I pushed that drawer shut and the top one bumped open.

Unlike the other drawers, this one held manila file folders haphazardly stacked on top of each other. The first two contained the resumes of law students. I pulled out a third folder where printed on the front in Keith's tiny print was "Judgeship and Partnership Notes." I slipped the pages out and found Sergeant Stone's guest list. But what interested me more, were the letters and a printed e-mail message marked "Priority":

Keith.

Pleased to advise that Joe, Frank, Walter and Edward have informed me that you did exceptionally well on your panel. Although not official, you will be appointed to the Supreme Court Bench. Congratulations, Son! An official announcement will be made in a couple of months. Other candidates need to be notified. We now need to consider whom we should make a partner. Jade's and Troy's names have been thrown around. I'm inclined to select Troy, even if Jade is Charles's daughter. I know you've always been sweet on Jade. Keep me updated on these two. Stop by the cabin this weekend and we can discuss it. Father.

Wow. Keith was going to become a judge. I checked the date

on the e-mail—one month before Jules's death. I slid that letter to the back and began reading the second message. It was about the scheduling of a golf game amongst the partners. I slid that message behind the other and began the third.

Keith.

Your last update on Jade troubles me. Jade's behaviour since Jules's murder has been most disturbing. One would have hoped that with the man killed, there would be an end to this heinous cycle. Anna was a whore. I'm relieved she's out of Olive's life. The Jade situation raises more concerns. She's asking too many questions. Your failure to rectify the situation leaves me no choice. If you won't stop her, I'll see to it that the Society will. I refuse to have that woman practising law in this firm. Troy will take her place. He will get the partnership. He won't hesitate to resort to extreme measures to achieve a satisfactory end. I'm not losing him to a dimwit girl who threatens to destroy all our lives, even yours. Father.

The pages crinkled in my grip. So that was the real reason for my losing the partnership. I checked the date on that message. A week before I had been run off the road. The partners had known that far back. Worse, Keith had known. So where were his loyalties? With his father, or with me? I glanced at the clock on top of the file cabinet—5:26. I gripped my shaken pride and slid that message behind the other. The next page was a three-column list of lawyers, judges and cops. Some of the lawyers had stars beside their names, others question marks. My name had a question mark beside it and had also been crossed out. Troy's name had a star. What was this? The lawyers's names were from a variety of law firms, some even from the mainland. I flipped the page and found James Aubischon's name starred, as well as Keith's, my father's, and Norman Bastine's—Noxzema Man. I flipped the page back and then it hit me.

A list of members.

Society members and potential members.

I leaned against the file cabinet. Jesus. Jules had been decapitated because he had threatened to expose the Society. I now held their members's list in my hands, which trembled as I flipped page after page. I only seemed to have half the list. I spotted Osmond's name, but there was no notation written by it. I ran a shaking hand through my hair. Should I take this to Osmond? Or leave it here?

The front door closed.

I froze.

Footsteps echoed down the hall.

I crammed the papers in the folder, shoved the folder into the cabinet, and slammed the drawer shut.

It got stuck.

Fu-u-u-ck. I restacked the file folders, slid the drawer shut and again it stuck. Heart pounding, a whirling in my ears, I pulled the cabinet all the way out, squeezed my arm along the top and reached back behind the last metal partition to get whatever was causing the jamb. My fingers touched a hard handle. I slid my arm out to find that I gripped a revolver.

"What the hell are you doing?"

I spun around. The revolver flew out of my hand and landed at a man's feet

23

Stand Off

Two loaded guns pointed in my direction. I was going to die.

Keith's black robes rustled in the uneasy silence as he bent down and retrieved the revolver. Briefcase in one hand, he turned the weapon over in his other, staring at it. He looked at me. "What the hell are you doing with this?"

I shakily stepped away from the open filing cabinet, bridging the distance between it and his leather office chair. Sweat seeped from my skin and the collar of my sweater seemed to squeeze my neck. I clutched the headrest. "M-my notes—"

"—Like Hell!" He flung his briefcase onto the armchair.

No plea of mercy was going to get me out of this mess.

"You couldn't leave things alone, could you?"

"No. Keith—" I attempted a smile "—I, I was—"

"Fuck, Jade!" He grabbed his briefcase and hurled it across the room. It hit the picture of great grandfather Justice Aubischon. Glass shattered and the picture popped off its hook. The briefcase fell open and amongst files and papers, a thumb drive dropped out.

I lurched and my feet tangled with the casters. I fell into the chair, crashing into the desk.

Keith turned, eyes cold. "Why the hell couldn't you leave things alone!"

Reason with him. "Who are you protecting? You're protecting somebody. Tell me. We can work something out."

Keith leaned his elbows on the back of the armchair, the revolver, black against the burgundy leather, dangled from his fingers.

"Your father? Olive? Who?"

He raised his head, all rage subsided, and calmly looked me in the eye. "No one, Jade. No one."

"That—" My chin trembled "—that can't be."

"It's my revolver—" he flicked open the chamber "—two bullets in it."

My heart pounded. Pressure built between my ears. This couldn't be happening. Not Keith.

"Come on, Jade—" he stood, undoing the tabs around his neck with his free hand "—ask me." He dropped the tab on the chair and loosened his shirt collar. "I know you're dying to. That's the reason why you're here."

Fear wormed its way into my conscience. I clutched the armrests.

"Ask me!"

I jumped again. I looked at his desk with its gold nameplate and gold pens. "Did you—" I closed my eyes. Unthinkable. He couldn't have. I took a deep breath "—Did you . . . k-kill him?"

"Who?"

He was toying with me. I glanced at the ceiling. "Jules."

He smiled. "Yes."

My throat tightened. His office blurred. I sniffed and wiped my hands across my cheeks.

"Anna too," he said, an arrogant tilt to his chin. "Pretty damn easy. She had no idea who I was, although I knew of her. Olive had once tried to introduce us, but I refused to have anything to do with my sister's *lovers*."

"What did Anna ever do to you?"

He sauntered between the armchair and the window. "That dyke was going to marry my sister."

"So you killed her?"

He whipped around, his black robes billowing. "She would have destroyed sixty years of honour. My great grandfather—" he pointed the gun at the wall where until moments ago Judge Aubischon's portrait had hung "—sat on the Brother John murder trial. My grandfather is a judge, my father is a judge, I'm going to be a judge. By marrying my sister, Anna would have soiled our reputation."

"You killed her—" my voice cracked "—because you were scared of what she would do to your *name*?"

"My name, my ancestor's name, future generations of Aubischons!"

"And what happens to Olive's next girlfriend? Are you going to kill her too?"

Keith smiled. He tapped the revolver against his leg as he looked out the window to the lit buildings next door. "That's not going to happen. Remember, Father's making Olive marry Troy. One lover killed, she'll think twice about taking another."

I stared, my body numb.

"Jade, don't look at me like that. The world is a cruel place. If the end justifies the means."

My cell phone vibrated in my suit pocket. I slowly rolled back the chair. If the end justified the means he'd kill me, with the gun I had thrown at him. My heart sank. I didn't want to die. I didn't want a bullet blowing me apart. I wanted to live. I had so much to live for. How did one reason with a killer? One didn't.

Jules had known. He had tried to warn me—after our win. The reason why he had wanted to meet me at the Aubischon party. "Jules found out, didn't he?" I said, my voice quiet.

Keith scoffed. "Jules swore he loved Olive. He wanted to protect her from the likes of us. Asshole." He rotated the gun around his finger as if to draw. "Jules was a Society member just like us. Father put up with him marrying Olive because at least their marriage would squash any rumours about her. But no, Jules had to dig. He realized the Society had approved my motion to eliminate Anna, and he had planned to expose what we had done. Stupid man. The Society will not be destroyed."

I thought about the members's list I had found. "You framed him for Anna's murder."

"Again, all with the Society's approval." He paced. "But then the asshole hired you. We didn't think you'd do it, having been five years since you last defended a criminal case, and then you won." Keith stood behind the armchair and rotated his shoulders. "We had an assassin waiting for him in jail, Jade." Keith cracked his neck. "It was all taken care of. Then you came along."

"All the more reason for my winning."

"You only prolonged Jules's life by a few hours."

I swallowed, trying to will back my tears, watching the gun swivel around his finger. I rolled back. "You have it all, Keith. A Cambridge law degree, you're a Q.C., you're going to be a judge, yet you killed two people because of your homophobic honour. What type of honour kills people?"

"The same honour that sends men to war. If Jules and Anna had any honour they would still be alive."

"You're blaming them!"

"Yes!"

My childhood friend—the young boy I used to play matchbox cars with—had turned into a cold-blooded murderer, and like every other criminal he blamed his victims for his actions. My friend. How could this have happened? When did it happen? The young boy had grown into a monster, and I had done nothing to stop it. "How could you? How could you watch them die?"

"I performed a public service."

"*A what*?"

"Honour, trust, respect. Fundamental principles of the Society, Jade, which people today lack. I believe in those principles. I acted on those principles. Because of those principles, I am who I am, and I'm where I am today."

"You are a murderer!" I hit my fist on the chair. "You killed two innocent people. Don't give me this crap about principles. You have no principles. You traded lives for your success."

His face paled. He again tapped the revolver against his leg. "Funny—" he looked at the revolver in his hand before looking at me "—Jules said the exact same thing before I shot him in the chest. Jack, the new recruit, whacked off his head."

I cringed. Keith was in control and my life was in his hands. I had to do something. I couldn't overpower him, I had to wait for that one mistake, that one window of opportunity and go for it. I wouldn't get another.

"Your ex wasn't so tough, Jade," Keith boasted, walking toward the desk. "I found him in the study, pissed out of his mind, arguing with Olive, trying to get her to put the engagement ring back on. I calmed Olive down, and I coaxed Jules outside for a scotch. Told him we would go check out where you and Sage used to play in the pagoda. He loved that idea. Maybe have a joint or two. Idiot."

I sat on the edge of my seat. "Who put his h-head on the buffet table? You? Olive?"

"Hell no. My sister slows down for squirrels. Olive was never involved." Keith stopped at the desk and began lining up his pens. "She caused all the trouble. First getting involved with Anna, then Jules, then she has to walk in on the new recruit as he's disposing of Jules's head. She went nuts, somehow managed to get Jules's blood on her hands. I calmed her down, again, told her to wash her hands and change her clothes. But did she listen? No. The bitch goes screaming out onto the deck. I take off after her. Jack heads back to the pagoda. I came back to double check everything and you walk in."

"Jack was the fourth chef?"

"Yes, and the mime who tried to take you out."

"You mutilated Jules, Keith. How could you do that?"

"I didn't. I shot him. I left the messy work to Jack. He's multi-talented: chef, mime, new recruit. I gave the order. Jules was a warning to anyone else thinking about double-crossing the Society." Keith stopped lining up his pens and looked at me, sadness in his eyes. "I never wanted you involved, Jade."

I rolled back the chair and banged into the cabinet.

Keith grabbed the arm and pulled me forward. "Out of two hundred lawyers, why did it have to be you? Why the hell did you have to walk into the study?"

Tears stung my eyes. "You told me you were trying to protect me. From who, Keith? Who the hell were you trying to protect me from!"

He dropped down to one knee. "Me." He pushed a strand of hair back from my face and with his thumb brushed a tear from my cheek. "You never saw a murderer when you looked into my eyes." His Adam's apple bobbed. "Now you do. I'm sorry, Jade." He thumbed the hammer back on his revolver. "This wasn't supposed to happen."

I drove my knee into his nose.

Keith screamed, toppling backwards, his hands cupped over his face. Blood gushed between his fingers and spotted his white shirt. The gun fell to the floor.

I leapt over him, landed on my sprained ankle and fell.

Keith grabbed my leg. "No!"

I swiveled onto my side and kicked at his bloody face. He grabbed the revolver and clubbed my sprained ankle. Fiery jabs shot up my leg and behind my knee. I screamed and curled into the fetal position.

Keith stumbled to his knees. "You *bitch*." He grabbed my arm. "Get up!"

His arm clamped around my waist. I hobbled onto my good foot. Another sharp jab shot up my calf. I buckled over.

"Stand up!"

"Shoot me here and you'll never get away with it. Try explaining all that blood and splattered brains to the cleaning woman."

"Who says I'm going to kill you here? We're going to your office, Jade. Overdose. You were depressed over your forced leave. Depressed over the death of your ex-husband. I'm sure you have a bottle of Vicodin in one of those boxes."

"No!"

He pushed me out the door.

I grabbed the door jamb. He hit my arm with the revolver. I cried out and cradled my arm to my body.

"You felt as if you had nothing to live for. I'm the co-worker and friend who finds your body. I'll make it look good, make the Society proud. They've been wanting me to do this for a long time."

"No!" I stumbled and fell to the floor.

Keith hauled me up. "Move."

"Let her go, Aubischon!"

I knew only one man with that voice.

Keith shoved the barrel of the gun against my temple, and his arm slipped around my throat. I gasped and clawed at the sleeve of his robes, the silk slipping through my fingers.

Dark hair, long leather coat, Osmond stood at the end of the hall, legs apart, both hands gripping his Smith & Wesson which was aimed our way. Two loaded guns pointed in my direction. I was going to die.

"Get out of here, Reeves!" Keith spat blood and tightened his grip. I gagged. Spots flashed before my eyes. "She wants to expose us. I have to get rid of her."

"Not Jade."

Keith pressed his face to the side of my head, his blood sticky on my skin.

"She knows too much."

Osmond advanced slowly. "Look at her. *Look at her*!" Osmond shouted.

I felt Keith's chin move against my head.

"Look at what you're doing to her. You love this girl. You've loved her since you were ten."

I heard a whispered curse. The gun muzzle scraped my skin.

"You don't want to kill Jade. We can arrange something, our own gag order. We'll make her leave the country. As for the Society, they'll think she's dead."

Tears and make-up pooled in my eyes, stinging. I pulled on Keith's arm.

"Come on, Aubischon. You can't do this to her."

Keith's lips pressed against my temple. "I'm sorry, Jade."

"*No.*" I pulled on his wrist. "Let me go, Keith. *Please*. Listen to Osmond. He's knows what he's talking about." I gasped again. "No one will know."

"We can have her disappear, Aubischon," Osmond said, edging closer.

"The Society wants action. They want to know why I haven't killed her. They're doubting my loyalties."

"Keith, please." I dug my nails into his wrists. "We can fix this, the three of us. I can disappear like Norman."

His grip loosened. "Disappear?"

"I'll hide. They'll never know."

"They won't know, Keith," Osmond continued. "We can do it. We can do anything."

I gasped. "They won't know, Keith. *Trust me.*"

His body sagged and his arm slipped from around my neck. I lurched forward.

"No!" He grabbed my hair, yanking my head back. I fell backwards. Keith slung his arm around my waist, propping me up against him as if in a romantic embrace. I clutched onto his robes. The revolver pointed at my head trembled in his hand.

"I can't risk it, Jade." Sweat ran down his forehead and into his eyes. He blinked, rubbed his eyes on his sleeve and blinked again. "They'll—" his voice cracked "—kill me."

"No, Keith," I whispered, looking up at his bloodied face. "They're making you a judge."

His dark eyes stared into mine, and for a brief moment I saw the fear of the young boy I used to know. That young boy, now a man, belonged to the Society, had a terrible secret, and was holding a gun to my head. Nothing would ever be the same.

Keith's face sagged. Tears trickled from his eyes, mixing with the blood on his cheeks. The hand holding the revolver dropped to his side.

"I'm sorry, Jade," he whispered.

I believed him.

He removed his arm from around my waist.

I collapsed, mashing my face in the carpet. I scrambled like a crab along the floor. The carpet blurred and I thudded into the wall and rolled onto my back.

"Jade. *Stay down*!"

Then I heard it.

The shot.

My body jolted and I curled onto my side, clutching my hands over my ears. Eyes closed, my mind reeled into blackness.

Running feet thundered on the carpet. Someone dropped. Hands grabbed onto my wrists.

"No!" I hid my face behind my arms. "No!"

The hands pried my arms apart.

"No!" I wailed, shaking my hands.

"Jade!"

Strong arms embraced me, my mouth muffled by a man's shirt.

"It's over, Jade. Over. He's dead. Keith's dead."

I turned my face to the side, trying to breathe.

"He's dead, Jade."

I pushed myself back.

Osmond held my face between his hands. "Keith's dead, Jade." He swallowed. "He shot himself."

I fell against Osmond and clutched onto his shirt lapel, staring at the dark hairs poking out from his collar, hearing him swallow. He caressed my hair as he spoke, but I only heard fragments, "—so sorry . . . risk a chance . . . hands sweating . . . arms shaking, scared shitless . . . kill you." He kissed me hard on the forehead.

I wiped my cheek and that's when I noticed the white transparent form kneeling over the heap of black robes.

Anna.

She looked at me and smiled. It was as if she had never been shot, her face whole—beautiful. She waved, blew me a kiss, and disappeared through Keith's door.

I sniffed, wiped my nose on the sleeve of my sweater, and looked once more at the lifeless form in the spreading pool of blood.

Keith.

His ultimate sacrifice for honour.

24

Fall Out

She was my conscience, not a drug-induced apparition.

THE YIROS IS my favourite Greek café, with its grand cherry oak counter, blue and white European tiled floor, and rows of red chickpea cans stacked along the back wall up to the thirty-foot ceiling. The lunch hour suit and tie crowd visit the little café regularly to incorporate a little hummus with their latest legal argument. Young opportunity-driven secretaries hang out at The Yiros sipping their lattes. The suits hope to catch mistress number two to replace mistress number one, which wife number three has just found out about. All socializing aside, the food at The Yiros is messy, spicy and loaded with garlic—excellent. Lunch for me is usually a three-napkin ordeal.

Today I had beaten the lunch hour rush and was sitting in my favourite spot at the wooden counter underneath the large green palm, overlooking the courtyard of Stamps Alley. I had already placed my order. The sizzling of lamb on the grill sounded like the percussion section in an orchestra of chattering patrons, banging pots, and shouted orders. Underneath this culinary opus, snippets of *La Traviata* floated from the overhead speaker.

Six weeks had passed since the horrific encounter with Keith. Aubischon senior, upon learning of his son's suicide, had suffered a nervous breakdown and been hospitalized.

Rumour had it that a Vancouver law firm was bringing about a search warrant application to search the offices of Aubischon, Thyme and Bastine. This would assist the RCMP Special Task Force created to expose the island chapter of the Society. Since I had discovered only half the members's list in Keith's office, the hunt was on to find the rest. Within twenty-four hours of my discovery of the list and the revolver used to shoot Anna and Jules, the RCMP had a second warrant to search the Aubischon residence. They confiscated two laptops, three boxes of Society paperwork, and a letter from a past president appointing Keith as one of two Society Recruiters. Bloodied rags were hidden in the cellar, which connected to the study by a service elevator also exhibiting blood splatters—how the new recruit was able to transport Jules's head without being seen.

The new recruit was the mime who had shot at me when Osmond and I found Nox. He had been arrested hours after that incident but refused to cooperate. The police kept him in custody until his next court date. When the mime found out that Keith had committed suicide, he began to cooperate.

One more Recruiter was still out there.

The Society, I learned, was organized in such a way that if part of the organization was taken down, the other part was left intact. Two independent entities, the island cell and the mainland cell made up the one chapter, making it twice as difficult for the RCMP. The Special Task Force didn't want the media or the public to know that Osmond or I had been involved with Keith's death. Osmond's name, as well as mine, had been part of the hold-back information. I hadn't seen much of Osmond since that night as he was immersed in the investigation—Operation Dragonboat, I had been told.

I was left clutching the broken pieces of friendships as more of my colleagues were implicated for having Society ties. A witch-hunt gripped Victoria and hysteria squeezed from its clutches. I was relieved that Jules's and Anna's murders had been solved, but I did not feel like a heroine. I felt conflicted. There was no tidy wind up like in the movies, no 'and they lived happily ever after.'

Day after day, as I stood in the morning line-up to get my coffee, newspaper headlines announced another lawyer charged, another conspiracy foiled. While the Mocha Cup employee would whip up my mocha, I would mentally beat myself up. I had turned against my colleagues. In my pursuit of justice, I had envisioned select individuals being exposed. I had never fathomed how far the Society's tentacles stretched. One lawyer could not be taken down without taking a slew of others.

Power firms such as Aubischon, Thyme and Bastine imploded—law practices folded, offices vacated. Turmoil was too weak a word to describe what was happening to Victoria's legal community. Lawyers, fresh out of law school, were being swarmed by hysterical clients whose previous counsel had either been arrested, or had abandoned them. I was no longer an employee of my father's firm, in fact I was one of many who had jumped ship, yet I wasn't at a loss for work—the reason why I was out in this part of the city. I had signed the lease for the nineteenth floor in the building across the street from The Yiros. Noxzema Man—Norman—and I would be forming a partnership and opening our law firm as soon as Nox pulled himself together and conquered his own demons. My demons, I was still wrestling with them.

No longer residing in an alley, Nox and his sardine cans had moved into a hostel. Social workers were assisting his re-integration into society as well as the work force—a scary feat for the sanest individual. By the time the renovations are done to our floor and to Nox's mind, we should be ready to open the doors of Thyme and Bastine.

Most of our work would be for the Crown. Bianca, still fighting lawsuits, and still in desperate search for a prosecutor, had designated us as her go-to ad hoc prosecutors. Norman and I would receive the ugly or "sensitive" cases that no one wanted to touch. Kate would remain my legal assistant, but she was also overseeing the renovations.

"One Caesar salad and lamb wrap."

I leaned back as the waitress placed my order in front of me. "Thank you."

A spring wind typical of Victoria whipped down Stamps Alley, rattling windowpanes and scattering orange and yellow leaves across the cobblestone courtyard.

I shivered and picked up my coffee mug, cradling its warmth as I watched men and women zip up jackets and tug on their coat collars. I took a tentative sip, then replaced my mug. I picked up my fork and stabbed a salad leaf. Signing the lease for the new office had been the best medicine.

I had nightmares about Keith. Missed him. Felt I had betrayed him, yet also felt betrayed by him. He had been my mentor and, at twelve, the first boy that had ever kissed me. He had been a driving force in invoking tougher laws for young offenders, and had provided the government with countless opinions regarding the national DNA databank legislation. He had served as president of the Law Society, and he had done so much for the local legal community.

He had been my assassin.

I had placed Keith on a pedestal, and now he lay dead at my feet along with my beliefs.

I put down my fork and took a bite of my wrap, when, as if a messenger from God, Sage walked towards The Yiros. Her long red hair flipping back in time to her long legged strides. She might as well have been on a catwalk. Leather jacket, tight jeans and knee-high boots, my sister was a superhero. She had a cloth bag in her hand. She saw me, smiled and pulled open the door of The Yiros. She sauntered over.

"Kate told me I'd find you here," she said.

"Have a seat."

Sage pulled over a stool and sat. "I can't stay long. Have you seen this?" She held up a real estate magazine.

"Houses for sale."

She flipped to a page. "Not just houses. Mansions." She held the magazine up and tapped a listing. "Dad's selling his castle."

I wiped my mouth and took the magazine from her hand. He really was doing it. The family home was for sale. "What about Edith?"

"I don't know what's going on with her. She hasn't returned my phone call."

I looked at the price. "It's cheap. I guess having the city mayor decapitated in your backyard and his body dumped in the lake doesn't help the curb appeal." I looked at Sage. "I could afford this if the price was about one–hundred thousand dollars cheaper."

"I could come up with the difference, maybe more."

"Legally?"

"Hey."

"That's a lot of money."

"I have investments."

"We'd have to get rid of the pagoda."

"Bulldoze that sucker down and build a new one."

I smiled. "Let's do it."

"Yes. I have an appointment with a realtor in forty minutes."

"But you didn't know if I'd be on board."

Sage smiled as she rested her elbow on the counter and slid the cloth bag towards me. "I knew I could convince you."

"You were going to bribe me? I can't be bought."

"At least look what's inside."

I opened the bag and pulled out a long plastic and pink box. A 1985 Astronaut Barbie. I laughed. "Well played little sister. Well played."

We both laughed.

"Where the heck did you find her?"

"Ebay."

It was the sweetest thing anyone had ever done for me. "Thank you." I placed Astronaut Barbie on the counter.

"We'll keep her away from the lake," Sage said. "So what's on your agenda this afternoon?"

"Osmond is meeting me."

She raised an eyebrow. "You two sleeping together yet?"

I choked on my coffee and sputtered. "*Sage*."

"Obviously not. Oh, and here comes your guy."

Osmond stepped out from underneath a green striped awning in his usual attire of bluejeans and leather coat. Businessmen and all the varied street people of Stamps Alley parted before him as the Red Sea had parted for Moses.

Sage stood. "I'll text you what the realtor says. Have fun with him."

"When my ankle's better, we'll go for that ride."

Sage winked at me and nodded at Osmond as he walked into The Yiros. Sage waved and headed out.

Osmond joined the food line-up and was soon placing his order. He paid and with coffee cup in hand, squeezed through patrons.

"Counsellor," he said. "Barbie?"

"Long story. How are you?" I asked.

He placed his hand on my back as he slid onto the stool beside me, glancing at my short skirt. "Going crazy." He arched one eyebrow and looked at me with those eyes. "You want to join me?"

I smiled. "Not today, maybe tomorrow. I already have an appointment."

He smiled. "I thought I saw Sage."

"Yes. She has an appointment too."

"You're looking better. How's your ankle?"

"I won't be wearing my Jimmy Choos for awhile, but . . . I'm alive."

He winked as he reached for the bowl of artificial sweeteners. He picked up a packet and frowned. "Don't they have any real sugar in here?"

I stretched to my right for the glass sugar dispenser. "Here."

Osmond took it and poured a steady stream of sugar into his coffee. "So did you hear? Sergeant Stone is being transferred to Tofino."

"Really? And hopefully transferring out of Bianca's life. I swear he was using her for information and . . . I don't want to think of what else."

Osmond placed the dispenser on the counter. "Maybe *she* was using him."

I stared.

"The other Recruiter." He winked again.

"Oh my God. Bianca was the other Recruiter?"

"Yes. She was working for us though, providing information about cops in the Society."

"Through her connections with Stone."

"Yes. Stone's not a bad guy. I know he's trying to do his job, but he's the most out of the loop cop I've ever worked with." Osmond sipped his coffee, paused, sipped again.

It must have tasted all right for he placed the cup on the saucer.

"The forensic lab emailed me their report on the DNA found in the blood on Keith's robes compared to the DNA found in a hair sample at the base of Jules's neck."

"Did it match?"

"Perfectly. The hair sample belonged to Keith."

"We'd have a case if Keith was still alive."

Osmond nodded before taking another drink. "Yeah, but tell me, Jade—" he looked me straight in the eye "—would you have testified against him? Or would I have had to get a witness warrant for you?"

I looked down at my salad and wrap.

"That's what I thought," Osmond said, slugging back a gulp of coffee.

Shame burned my cheeks. I placed my fork on my plate and picked up my mug. Osmond had been speaking to the forensic analyst about another case, when he learned about the matching DNA samples on Jules's case.

DNA samples from a female and a male had also been found on the tablecloth and punch bowl. Olive's DNA matched, but it was that of the unknown male which caused Osmond to visit Olive again. She'd broken down and admitted that Keith had been in the room with her when she and Jules had their fight, and that Keith coerced Jules to smoke a joint in my parents's pagoda, away from the party. Concerned about my safety and unable to reach me by phone, Osmond decided to check on me at work. Thank God. He saved my life.

"The forensic guys," he continued, "are comparing the shell casing found in Anna's apartment to the shell casings found in the pagoda. I have no doubt they'll match."

"How's James taking all of this? Is he still hospitalized?"

Osmond tapped the stir stick against the counter. "Yes, but because of the scandal and his associations with the Society, he's stepped down from the bench."

"Serves him right. The two of them . . . he and Keith . . . they destroyed so many lives. How's Olive?"

Osmond smiled. "You haven't heard?"

"Heard what?"

"Olive has taken the two-hundred and fifty thousand and flown to Sweden."

"I thought the money was missing?"

"Olive had a second safety deposit box. After Anna was killed, Olive moved the money."

I smiled. "Good for her. I hope she can find peace and happiness. Because no matter what we do—prosecute, throw Society members in jail, none of that will bring Jules and Anna back."

Osmond rubbed my shoulder. "No, but think about the lives you've saved without even knowing it. Do you think the Society was going to stop with you?"

I sloshed the coffee around in my cup. "No."

Osmond leaned forward. "With your help and your father's, we'll bring them down—one cell, one chapter at a time. Cracking this cell has been a coup for us."

I looked into Osmond's deep green eyes, trying to convince myself of his convictions. At that moment a waitress coughed loudly behind us.

Osmond leaned back.

She placed his Greek salad before him along with a receipt with a phone number written on it. She brushed past him onto the next customer.

"If that isn't obvious," I mumbled.

Osmond smiled.

"My father's assisting the investigation?"

"Quite a bit." He unwrapped his utensils from his napkin. "He was never one of the bad guys, Jade."

"How can you say that? He never told me anything."

Osmond looked at me. "He was helpful with the dive team when they recovered Jules's body from the lake. He had no objection to the pagoda being searched."

Where Jules had been shot and decapitated. The axe and Jules's cell phone had been found under the pagoda. "He's selling the house now." I sloshed back a mouthful of coffee.

Osmond nodded toward my plate. "Your wrap is getting cold."

I pushed a tomato slice through a puddle of sauce with my fork.

"Have you spoken to your father recently?" Osmond asked, munching on his salad.

"No. Did he tell you who ran me off the road and chased me at the lake?"

"Actually, he did."

My head whipped around. "No! Who?"

"Jade—" he eyed me as he ripped off a chunk of garlic bread "—you know I can't tell you that."

"Oh, come on."

Osmond looked at me from the corner of his eyes, a hint of a smile on his face. "Troy."

I banged my fist on the counter. "I knew it!"

He picked up his fork. "Although he denies that he was going to drown you. What did you hit him with? You broke his nose."

"My motorcycle helmet. I am more than willing to testify against him."

"Actually, and don't lose it on me, we're not pressing charges against Troy."

"Why not?"

"Because of the evidence he's giving us on the Society."

"Really?"

"The man's a survivor, Jade. He knows what wheel to grease." He took a sip of his coffee. "Troy is the only person who will talk." Osmond placed the mug on its saucer. "The Society put the fear of God into thousands of lawyers. The older generation is petrified that I'll show up at their door and slap on handcuffs, or that an assassin will greet them with a semi-automatic. The younger generation that's been trying to oust the old and clean up the Society will testify in court, but only if I can get them into the witness protection program. The RCMP does not have the money to protect that many lawyers, but we can protect Troy."

"So what's next?"

"On the orders of my superior, get out of the country. Despite all our efforts, my face has become known. How are you doing?"

"I'm still having nightmares, still cowering at loud bangs, still double-checking the locks on my doors." *Still expecting to see Anna's ghost and wondering when Keith's will make a first appearance.* "The destruction hasn't stopped. It's snowballing. More lives are being destroyed. Jules's and Anna's murders have been solved, but they were just the tip of the iceberg. I still feel . . . alone . . . betrayed. I want closure but I'm not getting it. Murderers are supposed to be monsters, Osmond. Not best friends."

Osmond gripped my shoulder. "Keith killed Anna and Jules for his own selfish reasons. And he just didn't kill, Jade, he mutilated. He ordered a new recruit to cut off Jules's head and then display it. His twisted allegiance was to the Society and what it would do for *him*. He was not a good person, Jade Thyme. He held a gun to your head, and he would have killed you. Don't you *ever* forget that!"

The anger in Osmond's voice startled me. I looked down at my half-eaten wrap. The Society in all its glory had turned enemies into friends, and friends into enemies.

He glanced at me, a sheepish look on his face. "I didn't mean to get mad at you. It's just—" he put his fork down and looked outside "—the Special Task Force has been trying to crack the

Island Chapter for years. The only reason why we were successful this time is because of Keith's arrogance. If Keith hadn't displayed Jules's head on that buffet table, we wouldn't have had a murder because we wouldn't have had a body. Jules would have been regarded as a missing person, a suspected homicide. That's it." He placed his hand on my shoulder and gave me a little shake. "You played too damn close to that monster, Jade."

I looked long and hard at him. I had a strong feeling that my mother would approve of Osmond, although she would disapprove of his long hair and my strong feelings for him.

"What's on your mind, counsellor?" he asked.

I looked out the window, then at him. God help me. "During this entire investigation, actually since Jules's trial, I've been seeing—" I couldn't believe I was telling him this.

"—Seeing."

I sighed. "—Anna's ghost."

His expression remained neutral.

"Now that Keith's dead," I blundered on, "and the murders are solved, I haven't seen her. Was she a ghost? Was I hallucinating? Am I going crazy? Or will I soon be loitering in some alley eating sardines out of a Nivea cream jar?"

Osmond looked out over the courtyard. His gaze rested on a bedraggled street person picking up red and orange maple leaves and joyfully throwing them in the air. Osmond turned his green eyes on me. "Well, you've already done the sardine thing. Do you think he's seeing a ghost?" He pointed at the street person.

"No. Good drugs."

Osmond smiled. "I don't believe in ghosts, Jade."

I bit my lip. Now he thought me a nut-case. "So, I was hallucinating."

"Maybe." His expression softened. "You're not going to like my answer."

"Say it. I can take it."

His hand slipped over mine, covering it. "Vicodin induced."

I tried to make light of what I was about to say. "I am seeing a counsellor."

"Given the crap you've been through, smart move."

I looked at the rows of tomato cans against the wall. Remove one can from the bottom and the whole thing would topple. How my life felt at the moment. I was always in control. I wasn't an addict. I wasn't snorting cocaine. I had never smoked pot, and now it was legal.

I thought of my last day at work, when Anna had appeared outside the office window just after Keith had left me. She had slammed her bloody hand against the windowpane. She was my conscience, not a drug-induced apparition. She had been trying to tell me that Keith had her blood on his hands.

Osmond slid his hand to the back of my neck. "You told me that Keith had planned to murder you by making you overdose on your Vicodin prescription."

I forgot I had told him about that.

"What scares me is if I hadn't been there, he would have gotten away with it."

Osmond was right.

"Be honest with yourself, Jade. When was the last time you had Vicodin?"

"I'm not an addict."

"When was the last time you had Vicodin?"

"It's not like I have a problem."

"When was the last time you had Vicodin?"

I glanced at the street person tossing more leaves into the air. "This morning with my iron pill."

"Oh, Jade." He rubbed my shoulder.

"When I take Vicodin I'm fine. I'm like a machine, no one knows the difference. I'm productive. But when I don't take any, I lose my shit."

"You're stronger than this."

I pivoted the little wooden stir stick from end to end. "I have a problem, don't I?"

He nodded then pulled me toward him and kissed me long and

slow, the rough hairs of his goatee scratching my skin. He leaned back.

The crash of a dropped plate shattered our reverie.

"So are you ever going to tell me why you have a Barbie?"

I smiled. "Gift from Sage." I glanced at Astronaut Barbie's space helmet and fuchsia-coloured boots and space suit. If Barbie could go to the moon, I could beat Vicodin.

About the Author

Joanna Vander Vlugt is an illustrator and book designer at The Self-Publishing Agency (TSPA). As a teenager, she drew charcoal portraits and wrote mysteries. It would be some years later before she would draw again. Joanna became a fitness instructor and personal trainer. During this time, under the pseudonym J.C. Szasz, her short mysteries *Egyptian Queen* and *The Parrot and Wild Mushroom Stuffing* were published in a Canadian mystery anthology. Her personal essay, *No Beatles Reunion* was published in the Dropped Threads 3: Beyond the Small Circle anthology. When Joanna retired from the fitness profession, she began drawing again, intrigued by fashion illustrations. Instead of charcoal pencils, she switched mediums and now creates fashion and motorcycle illustrations using Copic markers. Joanna has been commissioned to create motorcycle and car illustrations. Her art is collected by private collectors world-wide. Her next project is her motorcycle illustration book.

Photo courtesy of Posy Photography

42

10,000
2400
3000
2100
1400
18900